A ..... Place

The fit young mechanic pressed himself against Maddie and his fingers slipped under the waistband of her panties. Maddie willed them to dip deeper beneath the material but they stayed frustratingly out of reach. Then he crushed her up close to him. She could feel the knot of his overalls digging into her bare skin as he pushed her against the bonnet of her car. Below that she could feel a different pressure. She could feel him thickening and knew there was no going back.

A Secret Place

ELLA BROUSSARD

Black Lace novels are sexual fantasies.
In real life, make sure you practise safe sex.

First published in 1998 by
Black Lace
Thames Wharf Studios,
Rainville Road, London W6 9HT

Typeset by SetSystems Ltd, Saffron Walden, Essex
Printed and bound by Mackays of Chatham PLC

ISBN 0 352 33307 3

Chapter One

*T*ap tap tap. Then louder, and more insistent this time: TAP TAP TAP TAP TAP.

Maddie looked up from her paperwork and scanned the room, seeking out the source of the noise. Her gaze settled on Polly, the secretary, who was standing up behind her desk and signalling urgently to Maddie through the glass partition in the office. Polly's head was tilted at an awkward angle, with the phone receiver cradled between her chin and her shoulder. She was frantically scribbling something on a pad with one hand and gesturing to Maddie's phone with the other. Maddie raised her eyes to the ceiling.

'Oh, good grief, this is ridiculous! When on earth is Freya going to fork the money out to get the phone fixed?' she muttered to herself. 'This is hardly the way to run a business.' The hold-and-transfer facility between Maddie's and Polly's phones had been working erratically for the past few months, and Freya had yet to authorise Polly to spend the money

1

on getting them mended. Polly could put calls through to Maddie, but this outlandish pantomime was the only way that she could let Maddie know who was calling beforehand.

Polly held up the piece of paper against the glass for Maddie to see. On it, in large and wobbly capitals, underlined three times, was written 'SAM PASCALI!!!'

Maddie was dumbstruck, experiencing a sudden simultaneous rush of disbelief and elation and panic. Sam Pascali? Ringing her? But before she had time to gather herself, the phone on her desk rang. She looked across to Polly again, who was grinning and nodding so enthusiastically it seemed to Maddie that the secretary's head might bounce its way off her neck and on to the floor at any moment. Maddie reached for the phone.

'Hello. Maddie Campion speaking.'

'Hi there, Maddie. Sam Pascali here. Just thought I'd call and run an idea by you. I just got back from the Sundance Film Festival. Saw *The Great North Road* there. Fabulous movie, great locations. You did a fine job. Wanna tell me something about yourself?'

Sam spoke in an abbreviated form of telegraphese and so fast that it took Maddie a little time to catch up with him, and only then did the possible implications of what he was saying start to sink in. Was Sam asking her to pitch for a job?

'Hey? Maddie? You still there?'

'Oh, yes, I'm sorry, Mr Pascali,' Maddie stuttered.

'Nah. Sam: call me Sam. So, Maddie, tell me all about yourself. You know the kind of thing: movies you've worked on, directors you've worked with.'

Maddie took a deep breath and tried to compose herself. 'Um, OK, Sam. Let me think.' Maddie

2

struggled desperately to collect her careening thoughts. 'Well, I started out as location manager on several television series; and then I moved on to films – all British. I must have done about fourteen or fifteen of them now. Mainly small, independent movies: Channel Four Films, that sort of thing. I don't suppose you would have heard of any of them. I think *The Great North Road* is the only one that has been distributed in the States.'

'You got copies of any of them?'

'Er, yes, a few. Would you like me to send them to you?'

'You bet. Courier them to me overnight. Tapes, reels, whatever: don't worry about the format. I can cope with whatever you throw at me. Got a pen? Here's my address: home, not office.'

Maddie quickly jotted down some notes, trying to keep up with Sam's rapid-fire speech. It all seemed slightly unreal; especially so as she wrote down Sam's address in Beverly Hills.

'So, I want to ask you Maddie: if I like the rest of your work, do you want to join my next movie? It's my baby, been a long time in the works. I wrote it and sure as hell won't trust anyone else with it, so no prizes for guessing who's producing and directing it, too. It's called *D-Day Dawn*: a Second World War movie, 'bout GIs stationed in England and the lead-up to the Allied invasion. I need a Brit to find the locations – kind of like a native guide, I guess. We're scheduled to start shooting in the second week of September, so if I OK you, I need you to start looking for locations right now.'

Clearly, as far as Sam was concerned, there was no possibility that she might not be available, and Maddie guessed that Sam wasn't used to being

3

turned down. She was agog. It was early June, and that didn't give her long to get things sorted out, especially for a major picture which was bound to require a lot of different locations. But she was damn sure that she would make herself free for Sam Pascali.

'Um, sure, Sam. I'd love to.'

'Great. I'll get the outline details faxed through to you straightaway, and my secretary will let you know sometime in the next couple of days if you've got the gig, OK?'

'That's terrific, Sam. Thank you.' By the time Maddie had finished speaking, the other end of the line had gone dead. Sam Pascali was obviously a very busy man.

Maddie looked up in a daze. Polly had come through from her part of the office and was now standing next to Maddie, hopping from foot to foot in her excitement. She reminded Maddie of an excited schoolgirl.

'I can't believe it. I spoke to Sam Pascali. Oh, my God. Sam Pascali. Wait 'til I tell my friends,' Polly said breathlessly. 'Well? C'mon, spill the beans! What was he ringing about?'

'He wants me to work on his next movie; at least, that's if he likes my previous work. Hell, I'd better get the tapes sent off to him straightaway.'

'Oh, my God; oh, my God,' wailed Polly. 'You mean, you're going to the States to work with Sam Pascali? This is too much.'

'No, Pol, he'd use an American scout for that, wouldn't he? What do I know about American locations?' Maddie explained. Polly wasn't the most on-the-ball secretary sometimes. 'He's filming over here later this summer. Now where are the tapes of those last three films I worked on for Channel Four?'

Polly went over to one of the shelves behind her desk and pulled them out.

'Great. Can you courier them over to this address in the States straightaway? Make sure they go by priority service, please – they've got to get there as soon as possible.'

'Yes, boss,' said Polly, suddenly and unfamiliarly business-like.

Just then, clearly alerted by the commotion, Freya came into the office. 'What's all the hollering about?' she asked, peering over the top of her half-moon glasses like a stern schoolmistress.

'Maddie just got a call from Sam Pascali,' Polly blabbed, before Maddie had a chance to say a word.

'Oh, did you now?' said Freya. 'Come into my office and tell me all about it.'

Maddie followed Freya into her office, a small room across the hallway. Despite her exasperation with Freya's way of doing business, Maddie liked her boss. Freya was maybe fifty, maybe a bit older. She was a kind but sometimes sharp-tongued woman, and one of the few true eccentrics that Maddie had ever met. Her three main passions in life were work, cats and classic sports cars; she owned four of the latter. As if this wasn't enough, she was always looking to add another car to her collection.

Freya had started the business, finding and securing locations for television and film productions, in the 1960s, and for a long time she had worked on her own. She had taken on Maddie some years previously when the workload had become too great for her to manage on her own. Freya had recently added three more staff to the payroll: Polly; Miles, another location manager, and Greg, an assistant. Business was booming, largely due to the renaissance of the British film industry over the previous decade or so.

Freya's work was such that she was now almost completely office-bound with administration. Maddie mused that this was probably a good thing: she dreaded to think how Freya and her hair would manage in the great windy outdoors. Freya's long, thick grey hair was always put up in a messy bun on the top of her head. Even first thing in the morning, strands of hair would be escaping from the numerous clips and grips which held the whole teetering edifice up; and Maddie could watch the gravity-defying spectacle that was Freya's bun for hours, waiting for it to topple. Inevitably it would start its collapse and, without interrupting whatever it was that she was doing, Freya would nonchalantly hoik the whole lot up again and secure it (if that was the word) with yet more grips and pins fished out of a drawer or a handbag or a pocket.

'So,' said Freya, sitting down behind her paper-strewn desk. 'Sam Pascali, eh? Tell all.'

'So. Sam Pascali, eh? Tell all.'

Maddie squinted into the sunlight and looked up at Greg. The sun was behind him, and she could see the outline of his lithe torso silhouetted through his cotton shirt. She watched as he deftly wielded the punt pole, letting it fall in a controlled drop through his hands until it hit the river bed, and then pushing down and back on it to propel the punt lazily forward. A sharp twist released it from the sticky mud, and then he fed it back up through his hands and stood poised, ready to let it drop again. Greg had rolled the bottoms of his chinos up a little way, and his feet were bare to get a better grip on the flat backboard of the punt. Maddie gazed at them. They were nice feet: tanned and a fine shape, with neatly clipped toenails. You could tell a lot about a man from his feet, she reflected.

Maddie put her hand up over her eyes to shield them from the sun's glare. 'Yeah. I still can't believe it. Freya's cleared my schedule, and shunted all my odds and sods on to Miles so that I can get cracking on *D-Day Dawn* right away.'

'Old Miles isn't going to be very happy about that, is he?' Greg laughed. 'Still, too bad,' he said abruptly. Neither Greg nor Maddie was overly fond of Miles. 'But let's not talk about him, let's talk about you! What happens next?'

'I've got a bit of preparatory library and office work to do first, and then I'm off to scout for locations in Kent. Finding the right locations is going to be that bit more difficult, as it's a period film – can't have any anachronisms like motorways or electricity pylons in shot. I'm so looking forward to it. I can't wait to get started.'

Greg grinned. 'My congratulations, Miss Campion, it looks like you've hit the big time. Hollywood has come a-calling. Well done you. Who knows what this might lead to?'

'Let's hope. I can't get over the size of the budget for *D-Day Dawn*. It's massive: it must be as big as all the British films I've worked on put together. And Sam Pascali has never had a flop, has he?'

'Nope, you're right there. He's an A-list director, all right. One of the biggies.'

Maddie smiled contentedly, settled back into her

seat and let her fingers trail in the water as they drifted along the Backs, past the glorious architecture and grounds of the colleges. She loved Cambridge. Even though she had travelled all over the world and seen many beautiful cities, she felt that nowhere could beat Cambridge. It seemed full of beautiful people, too. Must be something to do with the student population, she thought: 'gilded youth' did indeed exist here in Cambridge. Every now and then, Maddie would have to stop and mentally pinch herself, to remind herself not to take things for granted, and to acknowledge how incredibly lucky she was to be living and working here. She had her dream job, based in a dream city.

'What time does the punt have to be back at Scudamore's?' she asked. She hoped that this idyll wasn't going to be cut short.

'We've got it all day,' Greg said. 'I thought you might like a picnic up by Grantchester.'

'You sweet man,' Maddie sighed, smiling up at him. She had worked with Greg for a year now, and their relationship had never developed beyond a gentle flirtatiousness. Looking at him now, Maddie couldn't work out why she had never made a move on him before. He looked good enough to eat. She lay back on the cushions and closed her eyes, thinking of her handsome companion. As she daydreamed, she heard the gentle splash and swish of the punt pole; the calls of the ducks, coots and moorhens from the river bank; and the far-off voices of people lounging on the grass or slowly walking by in the brilliant sunlight. To be here, in the sun with Greg, was the perfect way to spend her weekend.

Maddie had chosen her career for several reasons,

but one of the most compelling was that she adored being out-of-doors. She couldn't imagine having a job which kept her office-bound: preventing her from feeling the heat of the sun or the wispy breaths of a summer breeze on her skin, or leaving her unable to smell the rich aroma of freshly ploughed soil or newly mown hay meadows. She loved to watch great fluffy clouds scudding above her, or lowering storm clouds gathering on the horizon; to see a vivid sunset, or to walk in the monochrome world of a moonlit night. Maddie felt that the appeal of the outdoors to her was almost elemental, and she therefore accepted that it should also drive one of the most elemental urges within her: sex. When she was outdoors, she had an almost ever-present craving to make love somewhere in the open air, although she was not always lucky enough to have someone with her to help make the desire become a reality; when she was indoors, she spent most of her time wishing she was outside. Lying in the gently rocking punt, Maddie smiled to herself, thinking of Greg and the opportunities that might present themselves later on.

When Maddie finally opened her eyes again, she saw that they had travelled quite some distance and were well out of the city. Tall reeds flanked either side of the riverbank, and chestnut trees and oaks and willows formed a green canopy overhead, casting a dappled shade on to the surface of the water. Trails of green water weed swayed from side to side in the slowly flowing river. This is the life, Maddie thought to herself.

Maddie looked up at Greg, and was pleasantly surprised to see that he had taken his shirt off. 'God, I adore the summer,' she murmured. Not only for the weather and the beauty of the countryside, but for the opportunities it afforded her to look at semi-naked men. Bodies that had been concealed all winter were revealed at last, adding to Maddie's pleasure in her surroundings, and prompting even bawdier thoughts. Greg's body, or at least the part of it that she could see, was as brown as his feet, and even finer than she had guessed it to be. He had a lean, wiry body, reminding her of that of a well-honed lightweight boxer or a martial arts devotee. Maddie watched lazily as Greg punted steadily along, apparently unaware of her attention. She could feel herself drifting into sensual reverie as she admired the way the various muscles in his arms and chest moved in a slow rhythm. She couldn't deny it – Greg was looking good.

Maddie knew, with modest self-assuredness, that she too was more than attractive. She had had enough lovers for that to be beyond doubt; and whenever she glanced at herself in a mirror, that knowledge was confirmed. Maddie's Italian ancestry could be seen both in the colour of her skin, which appeared tanned even in the depths of an English winter, and in her strong, sensual facial features. She had large brown eyes with dark, curling lashes, a long, straight nose and full lips which, more often than not, were curved up into a mischievous smile. Her hair was a mane of chestnut-brown tresses, which reached half-way down her back when she wore it loose. She did not wear it loose during the daytime, as she found it could be a hindrance when she was working, the curls falling over her papers as she worked at a desk, or blowing around her face and obscuring her vision while she was outside. Maddie was proud of her hair, knowing it was her crowning glory; and accordingly she took great care of it, washing it every day and visiting the hair-dresser's once a fortnight. Today, she had piled it on the back of her head in a neat coil, with wispy tendrils escaping from their confines and framing her pretty face.

Maddie was wearing a long, thin white cotton dress: one which draped itself lightly over her curves as she lay back amongst the cushions. She also happened to know that, like Greg's shirt, the dress allowed the outline of her body to be seen through it when she was backlit by bright sunlight. She had made sure that she had been between Greg and the sun when she had got into the punt, and she hoped that this hadn't passed his notice. Beneath the dress she wore only a skimpy pair of knickers. She knew that Greg would be able to see the dark coloration of her nipples through the dress; and as she thought this, she could feel them reacting: tightening and hardening, and forcing the material up as they formed into two hard buds.

She gazed up at Greg again, and he smiled down at her, not taking his eyes off her as he propelled the punt forward. She shifted voluptuously and deliber-ately on the cushions, allowing the dress to settle even more closely over her body; and laid a hand over one breast and stroked it lightly. She knew it would appear to Greg as an unselfconscious gesture, but it was deliberately planned and executed in order to have an effect on him. She knew he would be wishing he could replace her hand with his own. Maddie smiled to herself as, right on cue, Greg suggested they moor the punt. He gestured ahead, and Maddie turned to see what it was he was pointing at.

11

'How about we picnic by that weeping willow over there?' Greg asked.

'Lovely,' she said dreamily, thinking of the possibilities that lay ahead.

Greg skilfully manoeuvred the punt until it was parallel to the river bank. He hopped out and made the punt fast by tying it to an old tree stump that was sticking out of the bank. Then he came back to help Maddie out, and handed her a rug, before returning once more to fetch the picnic hamper which had been stowed behind Maddie's seat in the punt.

Maddie, meanwhile, wandered over to the large weeping willow, and parted the soft leafy curtain of hanging branches. Peering into the shaded space beneath the canopy, she smiled to herself. 'Perfect,' she whispered. Under the draping foliage of the tree, the light was soft and diffuse; green-tinged through the leaves. The ground was covered with a spongy skim of fine mosses and grass. Standing in the interior of the tree, Maddie was reminded of being in a tepee or being sheltered under a huge umbrella. The world seemed excluded and far away.

Maddie spread the rug on the grassy ground, and called out to Greg, 'Come on in. It's gorgeous in here.'

Greg pushed his way though the branches and into the shady interior. He put the hamper down and looked around.

'Smart,' he said approvingly. Maddie wondered whether his thoughts had taken the rude turn that hers had.

'I used to love playing in places like this when I was a kid,' he said nostalgically. 'I had a den in just about every garden along my street. Half the fun was trying to sneak into them without the owners seeing.'

'Me too. I adore the sensation of being outside, but hidden away. In a special, secret place.'

Maddie walked up to Greg and took his hand, and guided him towards the rug. She had decided that she was going to give him a surprise. With a questioning look on his face, Greg allowed himself to be led without protest.

Maddie knew that Greg had a particular thing about her hair. It was not quite a fetish, but verging on it. One day, some months previously, she had overheard Greg telling Polly how attractive he thought Maddie's hair was, and that he had never seen her with her hair down. He had admitted to Polly that he desperately wanted to touch Maddie's hair, and sometimes had to restrain himself from reaching out and letting it down and caressing it when she was near to him. Polly had urged Greg to tell her, saying she was sure that Maddie wouldn't mind; but Greg had said that he was too embarrassed by it, and that Maddie might think him some kind of creep. It was only on overhearing all this that it had occurred to Maddie that Greg had indeed often previously commented on her hair; and that she had not fully understood the import of his compliments before that.

So now, standing in front of him, Maddie reached round behind her head and pulled out the large tortoiseshell comb that had been holding up her hair. She shook her head, releasing the long, coiling tendrils; and stood silently, allowing Greg to appreciate her.

'That's better,' she sighed. She looked at Greg,

who was staring at her with an almost hypnotic intensity. 'Do you like my hair, Greg?' she asked.

Greg bit his lower lip and nodded. 'Would you let me ... I mean, do you mind ... Can I touch it?' he asked tentatively, his voice a cracked whisper.

'Of course,' Maddie replied. 'As much as you like.'

Greg stepped towards her, and lightly placed his hands on her head, like a priest giving a blessing. Then he slowly ran his hands down her temples, past her ears and down her neck, gathering the curling locks into his hands as he did so, and playing them through his fingers as if he were lightly massaging skeins of the finest silk. Holding her hair with incredible gentleness, he bent his head down to bury his face in her tresses. With his eyes closed tight, he gently brushed her hair over his face; taking in the smell of it with slow, deep breaths. Maddie was a little taken aback by the strength of his reaction.

'You don't know how many times I've dreamt of doing this,' Greg whispered. 'It smells so good, it feels so good.'

Maddie said nothing in response. It was time for action. She drifted her hands over Greg's chest, then down to his stomach, and then down to the front of his trousers. As she had expected, her questing fingers met with a large and prominent bulge under the zip and the khaki material. She began a lazy stroking, light at first but increasing in pressure as Greg shifted on his feet in response. Despite his interest, which she could feel still growing under her fingers, Greg looked apprehensive.

'Isn't this a bit, um, public?' he asked.

Maddie smiled. 'Yes. That's the point,' she said. It amused her that Greg, normally so self-possessed, was reduced to this child-like state of agitated concern.

'But someone might come along,' he said lamely.

'So?' Maddie asked, undoing his belt.

Greg looked down at her, smiling in bemused disbelief at her forwardness. 'Do you make a habit of this?' he asked.

'Of what?'

'Seducing your friends in public places?'

'Only if they want to be seduced,' Maddie replied. She was now reaching to feel him through his flies. Greg could not quite stifle a low, animal-like groan, and Maddie was flattered to hear it. It signalled the strength of his desire.

'Oh, I want. Very much,' he said, and clamped his mouth over hers in a passionate kiss. She responded with equal ferocity, pressing her body against his and caressing his back and buttocks. With their mouths still locked and their arms wrapped round each other, Greg lowered Maddie on to the ground.

They lay side by side on the rug, kissing deeply and exploring each other's bodies with their hands. Maddie rolled over and pressed Greg back into the rug. He looked at her, clearly wondering what she was going to do next. In response, she swung her leg over him, straddling him at his groin, and her dress rode up her thighs as she did so. Her knees dug into the woollen rug, and she pressed her crotch down against Greg's, feeling his hardness against the centre of her own heat. Maddie's hair tumbled forwards over her shoulders, and Greg reached up to touch it again, before brushing it gently back as he reached for the straps of her dress. He took the fine straps in his hands and gently eased them off her shoulders. Maddie shook her hair as the dress fell down around

15

her, revealing her smooth flawless skin and her small brown breasts with their dark-tipped nipples. Her hair fell forward to obscure the upper part of her body, and Greg reached up and parted her tresses, feeling for her breasts. She gasped as she felt him cup them in his hands.

As she threw her head back, thrilling to his touch, Maddie remembered her earlier thought about Greg: that he looked good enough to eat. Smiling lasciviously, she took his hands in her own and removed them from her breasts, and placed them on his stomach. Greg looked at her curiously, and then, when it became clear what she was about to do, his quizzical expression was replaced by one of intense anticipation.

Still straddling him, Maddie shuffled backwards on her knees so that she was positioned lower down, over Greg's knees. She reached for his flies again. She could feel him straining beneath the zip and, as she undid it, his cock sprang out, brushing against her mouth as she was leaning so low and so close over him. Maddie took his prick in her hand and brushed her lips against the tip. Greg groaned, and reached down. He placed his hands on her head, gently pushing her down in an urgent reminder of what he wanted her to do. But Maddie was not to be rushed. She held his cock and rubbed it across her open lips, gently pulling his foreskin back and feeling the silky skin of his glans. Then she flicked her tongue over the domed tip, before lowering her mouth over him, encompassing him and taking him into her mouth. He gasped at this contact, but she was not yet finished. Flicking him with her tongue, she slowly engulfed yet more and more of his shaft. She felt his cock hardening at her touch, and Greg's hands were now grasping her shoulders gently, trying to make her take the last few inches of his length into her mouth and down into her throat.

Maddie moved her head back again, allowing her lips to slide slowly up his veined hardness. When she had all but drawn back from him, she gazed down at his cock, watching it twitch and jerk in her hand. She felt a rush of power, knowing that his pleasure was at her mercy. It was a gift she could equally give or withhold.

'Please,' Greg said in a quiet strangled voice. 'Please don't stop.'

She took pity on him, and returned to her rhythmic ministrations. It did not take Greg long to reach his orgasm. Still holding her, he thrust his buttocks off the ground, pushing Maddie's head upward as he did so. She could feel him tensing and bunching, and then felt the thick warm spurts of his come jetting into her mouth. He cried out, and fell back against the ground. She kept his penis in her mouth as it slowly returned to a more relaxed shape. Then she slowly licked him clean, enjoying the smell and taste of his fresh come. Greg smiled at her from beneath his half-closed eyelids.

'Where did you learn to do that?' he asked.

'That would be telling,' Maddie smiled. Now it was her turn. Her dress was still draped in a crumpled circle around her thighs, impeding her movements, and so she pulled it up and off and threw it aside in a single swift movement. Then, still kneeling over Greg, she moved back up his body. Her knickers were soaked with the juices of her arousal, and she allowed the dampness to graze over his body as she worked her way upwards, shuffling forwards first on one knee and then the other, pressing herself on to him. She would scent-mark him, lay claim to him like an animal. She anointed his navel, then his muscular torso, then his chest. Greg knew what was expected of him, and desired it also, and he threw his head back against the rug as she positioned her groin over his face.

Looking down at him, Maddie watched him nuzzling into the damp gusset of her knickers, breathing her scent right in. She reached down and pulled her panties to one side, revealing her neatly trimmed pubis and her slick pink quim. She slowly lowered her sex on to his mouth. Greg eagerly accepted it, dabbing her with gentle kisses, before moving inwards to her wet furrow and then to the centre of all her yearning: her clitoris. He gently took it between his lips, and started to caress it slowly, rolling it around and then sucking it.

Overcome by raw carnal desire, Maddie moved her hands to her breasts, and then down to feel Greg's face. She traced her fingers over his mouth and lips as he pleasured her with an increasing intensity. Greg took her clitoris between his front teeth and nipped it very gently, before returning to the incessant sucking and licking that Maddie knew she could not resist for much longer. Sure enough, she soon felt the slow, agonising build to her climax, and it came as a relief when she finally tipped over into the crashing descent of her orgasm, her tender bud still between Greg's lips. She fell forward, catching her weight on the palms of her hands, and gasped and shuddered as her orgasm wracked through her. For a few moments afterwards, she was incapable of movement. Her limbs felt like jelly.

Gradually recovering, Maddie moved off Greg and lay next to him. The two lovers lay in a gentle embrace as the birds sang in the branches above them. They still had all the afternoon for love. Beyond the green screen, Maddie could hear the sound of other people punting down the river nearby, ignorant of what was happening beneath the willow; and she smiled to herself.

During the next few days, Maddie was extremely busy. She had received the go-ahead from Sam's secretary, and was immediately impressed by Sam's way of doing things: she had received clear, precise and businesslike instructions from him about the type of locations he wanted. She knew that she was going to enjoy working for him. Maddie thought with a rueful smile how this contrasted with the shambolic methods of some of the other directors with whom she had worked in the past, and she reflected that perhaps ruthless efficiency was one of the secrets of Sam's success.

Once in receipt of her work orders, Maddie made all her accommodation and travel arrangements, and spent time in the local reference library, researching into Kent: its historic houses, which of the army bases in the county might permit filming on their property, and what ranges of scenery and types of coastal landscapes she could expect to find there. She also contacted the South-Eastern England Film Commission, who provided a lot of helpful information. They held a register of landowners and house owners who were willing to hire out their properties to a film or television production, and made this freely available to Maddie. She made preliminary enquiries by phone, and drew up a shortlist of some twenty properties that she was going to visit.

It was now the day before Maddie was leaving for

Kent. She arrived at the office at just after six that morning, as she had so much to do. An hour and a half later, Maddie heard Freya arrive, but she went straight into her office without popping in to see Maddie. The others came in at just after half past eight: first Maddie heard Polly's light skipping foot-steps up the stairs, then Miles's slow plodding steps, and finally Greg, who always ran up the stairs. She smiled to herself. Something had certainly put a spring in his step recently. The two men worked in an office next to Freya's across the hall but, as the coffee percolator was in Maddie's office, they always came in to see her first. There was the usual routine of gossip to be exchanged, coffee to be drunk and post to be collected from Polly before they settled down to work. Maddie smiled at Greg as he came in, but then put her head down and tried her best to ignore her workmates. She had a lot to do.

Maddie was looking in a nature reserve guide for places in Kent that might provide suitably unspoilt locations, when Polly came in from Freya's office. Maddie looked up. The clock on the wall showed that it was just after nine. Polly was holding an armful of files and papers, and had a pencil in her mouth.

'Freya wants to see you in her office,' she mumbled.

Maddie got up, somewhat peeved that Freya still felt it necessary to give her last-minute briefings when she knew her job inside out by now. Entering Freya's office, she was surprised to see that there was someone else sitting there: a man, probably about thirty-five or so, Maddie guessed. She hadn't heard him arrive.

Freya closed the door behind Maddie, and the

man stood up. He was exceptionally handsome, with dark hair and a lean hungry-looking face. His brown eyes darted over her face, as if trying to read her. He had the type of dark Celtic good looks that Maddie found irresistible, and she found herself entertaining indecent thoughts about this stranger within seconds of meeting him. Freya's sharp voice brought her back to reality.

'Maddie, this is Hugh Shepherd. I don't think you've met, have you?'

Hugh held out his hand, and Maddie shook it, and sat down in the chair next to him. She looked questioningly at Freya. What was all this about?

'Maddie. Mr Shepherd here has a proposition to put to you. Actually, I suppose it'd be more correct to say that he's got something to tell you rather than to ask you.'

Maddie turned in her chair to look at Hugh Shepherd. This was all very strange. He smiled genially at her.

'Hello, Maddie. I've been following your progress with interest over the years, and am so glad to finally have an opportunity to meet you and discuss working with you.'

Maddie was delighted with the compliment, but she glanced across at Freya. Had her boss organised something for her without discussing it with her? That wasn't on.

'I'd better tell you something about myself. I'm a director, but so far I've only notched up a couple of films, which I doubt you've heard of. I'm a good friend of Sam Pascali's.'

Bully for you, name-dropper. Am I supposed to be impressed? thought Maddie. She still didn't understand what was going on.

Hugh continued. 'I'm in pre-production for my next film, *Beneath the Hillfort*. It's a contemporary story, set in Dorset. Like Sam, I'm both directing and producing the film; but unlike Sam's efforts, it's extremely low-budget. Unfortunately, we just couldn't get the backing we were after. We've had to pare costs down to the absolute minimum: I've managed to persuade some of the actors to work for free, and we're keeping the crew as small as we can. We start filming in mid-July.'

Maddie's patience was wearing thin. Unlike his friend Sam Pascali, Hugh Shepherd was not very good at getting to the point. 'I'm sorry, Mr Shepherd, but I'm not clear why you're telling me all this. Of course I wish you the best of luck with your project, but I'll be busy working for Mr Pascali until September at the earliest.'

'Ah. That's what I've come here to see you about. Let me explain. My location manager has let me down. Seriously let me down: he dropped out yesterday, and was due to start work next week. I happened to mention this in passing when I was talking to Sam on the phone last night, and he said I could use you.'

'He said *what*?' Maddie spluttered.

'I need you for eight weeks. You've got three to find the locations, and then I need you during filming to check everything goes smoothly with the location arrangements, and also to perform some other duties.'

'Hang on. I already told you: I can't do it. Your schedule clashes with the period timetabled for *D-Day Dawn*.'

'Sam is happy for you to hand over to your associate, Miles. Miles can undertake the bulk of the work on *D-Day Dawn* and, after you finish working with me, you can rejoin Sam's production for the last couple of weeks of location scouting as Miles's assistant.'

Maddie bridled at this suggestion. 'No way. Hand over to Miles? Work as his assistant? You must be joking. *D-Day Dawn* is my project – Sam specifically asked for me. Why don't *you* use Miles?' she demanded.

'Because I want you,' Hugh said simply.

Maddie turned angrily to Freya. 'Why is Sam so willing to take on Miles all of a sudden? I bet he doesn't even know Miles's work. Well, does he?'

Freya shook her head. 'I don't think so.'

'Has he asked to see any of Miles's work?'

Again, Freya shook her head.

'I don't understand. I've got wads more experience than Miles; and Sam was so enthusiastic about us working together. It just doesn't make sense! Why is he willing to let me go?'

Freya looked down at her desk, and Hugh smiled awkwardly.

'Because I asked him,' he said.

Maddie flared. 'Well you can bloody well just un-ask him, then. *D-Day Dawn* was my job, and my first real chance at the big time. You think I want to pass it up to work on your poxy film?'

'Maddie!' Freya said sharply, but Maddie was at near boiling point. Nothing was going to stop her from having her say. She looked at Hugh, narrowing her eyes.

'What have you got on Sam, that he should do this for you?' she asked.

'Let's just say that he owes me a favour, and it was time to call that favour in,' said Hugh.

23

'And in the process, you screw up my career prospects. Thank you very much, Mr Shepherd. Thanks for absolutely bloody nothing.' Maddie got up and stormed out of the office.

Freya looked across at Hugh. 'Oh, dear. That went down even worse than I was expecting.'

Hugh shrugged. 'It doesn't bother me. As long as she's working for me, I'm happy. I've got the location manager I want.'

'And what are the "other duties" you mentioned?' asked Freya.

'Oh, she'll find out.'

In the meantime, Maddie had stomped back across the hallway, scowling at the closed door of Miles's office as she did so. 'Traitor,' she muttered. She barged into Polly's part of the office and crashed around in a fury, picking things up off Polly's desk, putting them down again and gesticulating wildly as she ranted at the bewildered secretary about Hugh Shepherd's duplicity. After about ten minutes, Maddie's fury had subsided somewhat, although it was by no means worked out.

Polly got up and fixed her a mug of coffee. 'Bad luck,' she said sympathetically.

'Luck had nothing to do with it. It was that interfering little pillock, Shepherd.'

'Oh, I wouldn't call him that. He seemed pretty tall to me,' Polly said.

'Give me strength,' Maddie muttered to herself as she raised her eyes to the ceiling.

The buzzer sounded on the intercom on Polly's desk.

'Polly, sweetheart. If Maddie is with you, can you send her in? And tell her that Hugh has left.'

Maddie shrugged and walked back to Freya's office. She glowered at her boss.

'There's no point in saying anything, Freya. You can't mollify me. I'm still furious.'

'Maddie. Please calm down. Look, I've just spoken to Sam Pascali, and he made it abundantly clear that you have to do *Beneath the Hillfort*. Refuse and not only will you forfeit *D-Day Dawn*, but you'll almost certainly blow any further chance of working with him in the future. You honestly don't have any option.'

'Well, if you woke him up in the middle of the night to ask him that, no wonder he was in a bad mood and refused to do anything about it,' Maddie snapped.

'It's 1 a.m. in Los Angeles, and Sam was fine about me ringing. He works long hours. That had no bearing on his decision. He said that he was honour-bound to comply with Hugh's wishes on this matter.'

Maddie was marching up and down the same track of carpet in front of Freya's desk.

'No doubt Hugh Shepherd won't be paying me the astronomical fee that Sam has offered?'

Freya shook her head.

'Oh, great. So not only do I fuck up my career by working with Mr Shepherd, but I also have to take a pay-cut for the pleasure.'

'Well, he did stress that it's a very low-budget production.'

'Hang on. He's not proposing that I work for nothing?'

Freya laughed uncomfortably. 'No, of course not. But the money isn't that good.'

'And I start next week?'

Freya nodded. She pushed a file across the desk to

Maddie. 'All the details of Hugh's requirements are in here, plus a copy of the shooting script. All the locations need to be within a thirty-mile radius of the Haddon Grange Hotel in Dorchester, where the crew and cast will be staying during shooting. Apparently, Hugh has negotiated a cheap deal with the proprietor.'

'I'll bet he has. He's probably got some dirt on every person he's ever dealt with; lots of little "favours" to be called in.'

'Oh, Maddie, try not to be too cynical. It'll be so much easier for you if you try to get on with Hugh. Remember that you're going to be working with him for the next two months.'

'Don't remind me,' Maddie snorted. She snatched the file from the desk and angrily flicked through it. 'So, let's see what Mr Shepherd requires.' She started to read out the list of locations: 'A maze (high-hedged, yew or box, with a central area at least three metres by three metres); Turkish baths (preferably Victorian-tiled, interior shots only); a furniture store (interior and exterior shots, must sell beds); an Iron Age hillfort; and a pub with accommodation (exterior and interior shots, plus several scenes in one of the bedrooms). The list goes on. Good grief! I'm supposed to find all these, and negotiate and secure the contracts in just three weeks?'

'It's a tough schedule, but I know you can do it. I think you should read Hugh's covering note as well.'

Maddie quickly scanned the roughly scribbled note in Hugh's spidery hand.

'Oh, come on, he doesn't really expect me to keep within that budget? He's mad. What he wants will cost ten times the amount he's specified.'

'It's all there is. There's absolutely no chance of the budget being increased.'

'Jesus, Freya.' Maddie sank into one of the chairs in irritated dejection. 'Let's be honest, here. We both know that some films are low-budget because, even though they're worthy projects, they can't find a backer; while others are low-budget simply because they are such a lousy proposition, such a stinker that no sensible backer would touch with a bargepole. Something tells me that dear Mr Shepherd's film falls squarely into the second category.'

'I don't think you should judge him or his project too hastily, Maddie,' said Freya. 'And you've worked on low-budget pictures before. You'll simply have to economise; use your initiative. You can do it.'

'Well, I'm glad you think so, because I'm not so sure.'

'Try to put a positive face on all this, Maddie.'

'I may have to lump it, but that doesn't mean I have to like it,' said Maddie stubbornly.

'Look. How about I lend you my MG, as a sweetener? I won't be needing it, and think how lovely it'll be driving round Dorset with the soft top down. Go on.' Freya smiled sweetly at Maddie.

Maddie thought for a moment, even though she already knew what the answer would be. Hugh had made quite sure that it would be impossible for her to turn this job down. And the promise of the MG was tempting, after all. Maddie had always admired it, and Freya knew this. 'OK. Thanks,' Maddie finally muttered, grouchily. Then she felt guilty at her churlishness – it wasn't Freya's fault, after all – and apologised.

'Don't worry, Maddie. I understand how you feel. Now, I think you'd better get to it. Hugh has got your mobile phone number, and will be in touch. Don't worry about the arrangements for *D-Day Dawn*. Miles has already taken them over.'

Maddie suppressed an irritated grimace, and left the office clutching the file. She went to the toilet to splash some cold water on her face and to try to calm down. When she got back to her desk, all the material on Kent that she had been working on and all her notes and contact lists had gone.

'Miles came and took them,' Polly explained unnecessarily.

Maddie's anger surged again, but there was nothing that she could do. It seemed that Hugh Shepherd truly had her over a barrel, and she had no choice but to comply with his wishes.

Chapter Two

Maddie was so angry that she left work early. She knew that, if she stayed around the office, she might say something to Freya that she would later regret. Still fretting over Hugh Shepherd and his little bombshell, she wheeled her bicycle up her front-garden path and leant it against the low iron railings between her house and the neighbouring one. She unwound the chain and padlock from around the saddle and secured the bike to the railings. When Maddie had first come to live in Cambridge, she had soon learnt that bicycles were a target much favoured by thieves. This was her third bike in four years, and she was determined not to have this one stolen as the previous two had been. She used to use her car for getting to the office, but it took almost three times as long to drive through the congested streets of Cambridge as to weave past the standing traffic on her bike, and so she rarely used it, choosing to rely on her trusty bike. Her car had sat unused on the street for so long that it now refused to start, and she didn't think it worth her while to get it fixed. At the same time, she couldn't bear to part with it as it was her first car, bought the day after she had passed her driving test, and the sentimental attachment overruled any financial or practical considerations. Now, when she needed a car for work, she rented one.

Maddie lived in a small Victorian terraced house in a quiet road not far from the river. It was a compact house, an old two-up, two-down: the front door opened straight into the living room. Beyond it was the kitchen, and the bathroom was in an extension beyond that. Upstairs were two bedrooms. Maddie rented it with her friend Kate, who worked in one of the many bookshops in the city centre. Today was one of Kate's days off, and Maddie could tell that Kate was already at home – the light in the living room was on and she could hear loud music pulsing through the walls.

She opened the front door and called out. 'Hi, Kate, it's me.'

There was no answer. The music was pounding from Kate's bedroom. Maddie looked up the stairs and could see that Kate's bedroom door was open. Maddie shrugged, dumped her bag on the sofa and went into the kitchen to put the kettle on. Then she had second thoughts and reached in the fridge for a beer. She felt she needed one, after the day's events.

As she leant back against the kitchen counter and took a long pull from the beer bottle, she thought she could hear low moans above the music. She paused, listening until she heard them again. They were coming from the bathroom.

'Are you OK, Kate?' she asked, pushing the bathroom door open. Her immediate thoughts were that

Kate might have slipped on the tiles and hurt herself, or that maybe she was suffering from food poisoning as, despite Maddie's warnings, Kate had eaten a reheated prawn biryani the night before. In her concern, Maddie didn't stop to think whether Kate might be decent in the bathroom, and besides, she and Kate were used to seeing each other in the nude. They would try on outfits together prior to an evening out, and they would often have conversations in the bathroom, one perched on the closed lid of the lavatory while the other took a bath.

What Maddie saw when she opened the door made her instinctively close it hurriedly. But then her curiosity got the better of her and she slowly pushed it open again.

Kate was standing in the shower stall. The sliding door of the shower stall was open and water was spattering over the bathroom floor, but Kate was far from caring. She was leaning back with eyes closed against a tall man, whose blond hair was plastered to his head by the force of the shower jet. Maddie didn't recognise the man. Kate was covered with soapy bubbles, and Maddie could see the traces in the suds where the man's hands had travelled over her body. The man's head was bent over Kate as he kissed her neck. One hand was cupping her left breast, fondling the plump fullness and playing the hard pink nipple between his fingers; and the other hand was slowly, rhythmically working up and down over Kate's crotch. Maddie could see that the palm of his hand was cupped over her pubic hair, and that his fingers were slipping down between the lips of Kate's sex. The man was masturbating Kate slowly and deliberately, and she was pressing back

31

against him, shifting her hips and writhing under the exquisite pressure.

The man looked up and saw Maddie in the doorway, her mouth an O of surprise. Instead of reacting with shame or confusion and breaking free, he held Maddie's gaze as he continued to caress Kate. He was clearly unperturbed by Maddie's presence, and he proceeded to stimulate Kate more ardently, all the while looking at Maddie. Kate's head had now flopped forward, and her eyes were still closed, and she moaned more loudly as the man was bringing her steadily towards her orgasm.

Maddie could not pull her gaze away from the scene in front of her. She looked at the man's legs, firm and well muscled, and the hollow of his haunch, at the side of his buttocks. The golden hairs on his thighs and lower legs were pressed against his skin as rivulets of water ran through them. She couldn't see his crotch, as Kate was pressed back against him, but she could see the side of his stomach, and the edges of his abdominal muscles. His hand was still busily working at Kate's groin, his fingers fluttering in and out of her sex and then rubbing and pressing her clitoris, which Maddie could see now as a hard, raised red bead. Maddie looked away, ashamed.

Maddie was used to seeing Kate naked, but had never seen or thought of her housemate in a sexual way. This new facet of her friend's personality was intriguing. She wondered how Kate would react if she knew that she was being watched, and that her wanton performance was stimulating an unashamedly sexual reaction in her best friend.

The man was aware of Maddie's close scrutiny. He mouthed at her, 'Join us.' Maddie shook her head, but still did not leave. She watched as the man brought both hands down to Kate's sex, spreading and opening her lips with one hand and flicking over her clitoris with an increasing, incessant rhythm with the other.

'You like this, don't you?' he asked, looking directly at Maddie. Kate, her eyes still closed, moaned and threw her head back against him. 'Oh, God, yes, you're so good,' she said. Maddie held the man's gaze. It was almost as if she couldn't look away, as if she were powerless and could not resist the urge to watch. The man seemed to understand this.

'I want to make you come,' he whispered into Kate's ear, still looking at Maddie.

These words seemed to trigger something in Kate. She strained and arched up on to tiptoes, pressing back into the man. She floundered out with one hand, blindly searching for and finding the pole that supported the shower head. She grasped on to it, her knuckles whitening, as she called out, her eyes screwed shut. Her legs were shaking, and her head first jerked right back and then fell forward as she shook and juddered with the power of her orgasm. The man smiled, as if satisfied at a job well done, and looked at Maddie.

'You next,' the man mouthed. Maddie smiled, shook her head and quietly left the bathroom, closing the door behind her. She wanted to leave before Kate recovered and opened her eyes.

Maddie was sitting at the kitchen table, reading the paper, when Kate and the man finally emerged from the bathroom. Kate had a towel around her, and her cheeks were flushed pink. The man had a small towel wrapped around his waist. Maddie could see the tempting bulging contours that hinted at what lay beneath. Kate was surprised to see Maddie.

'Oh, hi, Maddie. I wasn't expecting you home yet.' She giggled. 'Caught red-handed! This is Tony.'

Tony walked up to Maddie and put out his hand. 'Hi,' he said. 'Nice to meet you.'

Maddie shook hands with him, thinking how bizarre this formality seemed, in view of what had gone before. Tony gave her hand a little squeeze. She noticed the beads of water still sitting on his shoulders. 'You missed a bit,' she said, smiling at him.

Kate laughed. 'That's my fault. Didn't dry him off properly – I had other things on my mind. You know how it is.' Kate laughed again and picked up a tea towel, and she didn't notice the look that Tony gave Maddie as she dabbed up the moisture on his skin. Then Kate took his hand and started to drag him impatiently out of the kitchen.

'Come on, let's go up to my room. I haven't finished with you, yet.' She looked over her shoulder at Maddie. 'See you later,' she grinned, and turned to carry on trying to drag Tony towards the stairs.

Tony turned to look at Maddie. 'See you later?' he murmured quietly, the inflection slightly different, making it a question rather than a statement.

Maddie shook her head. She was flattered by his interest, but screwing her best friend's lover was not her style – that was, unless Kate wanted it, and Kate never had. Not yet, at least.

'Have fun,' Maddie said, knowing that she wouldn't see them for a good few hours. When it came to sex, Kate was almost as insatiable as her housemate; and between them, the two women were seldom bereft of male company. Girls behaving badly wasn't the half of it.

Back in the office the next day, Maddie reluctantly decided that she should follow Freya's advice and try to make the best of her time on Hugh's project. Her first undertaking was the same as for any other project: she sat down and read the shooting script, making notes of the precise location requirements for each scene.

Maddie read the script with mounting incredulity. The action of *Beneath the Hillfort* started off as a grittily realistic depiction of the rigours of contemporary rural life, and then veered off at a tangent which became increasingly bizarre. First there was the appearance of a mysterious crop circle; and then, at the film's climax, the three protagonists had an encounter with an alien spacecraft on the top of an Iron Age hillfort. Or at least, they thought they had – it might have all been a figment of their drug-influenced perception. Maddie guessed that this ambiguity in the storyline was a direct result of the finances of the film. Special effects were obviously out of the question, given the meagre budget; and making it all in the minds of the characters, suggested rather than shown, was a cheap way of avoiding such expenses.

In Maddie's experienced judgement, the script was first-class tripe, and it was the sort of project to which, normally, she would not have given a moment's consideration. But of course, her circumstances at the moment were anything but normal. She was hamstrung by happenstance; shunted helplessly along the fixed tracks of someone else's chosen journey into the future. Maddie was frustrated that, for the first time in her career, her situation was totally beyond her control. She didn't want to undertake this job, but she could do nothing about it. Her only way out would be to hand in her notice, and Maddie knew that she couldn't afford to make such a grand, not to mention financially damaging, gesture.

But despite Maddie's annoyance at Hugh, and all her misgivings about the script, her professional pride meant that she was determined to do as good a job as she could on his film. She decided to keep her head down and get on with the job. And so, on a sunny Wednesday morning at the end of June, less than a week after Hugh had come to see her in the office, Maddie loaded her suitcase and carpet-bag into the boot of Freya's MG, and set off for Dorset.

It was a glorious summer's day. Maddie drove with the soft top down, enjoying the warm wind on her face. Although it looked sporty, with its wire wheels and pristine paint job in British racing green, Freya's MG was old and rather tired, and could only manage a top speed of just over fifty miles an hour. Freya had neglected to mention this, but Maddie didn't mind: it gave her more time to look around and take in her surroundings. Maddie could never quite switch off from work, and would always be making mental notes about the scenery through which she was passing: a particular vista, or an unspoilt-looking village, or a clear fast-flowing river, or a meadow full of poppies; they all might prove useful for her future work. As Maddie could not drive at motorway speeds, she chose a slower cross-country route, using the network of minor roads to get her to Dorset.

By late afternoon Maddie finally saw the name she

wanted on a road sign: Winterborne St Giles, about ten miles from Dorchester. She had learnt from previous experience not to trust country signposts, and so she checked her map again, took a couple of turns down some tiny country lanes, and the cottages of the village soon came into view.

Winterborne St Giles was a pretty village, with flint and stone-built cottages, some thatched and some with old weathered-stone roof tiles. Each front garden of each cottage was lovingly tended; and in the centre of the village was a green, complete with duck pond, a large oak tree giving welcome shade and a wooden bench for sitting and taking in the pleasant view. Even the bus shelter, a small wooden open-fronted structure with a thatched roof, was attractive in a self-consciously twee way. Maddie filed away another mental note. This village was another possible location, and a perfect one should a film adaptation of a Thomas Hardy novel come her way; and this was a definite possibility as such films seemed to be all the rage at the moment. Yes, Winterborne St Giles would serve nicely, Maddie thought. Put some straw down to cover the tarmac of the lanes, take down the television aerials and there you are, bang in the middle of nineteenth-century rural Dorset. Little seemed to have changed over the years, and the village was free of the modern developments and refurbishments that usually made her life difficult when working on a period film: there were no uPVC windows, no breezeblock extensions, and no bungalows.

She pulled up outside a flint-built building. The swinging sign over the porch announced that it was the New Inn. This seemed to Maddie to be a bit of a misnomer, as the New Inn was evidently very old,

37

with an uneven and higgledy-piggledy tiled roof, and tiny windows punctuating the flint façade of the pub. The central porch shielded a wide studded door.

It was well past closing time for the lunchtime session, and the door of the pub was closed. Maddie tried it but, as she half-expected, it was locked. She knocked several times, but there was no reply. Frowning, she walked out of the porch and round to the front of the pub. She went up on tiptoes to peer in through one of the small windows. It was very dark inside, and there was no sign of any activity. Despite it being a hot summer's day, a log fire was burning down in the fireplace. Maddie looked through the window for a few moments, but there was no one about.

Maddie rummaged in her bag and pulled out her mobile phone and her notebook. She riffled through the pages until she found the telephone number of the pub and the name of the landlady: Grace Westoby. Feeling vaguely ridiculous, she dialled the number and could hear the telephone ringing inside the pub. She held the phone to her ear as she went up on tiptoes again and squinted into the gloom to see if anyone was coming to answer. She let it ring for a long time before reluctantly cutting off the call.

Maddie turned to see two elderly ladies looking at her from within the bus shelter across the road. They were sitting close together, and Maddie could tell from their steady scrutiny and inward-leaning heads that they were talking about her. She walked straight over to them, and smiled to herself as they registered her approach and instantaneously fell silent.

'Good afternoon, ladies. I wonder if you could tell me where I might find Mrs Westoby?'

'It's Wednesday, dear,' said one of them, and both ladies smiled at her, as if this self-evident truth should be sufficient explanation. Maddie waited for an elaboration. Realising this, the same lady spoke again. 'Oh, you're not from round here, are you?'

Ten out of ten for observation, thought Maddie.

'She's gone to Dorchester market,' the woman offered.

'Well, Mr Westoby, then? Is he about?'

'He's gone with her. She does the buying, he does the carrying.' The two old ladies looked at each other and smiled knowingly.

'Oh. I'm staying at the pub. Is there anyone else around who could let me in?'

'You could try Callum. In the garage over there.' The old lady gestured across the village green to a ramshackle-looking garage that Maddie had not noticed before. Now that she had seen it, she wondered how it could have escaped her attention, and she mentally crossed off the village from her list of possible locations. The garage was constructed, both roof and walls, of sheets of rusting corrugated iron. There was a single petrol pump standing in the small forecourt, next to a couple of battered car wrecks. The large double doors of the garage were open, and one of them was hanging askew, due to a missing hinge. But the open doors were a hopeful sign at least. Maddie thanked the ladies and walked over the immaculately kept green towards the scruffy eyesore.

As she approached, Maddie could hear banging inside. She leant in through the door and called out, 'Hello?'

The interior of the garage was harshly lit by fluorescent strip lighting. The lights hung precariously low over the work benches, and were swaying slightly in the breeze coming through the open doors. The walls were covered with posters for oils, tools, parts and tyres, and also with pictures of topless or naked women. Maddie smiled. It seemed that such decorations were compulsory: every garage she had ever been into seemed to come with its quota of girlie posters. There was a car up on a ramp in the centre of the garage, and Maddie heard noises emanating from beneath it. She called out again, and looked down into the inspection pit. She was met by a head bobbing out from under the front bumper of the car: a young man was grinning up at her. He had short cropped hair and large green eyes, and Maddie guessed that he must be in his mid-twenties. His face was covered by a combination of day-old stubble and smears of grease and oil from the car. Some of the dirt had worked its way deep into the creases around his eyes and mouth, and emphasised his crows'-feet as he smiled up at her.

It dawned on Maddie that, from his vantage point, the young man could probably see up her skirt. She made an effort, but a none-too-convincing one, to draw the material close around her legs. The young man grinned even more, and Maddie instantly knew that he had fully understood the subtext of this half-hearted attempt at propriety. Instead of saying 'don't look there', her action was, in fact, drawing more attention towards that very place, inviting him to look some more. The young man responded by putting his elbows on the edge of the pit, cupping his chin in his hands, leaning forwards and looking deliberately and brazenly up. Maddie hoped that he liked what he could see. Under her skirt she was wearing a tiny pair of thong knickers.

'Hello,' the young man said.

'Are you Callum?' Maddie asked. She hoped that he was, as she knew already that she would like an excuse to have further dealings with this young man. She was not at all averse to an encounter with a bit of rough, every now and then, and this bit of rough was looking very promising indeed. Her question seemed to animate the young man, and she watched as he ducked down under the car again, scrambled out of the pit and came round to stand next to her. He was broad-shouldered and fairly tall, and stood brushing down his oil-covered overalls before grabbing a grimy rag off the bonnet of the car and wiping his hands. Maddie wasn't sure which ended up the cleaner: his hands or the rag.

'I am,' he said. 'How can I help?' He looked at Maddie with an amused expectancy.

I can think of more than one way, thought Maddie, but she smiled at him and explained her more pressing need.

'I'm staying at the New Inn, only there's no one about to let me in. Those two ladies waiting at the bus shelter said that you might be able to help me.'

'Ah. They did, did they? Hang on a mo, and I'll get the key.' Maddie watched as Callum disappeared through a door at the back of the garage. Despite the baggy voluminousness of his overalls, she was willing to hazard a guess that beneath was a fit body. He had that look about him.

'They're not waiting, by the way,' he said as he reappeared with a large and clearly very old iron key.

'I'm sorry?' said Maddie.

'Those two ladies. They're not waiting for a bus. There's only two buses from here a week: one on

41

Mondays to Bridport and the one this morning to Dorchester. Those two old dears sit there all day, every day, and keep tabs on what's going on. Nothing escapes their notice; but if there's nothing going on, they don't let that stop them. They're more inventive than Tom Clancy or Jackie Collins, I tell you.'

'Oh,' said Maddie for want of better reply.

'The locals call them "The Watchers on the Green", although they've got a few other, ruder nicknames I won't mention,' Callum said.

Maddie laughed. '"The Watchers on the Green"? That sounds like the title of one of those old Hammer horror movies.'

Callum grinned. 'Hm, horror, eh? I hadn't thought of it like that before, but now that you mention it, I don't think you're too far from the truth!' He lowered his voice and muttered a stern mock warning. 'Don't let yourself be fooled by their outwardly respectable appearances.'

Maddie was pleased with the way this was going. Callum was fun, and that boded well.

He continued. 'They'll have sussed you out by now: what you're doing at Winterborne St Giles and why. And if we don't come out within another few minutes, they'll probably have decided that we're having torrid sex in here.'

'Oh,' said Maddie again. Perhaps he is thinking along my lines after all, she thought.

'Come on, then,' said Callum, heading towards the door. Then he stopped, turned and regarded her. 'What's your name, by the way?'

'Maddie Campion,' she replied, holding out her hand.

Callum grinned, and nodded down at his hands.

Maddie looked down, and felt foolish for forgetting that, despite his efforts with the rag, his hands were still black with grime and oil. Callum stuck out his elbow at her instead, and grinned as she grasped it and they shook an idiosyncratic greeting. Maddie could feel the firmness of his forearm through the coarse material of his overalls. She was pleased at this physical contact within a few minutes of meeting the man. Very promising indeed.

'Hang about,' Callum said. 'That reminds me. I'd better clean myself up if I'm going to the pub. Don't want to mess it up.' He went into the back room again, and Maddie heard the sound of water running. Maddie was impressed by his thoughtfulness. In barely a minute, Callum reappeared. His hands were clean and he had changed into a fresh pair of overalls.

Callum led the way back to the pub, and asked Maddie what she was doing in Winterborne St Giles. She explained briefly and, as they passed the bus shelter, Callum looked in and greeted the occupants.

'Afternoon, Mrs Rawson, afternoon, Mrs Hughes. This is Maddie Campion. She's an investigative journalist, researching a piece on the infamous Dorset Pensioners' Sex Ring Scandal. I've been filling her in on what little I know, and I think she may well want to interview you both later on.'

'Oh, my, oh, goodness,' spluttered the startled women, their eyes widening like those of two surprised owls. 'Is that the time?' said Mrs Rawson, the lady who had spoken to Maddie before. 'Bert will be expecting his tea.' She stood up and hurried off; and Mrs Hughes followed silently in her wake, though not without sneaking a shifty backward glance at Maddie first. Callum laughed.

43

'There they go: Radio Rawson and her trusty side-kick. Who needs a national broadcasting service when we've got those two?'

'You are terrible,' laughed Maddie. 'What will they think of me? "Investigating a sex ring." Honestly!'

'They were thinking it already, believe me,' said Callum. 'And it's always nice to be able to confirm people's expectations for them, isn't it?'

They crossed over to Maddie's car, and Callum took her suitcase off her as she tried to wrestle it out of the boot, carrying it as if it weighed nothing. He unlocked the pub door and pushed it open, standing back to allow Maddie to enter first. Again she was flattered by his polite manners, and mused that it just went to show the truth of the old adage about not judging a book by its cover. Rough he might be on the outside, but the inside was altogether different.

Callum went over to behind the bar, and pulled out a heavy old-fashioned ledger. He opened it at the page marker, and ran his finger down the entries. Maddie was a little surprised by his familiarity with the workings of the pub.

'Let's see. Maddie Campion. Yup, here you are. Bed and breakfast, a three-week stay. That's good,' he said, looking up at her with a grin. 'I'll have a chance to get to know you better.'

Better and better, thought Maddie, pleased by his interest.

'I'll show you to your room,' he said.

Maddie was a bit taken aback. She hadn't expected this level of service from the garage mechanic. Callum sensed her confusion.

'I should have explained. I'm Callum Westoby, Grace and Howard's son. They won't be back for a couple of hours. I don't live here any more, but I do know my way around at least. I keep a spare key in case of emergencies – you know, like running out of whisky at four in the morning!' He laughed, and then added, 'Only kidding!' in case Maddie had taken his comment seriously.

He picked up Maddie's suitcase and led her up a narrow dog-legged staircase. It opened out on to the middle of a narrow landing, and they walked along the creaking rug-covered floorboards to the room at the far end of the corridor. Callum opened the door and showed her into her room. Maddie was suddenly very aware of the great brass bed in the middle of the room, and wondered what Callum was thinking. Callum put her suitcase down and went over and sat on the bed. Maddie watched as the mattress depressed under his weight. He bounced up and down, grinning at her.

'Very comfy,' he said.

'That's good,' she said. 'I think I'm going to need my sleep. I've got a busy time ahead.'

Much as she fancied Callum, sex with him on the bed was the last thing on her mind. Maddie hadn't made love in a bedroom for years: it was far too prosaic for her sexual tastes. She just hoped that she could tempt Callum into a bit of experimentation, too.

'Well, I've got a car to fix,' he said. 'Make yourself at home. Bathroom's at the other end of the corridor. See you soon.'

She watched as he left the room. There was definite potential there, she felt.

A little later, Maddie had unpacked and settled into her small but comfortable room. She sat on the bed, looking at her diary, and then at the list of Hugh's requirements again. Everything had to be finalised in three weeks, and Maddie was having serious doubts about whether it was possible. She had not only to find the locations, but also to negotiate and secure the contracts with the landowners. Sometimes the landowners had land agents who would placate the tenants on her behalf, but other times Maddie was left to face the wrath of an irate tenant farmer herself: no enviable task when the tenant had just found out that his prime pasture was going to be given over to a flock of actors and film technicians for a couple of weeks, without his say-so. It could all prove very time-consuming; and, over the years, the demands of her work had meant that Maddie had developed a considerable talent for diplomacy and tact.

She looked at her watch. Although it was getting late, she had plenty of daylight left to scout out a few of the possible locations she had in mind. First on the list was the Iron Age hillfort. It had to be a hillfort, as some of the action in the script took place in the deep ditches and high earthen ramparts surrounding such prehistoric hill-top settlements; and then there was the grand finale when the alien spacecraft supposedly descended on to the top of the hillfort. She spread out a map of central and west Dorset on the bed. There were plenty of hillforts to choose from, more than she had expected, and they had wonderfully resonant names: Dungeon Hill, Maiden Castle, Lambert's Castle, Coney's Castle, Pilsdon Pen, Eggardon Hill.

Maddie quickly changed into more practical clothing: jeans and a loose sweatshirt and her hiking boots. There was a knock at the door and, before she could answer, a small, rotund and homely-looking woman poked her head around the door. The woman was wearing an apron over her dress, and her sleeves were rolled up over her elbows. From the amount of flour dusted about, Maddie guessed that she had been making bread. The woman smiled brightly at her. She spoke with a rich Dorset burr.

'Hello, I'm Mrs Westoby. Call me Grace. I got in a little while ago, but I didn't know you were here. Callum's just rung and told me, so I thought I'd pop up and see how you're settling in. I'm sorry that I wasn't here when you arrived earlier on, but I gather that Callum saw to you.'

I wish he had, Maddie thought ruefully. I could do with a good seeing to, especially from him.

Grace continued. 'I want you to make yourself at home here. If there's anything you need, just give me a call. Callum tells me that you're looking for locations for a film – how exciting. I've lived round here all my life, so if I can be of any help, just come downstairs and pick my brains.'

'Actually, there *was* something I wanted to ask,' said Maddie. 'I need to find a farmer with a farm and a large wheat field that he would be willing to let us film in. Can you think of anyone locally who might be able to help?'

'You could try Ben Hudson over at Home Farm. He's a lovely man – very friendly. Give him a try.' Grace took a pencil stub and a small notepad out of her apron pocket and wrote down a telephone number.

'Is he the landowner, or the tenant farmer?' asked Maddie. These small, irritating details were very important.

'Oh, he's the landowner, all right. He inherited it

47

off his Dad, which gave him a real leg up; but he's also done very well for himself. He's a bit of an entrepreneur, I guess you could say. He farms his own land, but he's got lots of other business undertakings – fingers in lots of pies, if you get my drift. Here's his number. Why don't you give him a call tomorrow? I'm sure he'd be most obliging, especially if there's a chance of making some money out of it.'

Maddie thanked Grace, thinking that her hostess's potted history of Ben Hudson was perhaps not the most discreet thing she'd ever heard, and she took the proffered piece of paper, which now had a light dusting of flour. She put it in her personal organiser, and folded up her map.

'Going anywhere nice?' asked Grace.

'I'm off hunting hillforts,' said Maddie with a smile. Grace seemed pretty curious about her, too. Perhaps nosiness was a village trait.

'Oh, that'll keep you busy,' Grace replied. 'Plenty to choose from round here.'

Grace was right. Maddie stayed out, driving from hillfort to hillfort and wandering around making notes and taking photographs until the light started to fade and brought her work to a reluctant close. She arrived back at the New Inn at nearly ten o'clock, and it was only when she stepped out of the car that she realised she hadn't had anything to eat since lunchtime and that she was feeling extremely hungry. She wondered if it was too late to get anything in the bar, but Grace seemed such a kindly person that she was sure she could prevail on her hostess not to let her go hungry.

As she walked into the pub, Maddie was relieved to see that Grace was behind the bar and that Callum was leaning against it on the other side; familiar faces in a mass of otherwise strange ones. Some of the locals turned to regard her as she entered, and she thought she heard 'journalist' and 'sex scandal' among the mutterings. News obviously travelled fast in these parts. She smiled, thinking that Mrs Rawson and Mrs Hughes did indeed live up to their colourful sobriquet.

Grace gave her a warm welcome, and introduced Maddie to her husband, a tall man who was also serving behind the bar. He gave a quick smile and nodded at Maddie but said nothing. She settled on a high bar stool next to Callum.

'Did you have a successful trip? Gather any useful information?' Callum asked with a broad smile and a wink, and in a voice that was distinctly louder than it needed to be. Maddie noticed that, on hearing Callum, some of the locals turned their heads slightly in her direction to listen to her reply.

Quick on the uptake, she played along with Callum. 'Very successful, thanks. I was surprised: there's a lot of them about – more than you might think at first. And I can't get over how old they are. I even took some photos.'

The heads turned back, and more low mutterings ensued, more animated this time. Maddie grinned at Callum and he winked back at her again. Maddie thought how sexy this wink was. It was a secret acknowledgement of their complicity, and gave a hint of the naughty, mischievous aspect of Callum's personality that she was growing to know and like more and more. She had always found a sense of humour a great aphrodisiac.

'Attagirl,' he said. 'Give 'em something to chew on.'

Grace was clearly used to her son's behaviour.

49

'Callum Westoby,' she laughingly chastised him, swatting him on the arm with a bar towel. 'I've heard from Mrs Rawson all about this supposed pensioners' sex ring. You'll get yourself into trouble one day, my boy. You shouldn't tease the locals. They won't like it when they find out that they're being made fools of.'

'Well, they shouldn't make it so easy for me then, should they?' Callum replied, shrugging his shoulders unconcernedly.

Grace turned to Maddie. 'Talking of something to chew on, have you eaten yet? Will rabbit casserole with fresh herb dumplings do you?'

Maddie nodded enthusiastically and gratefully. She could feel the gnawing hunger pangs once more as Grace disappeared off into the kitchen to heat up the food in the microwave.

Maddie swivelled slightly on her stool and regarded Callum with interest. He was looking very different from when she had last seen him. He was wearing jeans and a casual shirt, and he had showered recently – his short hair was still wet and he smelt of soap. Despite having cleaned himself up, he hadn't shaved; and his stubble gave him a rugged, rough appearance which Maddie found deeply attractive. She watched his Adam's apple bob up and down as he lifted his pint glass and drained the last of his beer. This, too, she found appealing in a way that she knew to be sexual more than anything else. Anything that emphasised a man's masculinity appealed to her: a bulging crotch, hard muscles, stubble or that peculiarly male musky smell that emanated from men when they had been working up a clean sweat.

Maddie accepted a drink from Callum, and was

pleased when he suggested that they go and sit at one of the tables in the corner of the bar. Maddie wasn't sure that even she was brazen enough to chat Callum up at the bar right in front of his parents. She sat opposite him across a narrow table which had once supported a foot-operated sewing machine. The word 'Singer' was worked in the pattern of the cast-iron footplate and, just for a moment, as she glanced down, Maddie thought it read 'Swinger'. She laughed out loud, wondering whether this might prove prophetic.

'What's the joke?' Callum asked. His knee brushed against hers underneath the table.

'I was thinking about the pensioners' sex ring,' Maddie dissembled, momentarily disconcerted by his proximity and by the unexpected contact.

'I probably wasn't that far off the truth,' Callum said. 'You'd be surprised what goes on in a village like this.' He rubbed against her knee again, deliberately this time, so that there was no mistaking his message.

With immaculate bad timing, Grace appeared from the kitchen with a steaming plate of food. Alongside the casserole and dumplings were carrots, broccoli and a baked potato. Callum withdrew his knee, and winked at Maddie.

'Hope you've got a good appetite,' he said. 'You're going to need it.'

Chapter Three

The next morning, Maddie was up by six. She had been woken by the noisy birdsong and was too buzzing with nervous energy to go back to sleep for another hour or so. She was always like this at the start of a new job, wondering how it would go, who she would meet and where she would go. As her location-finding work invariably involved activities such as clambering over gates, scrambling on her hands and knees through hedges, picking her way through muddy puddles and cow-pats, or wandering through dark, dirty and cobwebby outbuildings, Maddie dressed in her scruffiest clothes.

When she came downstairs to the kitchen, Maddie was surprised to find that Grace had already beaten her to it, despite the earliness of the hour. The kitchen was a large, welcoming room, painted in a pretty primrose colour. The decor had the effect of casting a yellowy light on to everything, making the room seem even lighter and airier. One end of the kitchen was kitted out with professional catering equipment – stainless-steel sinks and work surfaces, an enormous dishwasher, a large cooker and several microwave ovens; and the other end of the kitchen was a homely, family room, furnished with a solidly built refectory table, several chairs and a Welsh dresser decorated with lots of pieces of blue and white china. Freshly laundered pillow cases and tea towels hung over a clothes-drying rack overhead. Maddie saw that there was a series of signed, framed black and white photographs of film stars from the forties and fifties hanging on the wall. Grace noticed Maddie looking at them and laughed.

'I was a bit star-struck when I was young,' Grace explained. 'And that was quite a while ago now, I can tell you! I used to write fan letters all the time when I was a teenager – sometimes up to maybe ten a week. Occasionally I'd get a letter in reply, but more often one of these photos. That's my favourite,' she said, pointing at one of John Wayne astride a horse. 'Lovely man. A really *manly* man, do you know what I mean? Not like the film stars today – you can't tell the men from the women sometimes. But listen to me going on when I should be seeing to you. Sit yourself down and I'll get you some coffee. Oh, I almost forgot to ask. Did you sleep well?'

Maddie nodded. The silence in the village had taken some getting used to – she was more accustomed to falling asleep to traffic noise rather than the hooting of owls and occasional barks of a fox somewhere in the distance. And contrasting with her firm futon mattress on the floor at home, the mattress on her bed here was so soft and plump that she had sunk right into the bed, lying in a soft hollow as she drifted off to sleep.

'You were getting on very well with Callum

last night,' Grace observed, nudging her guest knowingly.

'Yes, I was, wasn't I?' Maddie laughed.

'I think he's taken quite a shine to you,' Grace said.

Maddie beamed with pleasure. 'It was a pity that he had to leave so suddenly.'

'Oh, I know,' Grace commiserated. 'He's always getting called out like that, usually at the most unsociable times. Still, it pays well, so you won't hear him complaining.'

Breakfast was laid on the large table, and Maddie was bewildered by the choice. After some dithering and plenty of prompting from Grace, she settled for a poached egg, followed by some toast and home-made marmalade. Grace proudly pointed out that the food was all home-produced, apart from the butter, which was from a nearby farm. Even the milk was fresh, and still warm from Grace's pet Friesian cow.

As Maddie ate her breakfast, Grace prepared her a packed lunch even though Maddie hadn't asked for one. She handed it to Maddie, saying, 'I know your type. You're so busy, you don't stop to eat, and that's no good. I don't want you wasting away while you're under my charge. Callum wouldn't thank me, either.'

Grace chuckled to herself as she plonked another piece of toast on Maddie's plate. Maddie looked up to protest, but Grace silenced her. 'No arguing. Eat it all up.'

Grace went over to the sink to begin on the washing up. Maddie watched as Grace started to scrub a frying pan vigorously, and she reflected that her hostess was clearly a close adherent to her doctrine of eating it all up. Grace's ample posterior shimmied with the movement, and the apron strings tied behind her back danced up and down over her buttocks. Maddie was pleased that her choice of the cheapest bed and breakfast that she could find in the area had been such a fortuitous one, for all sorts of reasons.

Breakfast over, the first thing Maddie did on leaving the pub was to ring Ben Hudson. She knew that the early hour would pose no inconvenience to a farmer; and, from the noise on the other end of the line, it sounded as if he were answering from within the cab of his tractor. His soft voice and relaxed manner instantly put Maddie at ease. She spelt out her requirements to him, and she was gratified that he didn't seem to think it was an outrageous request.

'Wait outside the pub. I'll take you to the field that I've got in mind, and then we can go and look at the farm buildings. I'll be right over,' Ben said, inadvertently giving Maddie a vivid mental image of being ferried across the fields while crammed alongside him in the cab of his tractor. Ten minutes later, a brand new Range Rover drove up outside the pub, and the horn parped, causing Maddie to jump. The driver beckoned at her, and she realised with a start that this must be Ben. It was not quite the entry that she had expected, and she was momentarily annoyed that she was dressed so scruffily. She went to the passenger door, and Ben leant across and opened it for her.

'Hello, there. Hop on in.'

'Hello to you, too,' Maddie grinned at him, and climbed into the plush interior of the Range Rover.

Maddie guessed that Ben Hudson was in his mid-twenties. This surprised her, as the land-owners that she dealt with generally tended to be much older than that. Ben's skin was weather-beaten to a deep brown, probably due to a combination of sun- and wind-burn, Maddie assumed. His black curly hair was partially concealed under a bandana, and he wore a gold hoop earring in one ear, giving him a rakish, piratical look. His blue eyes struck Maddie as surprising, given his dark hair and skin. Ben was wearing a scruffy, holed T-shirt and a pair of frayed denim shorts. Looking down, Maddie noticed that his ensemble was completed with a pair of mud-spattered black wellies. This, too, was not at all the conventional image that Maddie had expected. Most landowners that she dealt with were conservative in their dress, and largely seemed to adopt the same uniform: tweed-jacketed, corduroy-trousered and flat-capped almost to a man. Not so for Mr Hudson. She smiled to herself, thinking that Ben was going to be very interesting to get to know. What with Callum, and now Ben, she was looking forwards to her time at Winterborne St Giles with increasing anticipation.

'Glad to see you're sensibly dressed,' Ben said. He had been looking her over too.

'What did you expect me to be wearing? Stilettos and a sheath dress?' Maddie asked, pleased by his approval.

'You're closer to the truth than you might realise,' Ben laughed. 'Let's just say that townies don't always turn up wearing the most suitable clothing. But, thinking about it,' Ben said, slowly looking her up and down, 'I wouldn't complain if you had turned up in stilettos and a sheath dress.'

'Why, thank you!' Maddie laughed, pleased by this unabashed compliment. Then she thought she ought to get back to business. She didn't have time for distractions and flirtatious banter, and she wanted to impress Ben with her professionalism. For Maddie, there was nothing worse than not being taken seriously by others in her work. 'I may be a townie, but I've been doing this job for long enough to know the best way to dress for it. Believe me, this is a smart outfit compared to some I've worn. I once had to scout a sewage farm. That day, I wore an all-in-one disposable plastic coverall which went straight in the bin, the moment I'd finished.'

Chatting as if they were old friends, Maddie and Ben rattled and bumped their way across some pasture and then a fallow field, before arriving at the sloping wheat field. The crop was still green and stood at about calf-height, and the wheat-heads were just visible, forming within the green leaves.

From where they halted at the top edge of the field, the view was stunning. Maddie got out of the Range Rover and stood silently appreciating the vista across the valley to the gently rolling Dorset hills opposite, patterned with woods, fields and hedgerows. She knew immediately and instinctively that this would be a perfect setting for the crop circle scene. The slope of the land meant that the crop circle would be easily visible from the road that ran along the hills on the other side of the valley, an important requirement for some of the long shots called for in the script. The camera crew would set up on the road and film part of the scene from a distance.

Maddie turned to Ben. 'This is perfect.'

'So what are you proposing to do to my crop?' asked Ben.

'We need it when it's ripe, just before it's due to

be harvested. I'm afraid I can't tell you any more – not yet, anyhow. Trade secret, you could say. The director wants to keep it under wraps. He doesn't want any publicity during filming because it attracts sightseers, and they have an annoying habit of getting in the way. I anticipate the damage will extend to about a hectare, no more. We pay the standard rates of compensation for the damage to the crops, and these are built into the location fee that you'll receive. It's all set out in this contract here,' said Maddie, showing him the paperwork she had prepared beforehand.

'Sounds good to me. I'll look at the paperwork later. Shall we go and look at the farm?'

As they drove back to the farm, Maddie explained what she needed for the location shooting: there would be scenes shot in the farmhouse kitchen and a living room, a bedroom, the bathroom, the milking parlour and a barn. She also needed to negotiate the use of one of the tractors for several of the scenes. Maddie told Ben what times of the day the farm would be required, and over how many days. He didn't seem to think it would be a problem.

They drove into Home Farm and Maddie almost laughed out loud with delighted pleasure. It seemed perfect, from the exterior at least. It was clearly a working farm, messy and dilapidated in parts, with a muddy drive, pieces of rusting farm machinery scattered here and there, a tatty old pick-up parked carelessly by the farmhouse door, and with cats, chickens and geese ambling about. The farmyard was flanked on one side by a big old stone barn, on another by various outbuildings and some stables, and on the third side by the farmhouse. The farmhouse was a rambling building, and clearly very old. Ben showed her the inside of the farmhouse first.

Maddie was curious to see what sort of house this man lived in, a man who drove a brand new and extremely expensive vehicle in scruffy clothes and muddy gumboots. Ben led her into the kitchen, a long, low-ceilinged room which doubled up as the living room. It was as messy as the farmyard. There was not a clear surface in sight: every shelf, table, cupboard top and even chair arm was covered with invoices, bills and official-looking letters. At one end was a large sagging sofa. The cats had clearly used it to strop their claws, and the stuffing was hanging out in several places. At the other end was an old cast-iron range and a butler's sink. Washing-up was drying in an old wooden drainer. There was no oven – it seemed that Ben did all his cooking on the range. The kitchen wasn't dirty, just messy, and Maddie was surprised to find that this disarray pleased her, because it indicated that there was almost certainly no women in the house. She was already feeling a certain sort of possessiveness about Ben.

'Will it be a problem filming here?' Maddie asked. 'It's going to be pretty disruptive. They'll probably want to redecorate, or bring different furniture in, or move yours around, at the very least.' She was too polite to add, 'and give it a damn good tidy up.'

Ben nodded. 'No problem. There's just me and my brother living here, and he's away at agricultural college at the moment. Do what you want.'

Then Ben led Maddie out to the milking parlour, where the rows of milking gear hung down, waiting for the afternoon milking session. It was basic, but spotlessly clean. Ben then took her to the barns.

'We've got both types: an old-fashioned stonewalled barn and a more modern Dutch barn. Which are you after?'

Maddie explained that the barn was needed for a love scene in the hayloft, so it had to be the old-fashioned barn.

'Love scene in the hayloft, eh? I've had a few of those in my time. Can I watch them filming that?' Ben asked.

Maddie laughed at his open interest. 'If you're lucky, you might even be able to wangle a bit-part as an extra,' she teased.

'"Bit-part" being the operative phrase!' Ben joked. 'If I get to be in the love scene, I'll do it for free,' he offered.

Maddie laughed. 'I think you'll probably have to join the queue. I'm sure that most of the male crew will make that offer as well.' Grinning, she looked around her. 'This is perfect; exactly what we need.'

'How much are you offering?' Ben asked. Maddie was not surprised by his forthrightness. She had found over her years of dealing with farmers that they were especially good at getting to the nub of any deal. She warily mentioned a ridiculously low price, one which she was sure he would reject. However, it was all that the budget could afford, and if he pressed for a higher fee, she would have to make drastic cuts elsewhere.

'That's fine,' Ben said. 'I'll read the contracts later. I trust you, so where do I sign?'

Maddie was delighted. 'I don't think I've ever negotiated a location deal quite so quickly or painlessly.'

'Glad to oblige,' said Ben with a wry smile. 'Any time.'

'Let me give you my mobile number,' Maddie

said. 'In case you need to contact me about the contract,' she added, but she hoped that he might see through her ploy. She wrote out her name and number on a piece of paper and then tore it out of her personal organiser. Ben looked at it and then put it in his pocket.

'Can I have your number?' Maddie asked. 'In case there are any problems at my end,' she added limply. She was slightly peeved that she had had to ask. Ben borrowed her personal organiser, wrote his number out and handed it back to her.

'You can call me. Any time.' He smiled, placing a heavy emphasis on the last two words. Maddie's hopes began to rise as quickly as they had been deflated only seconds before. This roguishly attractive farmer did seem interested in her, after all.

Maddie's mobile rang just as Ben drove away after dropping her back at her car outside the pub. She fumbled in her bag and pulled the phone out.

'Hello?' she said. For a happy split-second she thought it might be Ben.

'Maddie. It's Hugh. You didn't ring me yesterday. I specifically asked you to ring me every evening with a full progress report on your day's work.' Maddie frowned. She hadn't thought that Hugh would want to be disturbed the previous evening, and besides, she didn't have much to tell him then. And now her first full day had hardly begun, and not only was he checking up on her already, but he was giving her a telling-off into the bargain.

'Well, are you going to tell me how you're getting on?'

Maddie bit her tongue. 'OK. Sorry about last night. I was busy working until very late.' She paused,

61

hoping that this disclosure would make Hugh feel guilty for being so sharp with her. There was silence from the other end; certainly no hint of an apology. Maddie continued. 'I've got the farm and the wheat field sorted; and I've found a good hillfort, but I haven't managed to get hold of the landowner yet.'

'What about the maze?'

Maddie's frown turned into a scowl. He didn't want much, this one. Not at all demanding, no, not in the slightest.

'Make sure you get it sorted soon,' Hugh continued. 'The maze scene is crucial and there's no way I can afford the time or the money to get the props department to build one. We need a maze. Make it your priority.'

Maddie noted that there were no pleases and no thank yous from Hugh. 'Yes,' she said curtly, and turned the phone off. If he rang back, she would say that she had been unaccountably cut off. She walked over to her car and tossed her bag on to the passenger seat. She had already prioritised the location requirements, and planned to spend the day checking out the three mazes in the vicinity, but she wasn't going to tell Hugh that. He would only think that her actions were due to his intervention rather than her own capable professionalism.

Knowing that she would be spending the rest of the day looking round formal gardens rather than rough countryside, Maddie nipped back up to her room and changed into some slightly smarter clothes. She slipped out of her jeans and shirt and put on a light sarong skirt, a cropped T-shirt and a cotton cardigan, and a pair of comfortable leather sandals. She looked at herself approvingly in the mirror: she was casually dressed and yet well presented, and the clothes were practical enough to allow her to check out the mazes in comfort. It was also already a scorchingly hot day, and the light clothing would help to keep her cool.

Outside again, Maddie had to put on her sunglasses to counter the sharp glare of the sunlight. She got into her car, and settled into the warm leather seat. Through her skirt, she could feel the heat that the seat had absorbed, warming her bottom and the backs of her thighs. She started the MG up, listening with pleasure to the deep growling rumble of the engine. Reaching over to her bag, she consulted her list of locations. First stop was Brigham House, a country house not far from Dorchester.

Two hours later, as Maddie drove away from Brigham House, she grinned with a mixture of relief and exhilaration. The maze was perfect for Hugh's requirements, and the owners had been more than amenable: they had seemed genuinely thrilled by the prospect of their property being used for a film shoot; and, as Maddie had measured the interior of the maze, made a plan for Hugh's reference and taken photographs from all angles, they had grilled her about who the stars were, who the director was and when the film would be released. Maddie had not been able to provide much in the way of answers, as she had no idea who would be starring in the film. But, given the budget, it would be no one famous, she was sure of that at least.

After the wheat field and the farmhouse, the maze was the third location that Maddie could knock off the list for certain, and she was pleased with the speed of her progress that morning. She had expected it to take much longer than this. Her high spirits were perfectly matched by the weather: a clear, blue sky and the intense, beating heat of the sun.

Maddie had driven barely five miles when the engine started misfiring. She looked at the fuel gauge, but the tank was still half-full. It was clear that there was something very wrong with the MG. It was losing power, and so she steered it over to a gateway at the side of the road and flipped on the hazard light switch. Maddie's knowledge of what went on under a car bonnet was fairly rudimentary. She knew how to change the spark plugs, check the oil and fill up the radiator, but that was about it. The sun had made the bonnet almost too hot to touch, and she had to wrap her silk scarf around her hand before she could open it. She looked at the engine, hoping that the problem would be something obvious, and with an even more unlikely hope that it would be something obvious that she could fix. She couldn't see what was wrong. Leaving the bonnet up, she tried the ignition again. The starter motor turned over a couple of times, but the engine was completely dead.

'Oh, Freya. Why didn't you warn me?' she muttered crossly to herself.

She had broken down on a very quiet road, and thought despondently that she would probably have to wait a long time before someone came by. Even then, there was no guarantee that they would be able to help her: it might be someone as mechanically inept as she was. She cursed herself that she hadn't renewed her membership with the car breakdown company the previous month. Just her luck. She had been a member for five years and had never called them out, and now that her car was off-road, she had determined that it was all a big waste of money and had let her membership lapse. And now, when she needed assistance, she had no-one to turn to.

Then a mental lightbulb flicked on, and Maddie smacked her forehead with the flat of her hand. How stupid could she get? Callum, of course. He had been called away to a breakdown from the pub the previous night; and she had glimpsed a tow-truck parked behind his garage. She rummaged around for her phone, which always seemed able to hide itself in the deepest recesses of her bag with a wilful regularity. She rang directory enquiries, and was relieved when the operator was able to give her the phone number of Westoby's Garage at Winterborne St Giles.

To her relief, Callum was working in the garage. She briefly explained her situation to him. He was concerned about her, and promised that he would get to her as quickly as he could. Maddie was not overly bothered about being speedily rescued. It was a gorgeous day, and she couldn't have wished for a more delightful spot to be stranded in. The road was on the crest of a ridge of chalk downland, and there were spectacular views of the farmland stretching out in all directions below her. The skylarks were singing overhead, and the sun was blazing. It was so hot that the tarmac of the road had started to melt slightly in the midday heat.

Maddie clambered over the gate and walked a little distance from the car up on to the short cropped grass of the downland. Rabbits had been busy excavating into the soil, and here and there were upcasts of soil and chalk, with scatterings of pebble-like droppings by the entrances to their warrens. A mass of wild flowers grew in among the grass. They were beautiful: small, due to the grazing of the sheep, but

65

worthy of close attention. Maddie undid her sandals, kicked them off and sat down amongst the flowers, peering at their miniature beauty. Delicate dusty blue harebells nodded on wiry stems, and the yellow and orange flowers of birdsfoot trefoil glowed in the brilliant light. Mats of low-growing thyme flowered next to her, and she crushed the tiny leaves between her fingers, releasing the concentrated aroma of the herb. Maddie sighed with contentment, and lay back on the grass. Resting her head on her hands, she watched the skylarks, tiny specks high in the sky.

She must have dozed off for, the next thing she knew, she was woken by a cloud falling across her face. She looked up to see that Callum was standing over her. He was wearing his familiar oil-smeared red overalls and a wide smile.

'Sleeping Beauty, I presume,' he said, looking down at her.

Lying prone beneath him, Maddie pushed herself up on to her elbows. 'What does that make you then?' she asked. 'Prince Charming?'

'Hardly. But I have my moments.'

I'll bet you do, thought Maddie.

'Let's see if we can find the problem then,' Callum said. Maddie was vaguely disappointed that he wanted to get straight down to business, but she scrambled up and put on her sandals, and led him over to the MG, explaining what had happened. He got to work straightaway, fetching his toolbox from the tow-truck and busily working under the bonnet. Maddie stood by Callum and silently watched his progress, admiring the sure-handed way he embarked on the task and his adroitness with the tools.

After ten minutes or so in the searing heat, Callum

stopped to undo the top few poppers on his overalls, and Maddie noticed that small sweat patches had started to form under his arms. She couldn't help looking through the open gap in his overalls at his chest, which was covered with a light fuzz of downy hair. As he leant forward over the engine, his overalls gaped open some more and she could see further down inside: two small, brown nipples pointing the muscular breadth of his chest, and the fuzz broadening and darkening down the centre of his stomach, where it covered a fine set of abdominal muscles. She could just see the top edge of the darker mat of his pubic hair.

Maddie's reverie was broken when Callum looked up at her from under the bonnet. 'Could you try the ignition for me?' he asked, the first time he had spoken to her since starting to work on the car.

As Maddie walked round behind him to get to the driver's seat, she glanced at Callum's buttocks to confirm what she suspected: that there would be no tell-tale lines of his underwear showing through the red material. She was pleased that there were none. It did indeed seem that Callum must be naked beneath his overalls, and this excited Maddie. She felt sure that before the day was out she would have confirmation of this. There was definitely something between her and this handsome mechanic, some unspoken attraction which they were both aware of. Maddie felt the shivering thrill of sexual anticipation.

Maddie tried the ignition, but there was still no response. Callum cursed under his breath, and Maddie came round to rejoin him. She could see the perspiration on his upper lip, and the glistening sheen of sweat over his neck and across his collarbones and the upper part of his chest; and she had the sudden urge to go over to him and lick the salty dew off him. She barely managed to contain herself.

'Would you like a drink of water?' she asked, ferreting in her bag for the small bottle of mineral water that she always carried with her.

'Thanks,' he said, and took the bottle from her. She watched as he tipped his head right back and drank deeply from the bottle.

'I've got another bottle. Finish it off,' she urged him, and he did just that.

'I needed that. It's so damn hot today,' he said, wiping his forehead. He looked down at his overalls. 'Do you mind?' he asked.

'Be my guest,' she smiled at him, inwardly elated at his request, and wondering how far he would go. She watched as Callum undid all the poppers down to his waist, and slipped out of the top half of his overalls. He tied the arms around his waist, forming a makeshift belt to hold his overalls up, and bent over the engine again. Maddie wondered if he was aware how much she had enjoyed this private show. Callum had a superb body, honed and muscular; and the sheen of sweat over it served to make him even more attractive in Maddie's eyes. It was good, honest, clean sweat; man-smell at its most potent and its most sexy.

'Did you say you've got another bottle going spare?' Callum asked.

Maddie nodded and fetched the bottle of water from the small cooler box she kept in the footwell of the passenger seat. She handed it to him, thinking that maybe the radiator needed topping up, and watched in electrified fascination as he undid the lid and, closing his eyes, he poured half the bottle over his head, rubbing it over the back of his neck and then his chest. The water glistened on his skin and soaked into his overalls at his waist.

When Callum wiped the water off his face and opened his eyes, he caught Maddie looking him over. He smiled. 'I'll be a little while,' he said. 'Why don't you go and lie down?'

Maddie wasn't sure if this was a suggestion or an invitation, but did as he said. She walked over to the flattened grass where she had been lying before and lay back again; but she kept a beady watch on him from under her nearly closed eyelids. She was pleased to see that he frequently glanced over at her. After a while, she heard the gentle slam of the bonnet, and looked across to see Callum walking towards her.

'All fixed,' he grinned. Maddie noticed that the water in his hair and on his overalls had completely evaporated in the heat, and he was sweating again. As he approached, he wiped the sweat from his face with a sweeping motion along the back of his forearm and his hand. Maddie could see the light brown hairs under his arms, and the muscles tensing along his side. She felt she could watch him for a long time.

Callum plonked himself down on the grass next to Maddie, and lay on one side, his head on his hand, regarding her. Maddie closed her eyes, waiting for his next move. Finally, Callum spoke. 'It's very quiet along this road, isn't it? No one's come past the whole time I've been here with you.'

'Mmm,' agreed Maddie. She was pleased by his reference to being with her. It might be an indication of the way his thoughts were running. 'It is very quiet, isn't it? It's a good job you came along to help me in my hour of distress. I would have been stranded, otherwise.' She smiled. 'How can I possibly repay you?' she asked archly.

Callum picked up on the loaded question. 'Oh, I'm sure I could think of something.' He reached over and lazily traced a line along Maddie's forearm.

'Payment in kind? Would that do?' she asked.

'I think that would be quite acceptable,' he said, and leant over and kissed her. She reached up and put her arms around his neck, and pulled him closer to her. His back was warm and slippery with perspiration. His lips tasted salty, and Maddie realised it must be sweat. She could hear his breathing loud in her ears, and feel his weight pressed against her. Their kiss lasted a long time, as they explored each other with their lips and tongues.

Callum finally broke free and drew back slightly from her. He gently placed his hand on the bare strip of skin at her midriff. He let it lay still for a moment, before starting to caress a lazy pattern around her navel. Maddie felt that her heart was in her mouth.

'Did you know that I could see right up your skirt yesterday?' Callum asked, gazing down at her.

'Yes,' she replied breathlessly. 'I let you.'

Callum smiled, and bent forwards to kiss her again.

'Did you know I could see down your overalls just now?' she asked him teasingly when their kiss ended.

'Yes,' he replied, grinning at her. 'I let you. Two can play at that game, you know.'

Callum's fingers swirled across her skin in an increasing spiral, soon brushing against the waist of her sarong. His fingertips slipped under the waistband and then away again at each pass. Maddie willed them to dip deeper beneath the material, but they stayed frustratingly out of range. Instead, Callum leant forwards again and kissed her, this time pressing himself hard against her, so that she was crushed up close to him. She could feel the knot of the arms of his overalls digging into the bare skin at her waist. Below that she could feel another, different pressure against her. It seemed that Callum did indeed share her penchant for love in the open-air.

A phone rang, and Maddie groaned. She looked at Callum, and he patted the pocket of his overalls and shook his head.

'Must be yours,' he whispered. 'Leave it.'

Maddie sighed. 'I can't. It might be something important.' She got up and walked over to the passenger seat of the car where she had left her mobile.

She flicked open the mouthpiece of the compact phone. 'Hello?' she asked, knowing who it would be before he had even spoken.

'Maddie. Hugh here. What have you done so far today?'

Maddie laughed. Hugh's timing was impeccable, and his inability to trust her to get on with the job was swiftly becoming all too apparent.

'Oh, this and that. I've found you your maze, by the way.'

'Excellent. Keep up the good work.'

'Oh, I will,' she said, taken aback by the unexpected compliment.

'Ring me this evening. Don't forget. And I'll ring tomorrow to see how you're doing.'

'There's a surprise,' Maddie muttered to herself as she put the phone away. Seeing that she had finished her call, Callum came over and stood by her.

'Come here,' he said, pulling Maddie round to the front of the car. She wondered what he was going to

71

do, but didn't protest. He put his arms around her and kissed her, at the same time positioning her so that the backs of her legs were against the bumper of the car. Through the material of her T-shirt, she could feel his naked chest pressing against her breasts. With a slight movement of one hand, Callum undid the knotted sleeves around his waist, and his overalls fell to the ground. He kicked them away, and was completely naked. Maddie gasped with pleasured shock and, as he drew her towards him again, she felt the narrow strip of her bare skin below her T-shirt come into burning contact: this time not with the rough material of his overalls but with his warm flesh.

He broke contact with her to reach down to the ground for his overalls. Maddie was confused, wondering why he was going to put them back on when he had only just taken them off. Instead, Callum reached behind her and spread them on the bonnet of the car. Then he kissed her again, and she could feel his hardness pressing urgently against her. He kissed her with a deeper passion, forcing her back so that she was sitting on the bonnet. His overalls protected her from the blistering heat of the metalwork.

Callum feverishly felt for the split in Maddie's sarong and, finding it, pushed the skirt apart. He slowly insinuated his hand between her knees, and she willingly let them drift apart under his guidance. Spreading her legs yet further, he moved to stand between them. He ran his hand up the length of her inner thigh; and she felt his rough palm rasping on the soft cotton of her knickers, which were already damp with her excitement.

Maddie looked down to see Callum's cock rearing

up against his stomach. She reached to grasp his swollen and fierce-looking prick in her hand, holding it near the base of its shaft. His foreskin had slid right back to reveal the purply-red dome of his glans, and Maddie could see the lubricant oozing from the tip. She slid her hand up his rigid shaft and gently massaged the clear fluid over his glans with her fingertips. Callum closed his eyes and shuddered with barely repressed desire. Then he placed a firm hand on Maddie's shoulder and gently pushed her right over on to the bonnet of the car so that she was lying on her back. She could feel the heat of the metalwork radiating through his overalls and her clothes, warming her and adding to her increasing sensation of wantonness. She didn't care who might come along, who might see; and neither did Callum, it seemed.

Callum was fired up beyond her expectations, and moved with a speed that both surprised and thrilled her. With one swift movement, he put his hands round her hips and slid her down the bonnet towards him, drawing her legs up around his waist. Maddie hooked her feet together behind his back. Callum leant right over her and kissed her and, as he did so, she felt his prick pressing against her cloth-covered quim. He slipped a finger past the elastic of her panties, and soon found the slick open wetness he craved. He gently slid a finger, and then another into her, and Maddie grasped him tightly. He looked at her with a start: she had a very strong grip. Callum removed his fingers and replaced them with the tip of his cock, teasing her by pressing into her a small distance and then removing it again. Maddie soon ran out of patience with this. She wanted to feel him filling her completely, and nothing else would do. As he moved to press lightly into her again, she tightened the grip of her thighs around his waist and pushed against his back with her lower legs, driving him right into her. Callum quickly got the message, and began to thrust deep in her with an urgent desperation. She could feel him thickening with desire and, as she reached down to touch his balls, she felt his cock throb, and he moaned and collapsed over her in a ragged heap.

After a while, they had both collected themselves enough to be able to speak.

Maddie grinned up at him. 'You were in a bit of a hurry,' she teased.

'I'm not always like that. You drove me wild, and I got carried away. If you'll let me, I'll prove to you that I'm not the insensitive oaf you might think; that I do know what "foreplay" means.'

Maddie didn't mind in the slightest. She had wanted a quickie as much as Callum had. Sometimes the speed and intensity of this kind of love-making was all that she required.

'I might just give you another chance to redeem yourself,' she said, as they arranged their clothing. The road was still quiet, the only sound the song of the skylarks.

'Just say where and when.' He grinned at her. 'I'll be ready.'

Maddie looked at her watch. 'Damn! Look at the time! I had no idea it was so late.'

Callum checked his watch, too. 'I'd better get back to the garage now,' he said. He told Maddie that there was a car that he had to finish servicing by the next day, and it was promising to be a long job – made longer by the pleasant interruption of his rescue mission. He kissed her before getting back into his truck. 'Like I said,' he reminded her, 'just say where and when.'

Maddie smiled, and waved him off, wondering which exotic locale she would choose for their next assignation. Then she got into the MG, and drove off in the opposite direction.

Maddie had some more locations to scout, and it was while she was driving between sites that she had had an idea about the pub and, the more she thought about it, the more she liked it. She pulled over into a lay-by and consulted her notes to make sure. For one of the locations, Hugh required a pub with accommodation. He needed exterior and interior shots, and one of the bedrooms would be used for several of the love scenes. The bedroom obviously had to be big enough to accommodate not only the two actors, but the cameraman, the sound-man and the director, at the very least. The other crew would have to squash on to the landing. The size criterion made her own bedroom out of the question, but she thought that if any of the other rooms in the pub were big enough, the New Inn would be the ideal setting.

Maddie got back to the pub at about five o'clock that afternoon. Grace had not yet opened up for the evening session, and Maddie let herself in through the back door with the key that Grace had given her. She went into the kitchen, where Grace and Alice, the cook, were busy preparing food. Maddie was suddenly reminded of how she and the land-lady's son had been energetically fucking not a couple of hours previously. She wondered if Grace could tell.

Grace looked up at Maddie's entrance and smiled. 'I was just telling Alice about you and your job. It's

75

very exciting.' Alice nodded enthusiastically, but said nothing.

'Could I have a word with you, Grace?' Maddie asked. 'It's a business proposition.'

'Of course, my dear,' said Grace, taking off her apron and ushering Maddie through to the bar. Grace looked at her watch and winked at Maddie. 'I do believe it's yard-arm time.' She motioned Maddie over to one of the tables, and went behind the bar and poured two generous gin and tonics. She came over and plonked herself down in one of the chairs, and lifted her glass to Maddie's.

'Cheers. I like to mix business with pleasure.'

Don't we all? thought Maddie. Your son and myself included.

Grace carried on, unaware of Maddie's indecent thoughts. 'So, what have you got in mind?'

Maddie explained her proposal, and Grace's face was enough to tell her that the landlady was delighted with the idea.

'Well, fancy! My pub starring in a film. What a lovely thought. It probably wouldn't do business any harm either. I read in *Publican's Weekly* that the hotel bedroom used in *Four Weddings and a Funeral* was booked up for two years solid after being featured in the film. You know, the room where Hugh Grant and – what's her name – that American woman have a bit of the other.'

'Andie MacDowell,' said Maddie. 'I think you mean Andie MacDowell.'

'Andie? Do I, dear? Are you sure? Andie. That's not a girl's name, is it?' Maddie wondered how Grace would cope with the news that John Wayne's real name was Marion Morrison, but decided to keep her counsel. Instead, she asked the question which had been on her mind for a bit. It wasn't an important question, but she was curious to know the answer.

'Talking of names, Grace, do you mind me asking why you chose a Scottish name for Callum? You're not Scottish, are you?'

'Good grief, no, with an accent like mine?' Grace laughed. 'No, there's a simple explanation. Callum was conceived in Scotland, on our honeymoon.'

'Ah, I see,' Maddie smiled.

Grace looked at her watch. 'Would you like to see all the bedrooms now, so that you can choose the right one? You're our only guest at the moment, so it's not a problem.'

The two women finished their drinks and went upstairs to look at the rooms. Apart from Grace and Howard's private rooms, there were six guest bedrooms, and three of them were ideal. One even had a four-poster bed, but Maddie wasn't sure if this would be called for in the script. But she knew that things often changed during shooting and, when Hugh saw the four-poster, he might just write one into the script.

Then they went back to the bar and concluded the deal over another large gin and tonic. Maddie felt guilty that the location fee was so small, but Grace was more than satisfied with it. Grace then excused herself, saying she had to finish up in the kitchen before opening time. Maddie sat back, feeling inordinately pleased with herself. It was the end of her first full day, and she already had several of the locations under contract. She decided to go upstairs and take a long relaxing bath. Then she would bring her notes down to the bar and work over her supper and a few drinks. This job was proving to be far more enjoyable than she had anticipated.

Chapter Four

*A*t half past eight that same evening, Maddie was still hard at work, sitting at one of the bar tables. She finished making a few notes and then folded up her map of the area. Then she reached into her bag for her contact notes, and started to make a list of everyone she had to get in touch with the next day. She was very organised; but in this job she had to be. She was so involved in her work that she didn't notice someone approaching her, and she jumped with shock as she felt a hand on her shoulder. She looked up, and was delighted to see that it was Ben.

'Mind if I join you?' he asked. Maddie smiled and grabbed the pile of brochures about local attractions, maps and her notes off the chair next to her so that he could sit down. 'Let me get you a drink,' he offered, and she accepted with pleasure. She watched him as he walked to the bar and leant against it. He chatted animatedly to Grace as she fixed a gin and tonic and then slowly poured a pint of Guinness, leaving it to settle on the bar before topping the glass up. Ben was wearing some faded narrow-cut jeans, which allowed Maddie to view his behind in satisfying detail. The prevailing fashion for baggy jeans infuriated Maddie, dedicated arse-watcher that she was. She regarded Ben with keen interest.

Maddie noticed that the rugby shirt Ben was wearing was the same colour as his eyes, and that it set them off beautifully. She wondered if this was an intentional bit of co-ordination, but then thought that from what she had gathered of Ben earlier in the day – that he was unselfconscious and seemingly unaware of his own good looks – it seemed unlikely. She could see that, now that it was freed from the restraint of the bandana, his hair was very curly, and reached to just below his ears. Not long enough to make him a hippy, but not short enough to mark him out as a respectable member of the landowning establishment. Ben clearly had his own way of doing things, unconcerned by what others might think of him, and Maddie liked him all the more because of that.

Maddie was pleased that Ben had sought her out, not least because, when she had casually enquired about him earlier that evening, Grace had told her that he didn't often come in to the New Inn, preferring to drink in the pub in the next village.

'Don't know what he sees in it,' Grace had sniffed. 'It's a rough sort of place. All sorts of shady characters go in there, so I've heard.'

Maddie hoped that Ben's sudden interest in the New Inn was down to her own presence there. She shook her head in bemusement, thinking that she had only been at Winterborne St Giles for just over a day, and she had already become involved – to a greater or lesser degree – with two attractive but very different men. Callum was good humoured and straightforward; Ben somehow darker, more complex. She felt she already knew Callum inside out, but that there was still a lot to discover about Ben, and not just sexually.

Ben turned and walked back towards her with a drink in either hand, and smiled at her when he saw that she was looking at him. 'Have you eaten yet?' he asked, placing the drinks on the table and sitting down next to her.

Maddie shook her head. 'No, not yet.'

'Wanted to get your work out of the way first – very commendable. Would you like to come out for a meal with me? I know a great little restaurant in Beaminster – it won't take long to drive over there.'

Maddie beamed with pleasure. 'I'd love to. Give me five minutes to get changed into something a bit smarter.'

Ben looked down at his own clothes and laughed. 'I've hardly made an effort, so don't feel you have to on my account.'

Maddie grinned, and got up from the table. 'Back in five,' she murmured, and hurried up to her room. She quickly sorted through her clothes, trying to decide which she was going to wear. She was desperately attracted to Ben, and hoped that something might happen between them. Things might move a little more quickly if she dressed for the part, and so she chose a white body with a scoop neck, over which she wore a pale blue silk shirt which she left undone; and a pair of khaki deck chinos. Not so smart that Ben would feel underdressed, but sexy enough. The body was fairly clinging and Maddie wasn't wearing a bra underneath. Ben couldn't fail to notice that, she thought with a smile, giving her nipples a little tweak through the material to pucker them up. She threaded a narrow leather belt through the loops in the chinos and cinched it in round her slender waist, and then gave a quick turn in front of the mirror. Satisfied by what she saw, she went back down to the bar.

Ben stood up as Maddie approached the table. 'You look great,' he said, slowly looking her up and down. She blushed with pleasure. 'Let's go,' he said, guiding her out of the pub with a hand placed on the small of her back. Maddie was acutely aware of the pressure of Ben's hand, and could sense exactly where each finger was: even where the ball of his thumb rested against her.

Ben opened the passenger door of the Range Rover and helped her in to the high vehicle, offering her his hand to steady herself. Maddie felt this contact even more keenly. His palm was rough and, as she placed more of her weight on his hand as she climbed up, she felt him tense and support her effortlessly. His fingers felt so much larger than hers. He gave her a little squeeze just before he let go of her hand. Maddie was glad that it was dark and he could not see her blushing like a love-struck and inexperienced teenager.

Maddie could feel a sexual charge, a tension between her and Ben, and almost everything he said to her was spoken with a knowing smile or carried some double meaning. It was as if he was testing her, to see what her reaction would be, to see whether she would rise to the bait. Maddie enjoyed parrying his questions with equally ambiguous answers, not letting him know for sure whether she was genuinely interested or merely teasing him. She enjoyed this kind of flirtation.

Ben drove at great speed down the twisting country lanes, so fast that Maddie was more than a little concerned. He clearly knew the roads well, but she was worried that they might meet another vehicle coming just as fast in the opposite direction along the narrow lanes. Ben seemed to sense her alarm, as he slowed down to a more sedate pace and apologised for alarming her.

Beaminster was a pretty town, and the restaurant was just off the main market square. Ben threw the Range Rover into a parking bay and, as Maddie got out, she saw that it was parked over two bays and was not fully pulled in. Ben seemed to have a very casual attitude to most things, and she liked this. If he was casual and devil-may-care in his living, she wondered if this attitude might also extend to his loving. The thought excited her.

Ben held the restaurant door for her, and they entered a darkly lit but welcoming room. The owner clearly knew Ben as a regular customer, and greeted them both warmly.

Over the meal they talked about many things, including Ben's farming and other businesses. It transpired that he also dealt in architectural salvage, buying up and selling old windows, roof tiles, fireplaces and doors: in fact, just about anything that could be removed from old houses before they were demolished or refurbished. He sold the pieces on to a dealer and made a tidy profit in the process. He intimated to Maddie that he also had several other, less acceptable business activities, but refrained from elaborating on the details. Maddie was quite relieved by this, as she didn't want to know. She had a feeling that, whatever these activities were, they almost certainly weren't legitimate. Maddie told Ben all about her work and how she had first got involved in location scouting, and explained the circumstances that had brought her to Dorset on this job.

'Am I right in thinking that you don't much like Hugh?' Ben asked, having heard her story.

Maddie laughed. 'Let's just say I'm about as keen on Hugh as I am on the idea of having my teeth pulled out one by one, with no anaesthetic. We didn't exactly get off to a good start, but he could have worked at getting me on his side. He hasn't made the slightest effort to be nice to me, and that riles me. It makes me antagonistic in response. I don't expect him to flatter me, but a little ordinary, everyday civility would be nice. But then again, I don't think the man knows the meaning of the word "civil".'

'Well, if you ever feel that he's getting to be too much for you, you know where you can come for comfort and a cuddle.' Maddie wondered if this was the nearest she was going to get to an unambiguous declaration of intent. Ben reached across the table and gently stroked the back of Maddie's hand. She sensed from Ben's body language, his gestures and his conversation that he was interested in her, but it seemed that he just wasn't going to make a move on her yet. She could wait.

Grace had clearly noticed her guest's departure from the pub with Ben the previous night, as she quizzed Maddie over the coffee and croissants that she served up for breakfast.

'You seemed to be getting on very well with Ben, yesterday evening. I won't tell Callum, if you're not going to. Next time that errant son of mine rings, I'll keep mum.' Then Grace laughed, amused by her unintentional pun.

Maddie was bemused. 'Don't tell me he telephones you when he only works a stone's throw away from here?'

'No, Maddie dear. He's gone away. He went off last night, up to some car show in the Midlands and then on to Scotland after that to see an old friend. He'll be away for a while – I've no idea how long for, as you never can tell with Callum. It's no way to run a business, but his customers all seem very understanding. They're far more loyal to him than I'd be if I were a customer of his.'

Maddie felt a momentary pang of jealousy. Callum hadn't told her he was going away, and she wondered who this old friend was. But then, she realised that this was an unreasonable emotion. After all, they had made no demands on each other, and she had spent the previous evening, albeit a chaste one, with another man.

Her feelings must have shown on her face, as Grace spoke up. 'What's the problem? Can't you make your mind up between them?'

Maddie was amused by Grace's good-natured maternal interest in her son's love life.

'They're both lovely men. Do you think I'm terrible?' Maddie wondered how Grace was going to react.

'Good grief, no. What a nice position to find yourself in, with two men after you at the same time. I'd have done the same when I was in my prime, if there had been the, you know, opportunity without consequence in those days. I think you should go ahead, play the field. Heaven knows, you're only young once.'

'And you're not cross with me on Callum's behalf?'

'Maddie, my dear, I'm his mother, not his keeper. He's a big boy now, and can look after himself. Just as long as no one gets hurt, you do what you want.'

Maddie smiled, wondering if she ever would get the opportunity to do exactly what she wanted with Callum and Ben. And as for Callum being a big boy ... Then she censored her thoughts. She knew that Grace couldn't read her mind but, even so, entertaining such thoughts when Callum's mother was sitting not four feet away seemed improper and made her vaguely uncomfortable.

Maddie made her excuses, and collected her bag from her room, ready to start another day's scouting. She had foregone her scruffy outdoor clothing for a light, summery dress and sandals. The MG roared into life, and it seemed that Callum had fixed whatever the problem had been. Funny, she hadn't thought to ask what had been wrong at the time. Maddie smiled, remembering the feeling of the hard metal of the bonnet, cushioned a little by Callum's overalls against her back; and the song of the skylarks overhead as they had made love.

But a little later, as she rattled along the country lanes after visiting a small village school, the first location of the morning, Maddie started to get more and more frustrated with the car. She had a lot of travelling to do that day and the MG was proving painfully slow. She was starting to think that borrowing Freya's car had been a serious mistake. It was slow and had already proved itself to be unreliable – the last thing she needed when she was working to a tight schedule. She would do much better to hire a cheap car and charge it to the project.

Knowing that Hugh's tight reins on the finances wouldn't allow her to make this decision without referring to him, she decided to ring up Hugh and get his go-ahead. It was best to do things by the book so as not to antagonise him, she thought.

Maddie pulled over into a layby to make the call. Hugh's phone rang a couple of times, and then his voice snapped on the other end of the line. 'What?'

Nice phone manner, Hugh, thought Maddie, before she spoke. She wondered if his phone had displayed the caller's number, making him terse because he already knew it was her. Probably not, she mused. She sensed that he was like that with most people. Maddie greeted him as cheerfully as she could manage, and then carefully explained her situation to him. She told him that she was wasting a lot of time because the vehicle was so slow and unreliable, and asked if she could rent a car on the film's budget. This was not such an unusual request, as she had frequently charged hire cars to the projects she had worked on in the past.

'No,' Hugh replied curtly.

'I'm sorry?' Maddie wasn't sure that she had heard him correctly.

'The answer's no.'

'But Hugh, it's a false economy. Think of the amount of time I'm wasting. I could get so much more done with a faster car. Even the cheapest hire car is bound to be faster and more reliable than this one.'

'That's your problem,' said Hugh, and the line went dead.

Well, sod you, too, thought Maddie angrily. She sat, trying to calm herself down by closing her eyes and telling herself not to allow Hugh to get to her.

She thought how sharp the contrast was between Hugh's attractive appearance and his deeply unattractive personality.

Once she had calmed herself, Maddie got on with her work. The MG was her mobile office, and she would often park and make calls in between appointments and journeys to locations. She had a lot of calls to make, enquiring about the possibility of using locations, organising meetings and confirming details. She reckoned that usually, for every location she was after, she would make enquiries about an average of some five or six different ones before she got lucky. Today she was on the trail of a furniture store selling beds that would be willing to allow filming on the sales floor. She knew that this was likely to be a tricky one to organise, as filming would disrupt the store and adversely affect selling. One solution would be to film at night, after the store had closed. She had a list of stores in all the market towns within a thirty-mile radius of Dorchester – Hugh's prescribed travelling limit – and there weren't that many.

Half an hour later, she had exhausted her list. A lot of the stores didn't sell beds, saying it was too specialised a market; and, of those that did sell beds, most had refused permission outright. The only possibility was a store in Bournemouth, but the manager of the store was away on holiday and the assistant manager didn't feel that he could authorise such a deal in her absence. Maddie made a note to visit the store the next day to check that it was suitable, and arranged an appointment with the manager as soon as she returned from her holiday. Maddie was fretting as, if the store refused permission to film, she would have a problem in finding another. Still, that was her job, and she was sure something would come up. It usually did.

Once again she tried the number of the man who owned the land on which the hillfort stood. She had been ringing his number regularly, but he was always either engaged or not answering the phone. To her surprise, this time the phone was answered. Maddie explained her proposal, and the man refused point blank even to contemplate allowing filming on his land. This was a great blow to Maddie. His hillfort was by far and away the most suitable of all those she had looked at. She knew there were more that she hadn't yet been to, and she sighed. There was nothing for it; she would have to start looking again. But not right away – she had business in Bridport, checking out the High Street on its market day as a possible location, and talking to the local officials to arrange permits, access and other details.

Maddie settled back in to the leather seat of the MG as she drove towards Bridport and looked around her. Dorset certainly was a beautiful county, and the road from Dorchester to Bridport ran through some stunning scenery, part of it running along a high ridge. From the ridge, Maddie could see for miles. To her left, beyond the hills, was the sparkling blue of the sea, to her right was the lush and rolling greenery of inland Dorset, and in front of her were the distant hills of Devon.

Maddie shifted slightly on the warm seat and looked down. Her short cotton floral print strap dress had ridden up her thighs as she was driving, and with each gear change and gust of the wind it seemed to slip higher up. She was going to pull it down again, but then thought better of it. It was nice to feel the cooling breeze on her legs, and she also liked to look at them. She had good legs, toned and bronzed by exercise and regular sessions on the sun bed at the gym. She knew it was narcissistic, but it gave her pleasure to view herself like this.

The road turned into a dual carriageway, and Maddie saw in her rear-view mirror that, behind her, a truck was accelerating to overtake. She could see that it was a cab unit with two men inside and without its trailer, and knew that it would be capable of going much faster than she was. As the cab drew level, she glanced up and saw that one of the men was leaning out of the passenger window, looking down at her. She smiled up at him. The man turned to his right and said something to the driver and, instead of overtaking her, the cab kept the same speed as her car. They drove parallel for a little while before Maddie looked up again. The man in the passenger seat looked down and shouted above the noise of the engines and the wind.

'Nice legs. Want to show me some more?'

What the hell, thought Maddie. I'm never going to see him again. Let's make his day.

She looked up and smiled again, and then took her left hand off the steering wheel and placed it on the hem of her dress. She slowly started to draw the dress upwards, shifting on the seat to move her legs slightly apart as she did so. She looked up again. The man was staring down intently.

'Go on,' he shouted to her. 'More.'

Maddie hitched her dress up a bit further. Looking down, she could see that the white gusset of her knickers was just visible. She could feel herself dampening. The man was cheering her on now.

Emboldened, she slipped the middle finger of her left hand between her legs and rubbed it gently against the soft cotton of her knickers. She could feel the dampness against her fingertip.

'Jesus Christ,' she heard the man shout above the noise. She slipped her finger lower, feeling the contours of her sex against the cotton – the slight furrows between her outer and inner lips, and the deeper, damper furrow at the centre. She lifted her damp finger and sucked it, turning her head to look at the man. It tasted of clean freshly washed cotton and just a hint of her own distinctive taste. The man was thumping the side of the cab door with the flat of his hand. 'Go on. Do it. Do it to yourself.' Maddie noticed that he had tattoos up his arm.

Maddie was turned on, but she knew this was only partly due to the attentions of the trucker's mate. She had been seriously frustrated by her lack of progress with Ben the previous night. He had shown her, in lots of little ways, that he was interested in her, but had failed to capitalise on it. And she too had held back from making the first move. Their flirtation had continued all night, becoming more and more explicit, but nothing had happened. Thinking of Ben, she slid her finger back to the warm damp cotton, and gently wormed her finger under the side of her knickers. She slowly slipped it towards her opening, which she knew would be slick and hot to the touch. She rubbed her finger gently over the slippery wetness, and then brought it up to her hard pulsing clitoris. But this was too much. There was no way she could control the car while she was having an orgasm. Maddie smiled up at the man once more, removed her finger and brought it up to her mouth, slowly pressing it between her lips.

'You beautiful, dirty tease,' he shouted at her.

Maddie looked ahead. The dual carriageway was

ending. She took her foot slightly off the accelerator, allowing the MG to slow down so that the lorry could easily pull in front of her. Looking in her mirror, she could see a long queue of traffic behind the lorry, the drivers clearly annoyed that it had been blocking their passage. The car immediately behind the lorry was flashing its lights. The lorry drew away from her, and Maddie laughed to herself. That would give them a story to tell at the next truck stop.

She drove into Bridport, down the main street along which the market stalls were ranged, and turned left into another street, following the signs for a car park. She parked and wandered back up South Street, looking at the stalls that lined this road too. She stopped by one that sold second-hand tools, fascinated by the gleaming polished brass on display and wondering what most of them were for. Then she walked on, following the instructions she had been given about reaching the council offices.

Four hours later, Maddie was pleased with the way the meeting had gone. After an extensive walk-about round the town with the official, and more time spent explaining her requirements, she had secured permission to film on the market day, and the town-council official had waived the fees as he felt that it would be positive promotion of the town for it to appear in a film. Maddie wondered whether he might think so had he seen the script; but she decided not to say anything. She had a job to do, after all. Any misgivings about the film's artistic merits were extraneous to that.

Maddie's mobile went just as she was walking back to the car park. She had a feeling that it was going to be Hugh. She answered brusquely, and was surprised to find that her caller was Ben instead.

'You sound grumpy. Everything all right?'

'Yes,' she sighed. 'Well, no, not really. My hillfort man has refused permission to film. His was the only one I've seen that fitted the bill closely enough. Hugh isn't going to be very pleased.'

'Have you checked out Dragon Hill?' Ben asked.

'No. I've not even heard of it. Where is it?'

'About eight or nine miles from Winterborne. It's on land owned by Simon Rayner, a friend of mine. I don't think he'd object to filming – anything to make a few extra quid. Want to go and have a look?'

Maddie whooped with delight. 'You star, Ben. You lovely, lovely man. Give me directions and I'll meet you there.'

Forty minutes later, Maddie pulled the MG up on to the road verge behind Ben's Range Rover. He got out and came over to her, and she noticed that he got a good look at her legs as she was undoing her seat belt.

'Yeah, I know,' she laughed. 'So much for being appropriately dressed for the job.'

'I'm not objecting,' he said, looking some more. 'I'll just have to make sure I'm behind you when you're climbing up the hill.'

Maddie laughed at the flattering rudeness of his comment and gave him a playful push. 'It's not that short,' she said, pleased by the contact.

'Short enough,' he replied with a smile. 'Come with me.'

Maddie put her mobile and her notebook into the small handbag she always carried in the depths of her larger bag, and slung it diagonally over her shoulder. The strap settled between her breasts and pressed the material of her dress closer to her, emphasising the shape of her breasts. Maddie was pleased with this accidental effect, and hoped that Ben had noticed. He was gazing up at the hill, however.

Maddie walked over to him and stood by his side. Ben was much taller than she was and, although she was not a short woman, she felt petite next to him. She coughed to attract his attention and quietly announced that she was ready. Ben looked down at her, smiled and started off up the path. He led her through a meadow and then up a narrow bridlepath that wound its way up the side of the hill through some scrubby bushes. The path was fairly overgrown and Ben had to hold back the branches of the black-thorn, brambles and dog roses while Maddie ducked around and under them. The ground was uneven where horse riders had churned up the ground when it was wet in the spring; and in the hot parched weather of the previous months, the ground had set to the consistency of concrete. It was hard work on Maddie's feet, as her sandals offered her ankles no support; and small pebbles kept rolling in under her feet, causing her to wince as they dug into the tender flesh of her soles. Ben saw that she was lagging further and further behind. He stood, hands on hips, shaking his head in amusement as he watched her catch him up.

'What was that you said to me when we first met about knowing the best way to dress for the job?' he asked.

Maddie smiled at this gentle teasing. 'Oh come on, that's not fair. When I got dressed this morning, I thought I was going to spend my day at a school, in Bridport and then checking out furniture stores, not clomping up another bloody hillfort.'

'OK, point taken.'

'My feet are killing me,' she muttered as she drew level with him.

'Want me to carry you, my poor wounded little lamb?' Ben asked facetiously.

In for a penny, in for a pound, thought Maddie. 'Yes, please,' she replied.

'OK, then,' Ben laughed, and turned so that his back was to Maddie. 'Piggyback,' he said, standing still, bending forward slightly at the waist and stretching both arms out behind him. Maddie grinned at the success of her ploy and, placing her hands on Ben's shoulders, she jumped up on to his back. She could feel his shoulder muscles under her hands, strong and solid. He crooked his arms under her knees, hitched her further up on to his back, and set off.

Ben walked briskly, bearing her weight with no trouble. Maddie sat back at first, not wanting to seem over-intimate; but soon she found it more comfortable to lean forward and rest her chest against his back, her arms loosely crossed about his neck as she looked over his right shoulder. He smelt good, and she was very aware of her whole body pressed against his. She hoped that he was feeling this, too. She could feel that her dress had ridden right up her thighs, and could also feel the coarse wiriness of the hairs on Ben's arms against the tender skin behind her knees. It tickled her and she squirmed slightly. This had the unintentional effect of rubbing her crotch against his back. Maddie froze with embarrassment, thinking that Ben might interpret this as some kind of unsubtle come-on, but he didn't appear to notice – or, at least, he pretended not to if he had. She covered her consternation with chat.

'Do you know why it's called Dragon Hill?' Maddie's face was so close to his that she could see the sun-bleached tips of his dark eyelashes and the fine downy hairs on his ear lobe.

Ben turned his head to one side to answer, and it brought his lips enticingly close to hers. She could smell a faint hint of mint, maybe the trace of toothpaste or chewing gum, on his breath. 'There's some old legend that a slumbering dragon is supposed to lie inside it,' he explained.

They continued for a little while in silence, and every now and then Ben would give a little upward jog with his arms to shift Maddie further up his back. He adjusted his grip on her so that now his hands were holding her behind the knee, partly encircling her leg. She felt this close contact of his flesh on hers, but more immediately she was focused on that small area of her crotch that was pressed against him; and the gentle up-and-down movement as Ben strode steadily up the path was adding to the concentration of all her sensations in that particular and very sensitive part of her body.

The path steepened as they neared the top of the hill. Maddie could feel herself slipping down Ben's back more quickly than before.

'Excuse me,' said Ben and, before Maddie had a chance to ask what it was that she should excuse, he stopped, hitched her up more powerfully than previously; and, as she settled down his back, he caught her behind in his hands.

Maddie gasped. Ben's hands were below the short skirt of her dress, so that there was only the tiny scrap of her knickers separating her flesh from his. She could feel his hands grasping her buttocks gently, the wide span of his hands covering them easily. It was such an intimate contact, but undertaken so matter-of-factly, that Maddie didn't want to comment on it, lest Ben be acting quite innocently. She didn't want to offend him, by accusing him of groping her; or, by that same accusation, make him think that she was some smutty-minded trollop.

I may well be, she thought to herself with a grin, but he doesn't need to know that yet. Perhaps he likes them virginal and pure instead. From what Maddie had learnt of him in the short time they had been acquainted, Ben certainly gave out the signals that he was more than attracted to her, and so she hoped to herself that his actions were deliberate. She also hoped he liked what he could feel.

Eventually the path opened out, and Maddie could see that they were almost nearing the summit. The wave-like earthworks that surrounded the crest of the hill were very impressive, and she wondered why this hillfort hadn't been mentioned in any of the sources she had consulted when she had been doing her preliminary research.

'Shall I put you down now?' Ben asked.

Maddie could have happily stayed on Ben's back for the rest of the day. She had not been this close to him before, physically at least, and she didn't want it to stop. 'Only if you're getting tired,' she replied. 'I'm enjoying this.' She stretched out her arm to indicate the view, but hoped that he might pick up on another meaning.

They followed the path round to one of the entrances through the massive grass-covered earthworks: a causeway which twisted through three sets of banks and ditches. Only when they finally reached the flat ground in the interior of the hillfort did Ben stop and gently lower Maddie to the ground.

'Let's walk over the other side,' Ben said. 'There's a great view.'

The grass was spongy beneath Maddie's feet, and an alarmed flock of sheep scattered as they approached. Maddie could see the dips and hollows in the ground surface that marked the site of the Iron Age huts which had once clustered on this exposed hilltop.

'Wow,' was all Maddie could say. The view from the hilltop was stunning. She could see the silvery sheet of the sea in the distance, and the patchwork of woods and fields stretched out below her, each field rimmed with a green strip of hedgerow. It was a perfect landscape, so different from the flat, prairie-like fields of the fens near Cambridge. There the fields were massive, bounded only by drainage ditches, and the landscape practically treeless: so unlike the small, intimate landscape in front of her now. It called out to her to come and explore, to wander through the meadows and dappled woods, across the shallow, meandering streams and past the hedgerows busy with butterflies and birds. Maddie sighed with contentment. She walked right to the edge of the ramparts and looked down. The inner rampart was the highest of the three, and the depth of the ditch below her was all the more staggering when she reminded herself that this had all been dug out by hand and piled on to the banks, over two millennia ago, and that the ditch had silted and was a fraction of its original depth.

'This hillfort would be great,' she said. 'There's only one problem. Getting all the filming gear up here is going to be a real drag.'

'There's a farm track that runs up the other side,' Ben said.

'You mean we could have driven up here? We could have saved quite a bit of time,' said Maddie, slightly peeved that Ben had failed to mention this. It would have saved her sore feet as well as time.

'Yes, but it wouldn't have been nearly so much fun, would it?' Ben looked at her and smiled knowingly.

'True,' she acknowledged.

'So, what do you reckon?' asked Ben.

'I think this will be perfect. Thank you so much. You've saved my skin.' She went up on tiptoes and kissed him on the cheek. Her lips grazed his rough chin, where the small prickles of his stubble were emerging. She was still taken aback when he turned his face, searching for her lips with his own. As they kissed, a gentle breeze blew up, ruffling Maddie's hair and the light cotton of her dress.

Ben broke the kiss, and looked down at her.

'How are your feet? Sore?'

Maddie nodded.

'Let me have a look at them,' Ben said. He took her by the hand and led her over to where a wind-blasted hawthorn tree was growing on the inner earthwork. He sat on the slope of the bank beneath the tree and pulled her down next to him. Then he reached over and undid her sandals.

'Lie back,' he said, taking her left foot in his hand. Maddie didn't need to be told twice. She lay back and closed her eyes, listening to the skylarks overhead and feeling the gentle, soothing pressure as Ben massaged her foot. He worked his thumbs over her heels, then the tender skin of her arches, and then the balls of her feet, before attending to her toes, one by one. He lightly rubbed them before sliding his fingers between her toes, one of Maddie's many secret sensitive spots on her body. She shifted slightly, and tried to pull her feet away as the sensation was almost too intense, but Ben held on and carried on massaging her. He certainly knew what he was doing. Maddie day-dreamed about what this could turn into. Ben liked her – he had made that clear enough, and she had not hidden her attraction for him either.

Maddie's phone rang. She cursed. It always seemed to ring at the most inopportune moments, and it always seemed to be Hugh, ringing with another set of nagging questions. 'Sorry,' she murmured to Ben. 'Duty calls.' She pulled the phone out of her bag and answered it; and, as she expected, it was Hugh.

'Maddie. I need to know exactly what you've got under contract, and what there is still to do,' Hugh said, without pausing for pleasantries.

Maddie grimaced at Ben, and mouthed 'Hugh'. Ben responded by making a crude gesture, suggesting that Hugh was given to the solitary pleasures of onanism, and Maddie had difficulty controlling her desire to laugh out loud. She struggled to carry on listing the locations to Hugh, as Ben carried out a silent pantomime depicting Hugh's various imagined sexual shortcomings. In the end, Maddie had to look away from Ben, as he was proving too distracting and she was finding it increasingly difficult to concentrate and sound suitably serious and business-like for Hugh.

Ben continued to massage her feet as she detailed her achievements to Hugh. She couldn't help noticing that Ben's hands seemed to be slipping higher up her ankles with each swooping stroke. Soon he was gently massaging her calves, which were aching from the walk. This caused her attention to wander from Hugh again, but for a different reason this time.

Then Hugh dropped his little bombshell. He wanted to come down to Dorset to see all the locations she had organised. He told her that he wanted her to prepare a detailed breakdown of the negotiated fees and for her to have all the signed contracts ready for inspection. Maddie had been expecting Hugh to want to see the locations, but normally the director would wait until she had finished her scouting before bothering her. The fact that she still had quite a few locations to find, and that he had given her so little time to do so in the first place, put her in a fluster, and she felt the familiar sensation of Hugh conspiring to make her life difficult yet again. Doubtless he would give her a roasting when he saw her for failing to complete her task ahead of schedule and under budget.

Maddie was about to say something to Hugh when she jerked her head back in a sudden surprised flinch. Ben's hand was now travelling much further up her leg than was required for a foot- and calf-massage. She tried to concentrate on what she had been about to say to Hugh, at the same time trying to drag her leg free from Ben's grasp. But Ben held her tightly, his hands encircling her leg just below the knee. Maddie could feel her instantaneous reaction to his touch: she could feel the gushing wetness gathering inside her. At last, her handsome farmer was making his move on her. She was finding it desperately difficult to carry on a conversation with Hugh while experiencing such tender attentions at the hands of Ben.

Hugh talked on, and then casually added another little surprise. He wanted two additional locations, ones which were not on her list. A couple of extra scenes had been added to the script since he had last spoken to her, and she needed to find locations for these, too.

'You must not fail. We need the locations; they're pivotal scenes, essential to the plot.'

Maddie made a herculean effort to pay attention to Hugh, but the sensations she was experiencing were too much. She was too engrossed by Ben's actions to feel even annoyance at the timing of Hugh's latest request. She lay back and closed her eyes, holding the phone to her ear as she felt Ben sliding a hand up the outside of either thigh, pushing her light dress up with them. Maddie managed to gather her wits enough to ask Hugh whether she would be given any additional budget for the extra location fee.

'No, you'll have to find it out of the existing budget,' Hugh replied. Despite the sharpness of his words, Maddie barely registered them. Ben had pushed her dress up around her waist, and was now sitting back on his haunches, looking down at her in rapt wonderment.

'But –' she whispered.

'No buts, Maddie. Just do it.'

Then Ben leant forwards again and hooked either side of her thin cotton panties with his fingers, slowly drawing them down.

'Oh, I will,' Maddie said softly into the phone, closing her eyes as she felt the waistband of her knickers slowly being drawn down over her pubic hairs, the elastic depressing the dark coils slightly before they sprang back. She felt Ben slipping them all the way down her legs, and lifted her ankles to help him take them off over her feet. Ben's hands then returned slowly up her legs, his fingers fanning out as he felt her soft skin. Slowly, deliberately, they crept higher. Maddie reacted by shifting her legs, to allow him better access. She bit her lip as he brushed his fingers lightly over the sensitive flesh of her inner thigh, then inwards towards her sex. He removed his right hand, spat on his fingertips, and returned them to Maddie's quim. Gently, he applied the lightest of pressures to her clitoris, dabbing and stroking as if it were some delicate creature that could be crushed by too harsh a touch.

Maddie held her breath as Ben worked deftly and surely, bringing her perilously close to the edge. She struggled inside to control herself. Ben seemed to realise this, and withdrew his hands, allowing her to recover.

'One more thing, Maddie,' Hugh commanded down the phone. His sharp tone caused Maddie to open her eyes again. She felt that this might be important. At that moment, Ben caught her eye. 'I'm going to lick you,' he whispered to Maddie.

'Mm?' she murmured into the phone. With her left hand, Maddie reached down and grasped Ben's head as he bent to caress her with his mouth. She played his curls through her fingers as she pushed him gently deeper into her.

'If I'm not happy with the locations, the implications for you will be serious.' The touch of Ben's hot tongue on her most sensitive parts caused her to gasp out loud. Maddie had barely heard what Hugh had just said, and cared even less. All her thoughts were concentrated on the agile, slick actions of Ben's able mouth and tongue, which were busily exploring her.

'You have every reason to be worried,' Hugh said.

He had clearly interpreted Maddie's gasp as one of alarm. With that, Hugh's end of the line went dead. But Maddie was past caring at that moment. Ben was as skilled and dextrous with his mouth as he had been with his hands, and she lay in the sun, allowing him to pleasure her without any effort to return the pleasure to him. She knew now, with certainty, that there would be plenty of time for that.

Chapter Five

Maddie had been in Dorset for about a week and a half, and her scouting had brought her to Weymouth. After driving round one of the town's car parks for a couple of circuits, Maddie finally spotted an empty bay. The good weather had ensured that Weymouth was thronging with visitors, and consequently parking spaces were at a premium. Maddie parked the MG and decided to put the soft top up. Even though the sky was a brilliant cloudless blue, she didn't want to risk the interior of Freya's car getting soaked by a sudden summer downpour. Maddie reached in her bag for the street guide to all the towns of Dorset, and turned to the relevant page. She checked the route and set off through the back streets.

Maddie had not visited Weymouth before, and was pleasantly surprised. She had expected it to be yet another tacky seaside town. It was a pretty place, with many small terraced Georgian houses, some with bow-fronted windows, others with bay windows on the first floor jutting out over the pavements, and what she had seen of the town was not overspoiled by unsympathetic modern developments. Families wandered past, the children juggling a confusion of buckets, spades and rapidly melting ice creams; and the adults carrying picnic boxes, folding chairs and bags full of swimming gear.

Maddie wandered through the narrow streets, where every other shop seemed to be a tea shop or to sell souvenirs, and her progress was slowed by the milling crowds of tourists. She eventually turned into Casterbridge Road. At the other end of the street, she could see a large building which she guessed must be the place she was looking for. She walked towards it, looking at the elaborate details of the architecture. She walked up the flight of steps to the front entrance, and looked at the elegantly painted sign below a large brass doorbell. It read:

MEMBERS ONLY. LADIES' SESSIONS MONDAY, WEDNESDAY AND FRIDAY; GENTLEMEN'S SESSIONS TUESDAY, THURSDAY AND SATURDAY. PLEASE RING FOR ATTENTION.

Maddie pressed the bell, but didn't hear anything. She wondered whether it had actually sounded deep in the bowels of the building, or whether it was broken. She pressed the bell again. She heard echoing footsteps on the other side of the door, and then it opened. A slim blonde-haired woman in a white tunic uniform and with a welcoming smile stood at the door. Maddie was briefly reminded of her school nurse from many years ago.

'Can I help you?' the woman asked.

'I have an appointment with the manager, Mr Babbage. My name is Maddie Campion.'

The woman smiled pleasantly, and asked Maddie to follow her. She led Maddie through an echoing hallway, up a broad stone staircase and along a corridor, before ushering her into what was clearly the vestibule of an office. Black leather couches lined two of the walls, a dusty plastic plant sat in one corner of the room, and a low coffee table bore copies of *Recreation Weekly*. The woman went over to another door, knocked and went inside. She reappeared, followed by a portly, avuncular-looking man, who smiled broadly at Maddie and walked towards her with his hand outstretched.

'Miss Campion. Delighted to meet you. Jack Babbage – please call me Jack. I'm intrigued by your proposition, but feel that it could be a most mutually agreeable arrangement. Let me show you around.'

As he led her back down the stairs, Jack related something of the history of Weymouth's Turkish baths. The baths had been built in the early Victorian period, at the height of the craze for all things oriental. They were the largest Turkish baths in the country, and had been operating continuously since they were first built.

'The baths have always closed on Sundays. It's a tradition, even though it would probably be our busiest day, should we choose to open. It gives the staff a much-needed day off each week. They work so hard here, and it's very physical work sometimes, as I am sure you can understand. So the baths will be free for your crew to use for filming on any Sunday you like.'

Jack led her through a swinging door and then up to another heavy dark wooden door. He opened the door and immediately Maddie felt the blast of warm air on her skin. She followed him into a small room, with a counter at one end and another door at the opposite end. Behind the counter were sets of shelves, each stacked with clean, plump white towels. A man was sitting behind the counter, reading a newspaper which had become slightly floppy in the humidity. Jack went up to him, spoke quietly to him and nodded. Maddie watched as the man reached under the counter and handed him a set of what looked like wooden clogs. Jack put them on and then went to the other door. Maddie moved to follow, but Jack gestured at her to remain.

'Just one moment, my dear. It's our gentlemen's day, and I have to ask if any of them object to you coming in.'

Jack disappeared inside. Maddie sat on one of the low benches and waited. Jack was gone for what seemed like an interminable period but Maddie guessed that there might be a lot of people in the baths to ask. The man behind the counter made no attempt at making conversation with her. She could hear him sniffing from behind his newspaper every now and then, and Maddie wondered with amusement at Jack's comments about his staff working so hard.

Jack eventually reappeared, just as Maddie had started to think that he must be meeting with some resistance to her proposed tour. She was heartened to see that he was smiling.

'No one objected, my dear. In fact, a couple of the gentlemen seemed rather tickled by the idea of a young lady visitor and made some rather risqué comments. They aren't used to seeing women in the baths. We don't have mixed sex sessions here – we're not as progressive as some other establishments. In fact, we rather pride ourselves on our old-fashioned

107

values. On the ladies' days we have a lady masseuse, and a male masseur for the gentlemen. It's all very proper here.'

Jack seemed to be at pains to portray the baths as a bastion of propriety. Maddie wondered why he felt compelled to do this. Jack coughed with embarrassment, and continued. 'I must warn you that some of the gentlemen will be naked.'

Maddie smiled at this well-intentioned warning. Jack Babbage seemed to be of the old school, one of those men who found it hard to believe that a woman might not only want to but also enjoy seeing a naked man.

He continued, 'I hope that won't offend you; but as you are the guest here and our members have every right to be naked, I could not ask them to cover themselves up.'

'Of course, I understand.'

'You will need to either be barefoot or wear a pair of our clogs.'

Maddie kicked off her sandals and followed Jack through the door, feeling the welcome cool of the tiles beneath her feet. They entered a long room, with wooden-panelled changing rooms ranged along three of the walls. Each changing room was about the size of a shower stall, decorated with carved side panels and with a velvet curtain across the front. Maddie went into one of the cubicles. There was a cushioned bench seat in matching velvet, three polished brass hooks and some hangers for clothes and a neat rack under the seat for shoes. There was also a mirror, decorated with an etched design of scrolls and swags. Opulence must have been the byword when the baths were being furnished all those years ago.

Jack watched Maddie's close scrutiny anxiously. She looked around and nodded. Having seen how soggy the attendant's newspaper had become, she had decided to make mental notes rather than struggling with her notebook. 'Now we go through into the relaxation and massage room,' Jack said, leading her through another door.

Maddie's senses were assailed. The air was much warmer than in the changing rooms and was scented with an oil: sandalwood, she thought. The room was spectacularly decorated with mosaics of tiny tiles arranged in arabesque flourishes and intricate Islamic patterns; on the floor, the walls and the domed ceiling. Just about every surface that could be decorated had been. Long couch beds were arranged down either side of the room, each covered with a large pristine white towel with another rolled up to form a bolster at the head. At the far end of the room was a raised massage table. The masseur was busy at work on a naked man, who was lying on the table like some kind of helpless beached seal. The man's eyes were screwed tight shut, but Maddie could not tell if it was in ecstasy or agony. The masseur was vigorously pummelling his back, and reminded Maddie of nothing so much as a butcher tenderising a piece of meat. The massage looked almost too violent to be enjoyable, she thought.

Then Jack gestured Maddie through to the next room, the warm room. There were about eight or nine men in this room. Some were seated on the cool tiled benches that stretched along the side of the room, and others were standing and chatting. All were naked. The men fell silent as Maddie entered, but none of them made any effort to cover themselves. This surprised Maddie, but fascinated her, too. She felt very much like an interloper in foreign territory, and was keenly aware that she was the only female present. She smiled an acknowledgement at the men, and she was pleased to see that they all responded. Some smiled back, others raised their hands in a small wave of greeting.

One man, a blond man of about thirty, caught Maddie's eye and smiled broadly at her; and, as she was looking around the room, he got up and walked slowly past her, so deliberately close that he brushed against her. She could not help but notice his body, which was lean, tanned and fit-looking. Jack, on the other hand, was so engrossed with showing her the recent and very expensive repairs to some of the tile mosaics that he didn't notice this blatant behaviour at all. As Jack was showing her the wonders of the Victorian plumbing and explaining how the room was heated, the man from the towel store entered the room. He apologised for interrupting, and told Jack that he was wanted urgently on the phone.

'Excuse me, my dear,' Jack said to Maddie. 'Do you mind finishing the tour on your own? The hot room is through there, and beyond that is the steam room, and the cool room with the plunge pool.' He gestured towards the other end of the room, where there was a large archway leading through to another area.

'I'll be fine,' answered Maddie. Jack and the man hurried out, the man animatedly explaining something to Jack as they went. Maddie gingerly opened the door to the hot room, and was greeted by a blast of hot, dry, oven-like air. The room was empty, but it was far too hot to look around it comfortably, dressed as she was. She glanced around, making quick mental notes, and closed the door again.

Maddie looked around her, and decided to follow where the blond man had gone. She walked through the archway into a small area where there were some beautiful carved marble basins with brass taps. On the floor beside each basin was a stack of beaten brass bowls. The blond man reappeared. He nodded at Maddie, and picked up a bowl and filled it under the tap, all the time looking intently at her. She found the intensity of his gaze intriguing. He was making his interest in her perfectly clear. The man stood before her and poured the water over his head, to cool off. Maddie watched wordlessly as the water trickled down his fine body, little beads trapped in his pubic hair and the rest gathering in a pool at his feet, before running off through the brass grille of the drain. She knew that this display was for her benefit, and she could see that his cock had grown a small amount: not so much that it might be thought obscene in company, but enough to ensure that it would draw admiring glances from the other men. And from Maddie.

'Coming into the steam room?' he asked.

He had the assured arrogance of a man who knows he is admired, and he behaved as if being naked in front of a complete stranger were the most natural thing in the world. Maddie followed him, thinking how incongruous it was for her to be in such a place fully dressed. She doubted she would be able to see much in the steam room, let alone stay in there for long. She also knew that the steam would have a disastrous effect on her hair and clothes, but that couldn't be helped. She watched the man walk ahead of her. He had a broad back and a good arse, with buttocks that were almost crying out to be cupped and fondled.

The wall of steam in the steam room was so dense that as she suspected, Maddie could see very little. She doubted whether filming would be possible under such conditions. It was a fairly small room, and she could see more mosaic-covered low benches along the walls, and there were three men sitting at the far end. The sweat was dripping off them. They were not talking, but sat silently, with their heads thrown back against the wall. Maddie thought this silence was probably because it would take too much effort to talk in such an atmosphere. The blond man sat on a side bench with his legs wide apart, and looked up at Maddie. She was intrigued by the brazenness of his invitation but, despite liking what she saw, Maddie decided that she had seen enough. Besides, it was too much being fully dressed in such an atmosphere.

Maddie left the steam room, and had a quick look around the cool room. Here there was a large, deep rectangular pool, like a small swimming pool. It too was decorated with tiny jewel-like tiles, and a set of brass ladder steps led down into the inviting blue water. Maddie knelt to feel the temperature. It was icy cold. She cupped her hand and splashed her forehead with the refreshing water, glad for some kind of relief. She looked up across the pool and saw that on the other side of the room was a brass shower. Like the ladder steps, it was highly polished; and Maddie guessed it was an original fitting, as it looked so old. She counted eight separate shower heads set at various heights and angles. As she watched, a young man, maybe eighteen or nineteen, entered the room and stepped into the shower. He hadn't noticed Maddie, and she in turn wondered how she could have missed seeing him before.

He was a handsome, lithe specimen, his body still filling out but already manly rather than boyish. He was hairless, apart from a dark spread of hair around his balls, and Maddie couldn't help noticing the impressive length of his cock. He was tanned, and she reckoned it was a much deeper tan than could have been achieved on a sun bed. His bleached hair also suggested he had recently been abroad, and Maddie noticed a thin braided bracelet around his wrist. She wondered if he were a student, maybe returned from a holiday spent bumming round the sunny beaches of Europe. The young man turned on the shower, and his entire body was blasted by the various jets. His back was turned to Maddie, and she viewed his pert rear with fascinated lust: all was taut, lean and youthful. She could imagine the boundless energy of such a young man in bed.

The young man turned a knob to decrease the force of the water, and then turned towards her, still unaware of her presence. He soaped himself with lazy abandon. Maddie decided that she must leave. This wasn't helping her work get done, and it was merely making her even hornier than she had been feeling before. Sexual frustration was one of her least favourite conditions. It always made her intensely irritable.

Just as Maddie was about to get up from by the pool and leave, the blond man she had followed earlier entered the room, and walked straight up to the young man in the shower. She was immediately reminded of the afternoon back in Cambridge when she had disturbed Kate, her housemate, in the shower with Tony. Maddie watched as the blond man wordlessly took the soap from the young man's hand and proceeded to soap him. The young man turned, and closed his eyes as hands busily worked their way down his back and over his buttocks.

Maddie felt she shouldn't, but she wanted to watch. She was fascinated to see what would happen next. She had never seen two men together before. She was about to leave when she noticed the blond man had slipped one soapy hand into the cleft of the young man's buttocks, and was working it up and down with a steady rhythm. The blond man then reached round with his other hand and grasped the young man, and Maddie watched in alarmed fascination as he began to masturbate his already-rigid cock.

Maddie didn't dare move, lest she should give her presence away, and watched silently as the blond man slowly worked the other man's prick with his hand. The young man was standing with his head thrown back in an attitude of one experiencing exquisite abandon. Maddie felt the rushing thrill of a voyeur, seeing for the first time that which is forbidden.

Suddenly, she remembered something. Maddie looked at her watch and cursed silently. It was already getting late in the morning, and she knew she could not stay and see this encounter through to its inevitable conclusion. She made her way back to the towel room, and put on her sandals. The man behind the counter was back in his position, buried in his newspaper, and she slipped out without him noticing. She returned to Mr Babbage's office, and swiftly concluded the deal: filming at the baths to take place on two consecutive Sundays, from six in the morning to ten at night. As a gesture of goodwill, Jack kindly made Maddie an honorary member of the baths for the duration of her stay in Dorset.

Maddie was pleased by this, as there were precious few perks in her job.

After leaving the baths, Maddie checked her watch again. She had arranged to meet Ben at midday, and there was still just enough time for one more task, as long as she was quick. She briskly walked through the back streets of Weymouth towards the beach. She wanted to check it as a possible location. The Esplanade, the long road which fronted the beach, was almost entirely taken up by tourist shops and hotels. At one end was a large and imposing statue of King George III, gaudily painted in bright colours with strategic applications of gilding. Maddie smiled, thinking how refreshing it was to see it like that, looking so unlike most statues, which were grim and grey in their stony nakedness. The statue of the king looked rather tacky and tasteless, and she liked it all the more for that. She walked down on to the sandy beach, and picked her way through the groups of people sitting on deck chairs and sunning themselves on large towels spread on the sand. The tide was out, and Maddie had a longish walk to the edge of the water. She took off her sandals and watched the way her footprints in the soft wet sand gradually filled with water. Then she walked into the shallow ripples of the sea, letting the waves lap gently at her ankles. She looked around her, sizing up the scenery.

To the west lay the bulk of the Isle of Portland, jutting out into the sea and creating part of the harbour protection against the open sea. To the east she could see the cliffs curving round in the distance, and the ranks of white mobile holiday homes in the fields above the cliffs. The beach was pretty, but sadly it was far too busy and popular to be suitable for filming. Maddie knew that there was nothing more likely to deflate the audience's belief in the fictional world on screen than seeing people in the background caught openly gawping at the camera. Children were screaming with excitement and splashing each other in the water, and Maddie was sorely tempted to go for a cooling swim. However, she had work to do.

When she got back to the car park, she was annoyed to see that someone had parked their car on part of the access lane immediately behind the MG. The offending vehicle was a large Volvo estate, and its bumper stuck out far enough across the end of her space to block her exit. The car park was still full, and cars were circling, the drivers eagerly scanning for the next space to become available. Obviously the driver of this particular car couldn't wait – the car was empty but the driver had left his indicator blinking to show that he would be back soon. Maddie looked around, but couldn't see anyone hurrying back towards it. There was a newsagents' shop across the road, and Maddie guessed that the driver might well be in there, buying some urgently needed item that he or she couldn't possibly do without. Maddie smiled, thinking that such emergency shopping stops were often the recourse of smokers or chocoholics, and as a closet chocoholic herself, she could easily sympathise with such an addiction.

Maddie peered inside the car. The keys were in the ignition. That decided it: she would move the car herself. She got in and started up the engine, and drove the car forward about three or four feet, to allow her the space to reverse the MG out of her parking spot. As she was getting out of the Volvo, she saw a man running towards her. She expected him to be angry for moving his car, but instead he was touchingly apologetic.

'Hell, I'm really sorry. I left the keys in case you might need to move it, but I was hoping I'd be gone before you got back to your car. Bad timing!'

Maddie looked at what he was carrying: a packet of matches. She noticed that on the lid there was a picture of the statue she had just seen, and she guessed that nicotine must be the man's weakness. He was about thirty, broad with short, blond hair and a kindly, smiling face.

'Allow me to introduce myself. Harry Gooder.' The man held out his hand and Maddie shook hands with him and introduced herself.

'That's a nice MG,' said Harry. 'Always wanted one myself.'

'It's not mine – my boss has lent it to me,' Maddie explained.

'You must have a very indulgent boss,' said Harry. 'What's your line of work?'

Maddie explained her job and what she was doing in Dorset. Harry seemed very interested, and she in turn asked what he did for a living.

'I run my own company – hot-air balloons. I do all sorts of work: promotional, weddings, anniversary trips, you name it. Mostly, though, people hire the balloon to drift over Dorset for a day, and I do the piloting.'

'God, that sounds divine,' said Maddie emphatically. She was feeling that she could do with a relaxing break like that.

'Here's my number, if you want to get in touch,' said Harry, handing her a small printed business card. 'I do very reasonable rates. I know Dorset like the back of my hand. I would offer to help you with

117

your work, but I guess you've got it all figured out by now. But take it, just in case your director wants to do some aerial shots. I'm far cheaper than a helicopter – not to mention quieter and steadier.'

'But not quite as easy to direct,' Maddie laughed.

'When all the countryside is as beautiful as it is in Dorset, it doesn't matter where we go,' Harry replied.

'True. Well, that's very kind of you, Harry. You never know, I might call on your expertise. If you don't mind, that is.'

'Of course not. Where are you staying?' Harry asked.

He's keen, thought Maddie. She was titillated by his interest. She told him about the New Inn and then her accommodation arrangements in Dorchester during filming.

'Might I give you a call?' Harry asked.

'Please do,' she replied, surprising even herself at how quickly she was organising an assignation with yet another man. Harry nodded happily as she wrote down her mobile number and gave it to him.

'I have to go now,' Maddie apologised, remembering again her meeting with Ben.

'I'll be in touch then, Maddie. It was a real pleasure meeting you. I mean that.' They shook hands again, and Maddie watched as Harry got in his car and drove off, giving her a little wave as he went. Maddie smiled to herself with satisfaction. It was always nice to be openly desired. As she drove away, she realised that there had been a cigarette lighter in the Volvo dashboard, and shook her head, amused. She would tease him about it next time she saw him. She felt certain there would be a next time.

Maddie's next port of call was Chesil Beach, the

long pebbly spit of shingle which stretches westwards from the Isle of Portland for some miles. She had arranged to meet Ben at the beach car park below the village of Abbotsbury. The beach was yet another location to check before their pub lunch, and she could only allow herself half an hour off for food because of the pressure of time on her work.

As she drove along the road above the coast, she reflected on the past few weeks. In that time, she had had three sexual partners, Greg, Callum and Ben; and it looked as if she might be about to add a fourth, Harry, to the list. She loved the feeling of being pursued and doing the pursuing herself, and it always had a snowball effect on her: the more sex she had, the more she wanted. Each man was a new experience, a new challenge, and she felt that her blood was up.

Maddie thought back to the blond man in the baths, who she was convinced was bisexual rather than gay. There had been something in the way he had looked at her, and displayed himself to her, and invited her to join him in the steam room in the baths. She wondered if the handsome young man was bisexual, too. Bisexuality intrigued her, mainly because of the possibilities and permutations it presented. The encounter in the baths had been swiftly followed by Harry's open interest in her, and the morning's events had left her feeling sexually charged and impatient. Maddie wanted sex – lots of it, and it was extraordinarily easy to get. She wasn't insatiable, but she wasn't far from it.

She was grateful for the ruffling breeze that blew in from the sea. It cooled her, and she certainly felt that she needed cooling off. The horizon was blurred by a misty haze, and the sky had an unforgiving appearance; unremitting in its searing, bleaching heat.

Maddie saw Ben's Range Rover in the car park and parked next to it. He was nowhere in sight, and she guessed that he might already be down by the water. She walked down to the beach, climbing up the high-mounded ridge of pebbles and then down towards the sea. The pebbles had been graded in size by the sea, with the largest ones tossed highest up the bank, and the smaller ones rattling back and forth under the waves. The beach was surprisingly empty, and in the distance Maddie could see a figure she was sure was Ben.

She walked slowly towards him, her progress slowed by the wearying effort it took to walk on the loose, shifting pebbles. It felt as if she was wading through treacle. The noise of the waves as they crashed on to the shingle was deafening, and as they receded they dragged the small stones back with them, creating yet another effect in the surging cycle of sound. A few seagulls wheeled overhead, on the lookout for scraps; and beneath them strands of beached seaweed lay at the high-water mark, tangled among lengths of bleached, fissured wood and other pieces of flotsam and jetsam.

Maddie sensed that the beach would be perfect for filming, although it was possible that the sound crew might have their work cut out muffling the noise of the sea so that the dialogue was clearly audible. That would be a small technical problem, but not an insurmountable one.

She finally caught up with Ben, who was skimming pebbles across the waves. He was wearing a loose T-shirt, baggy shorts that came to just above his knees and baseball boots. Maddie regarded his legs with a surge of lust. His calves were well muscled and surprisingly hairy. She hailed him, panting slightly from her exertions in reaching him.

'God, you sound like you need some exercise.' He grinned at her.

'No, thanks, not right now, darling,' Maddie said cheekily, clearly alluding to exercise of an intimate, two-person nature. 'I've just had more than enough. Can we walk back along the road?' she asked, gesturing to where the single-track tarmacked road which ran parallel to the beach lay concealed behind the shingle bank some distance away.

'Sure,' Ben laughed, and they walked up the bank and down to the road. Maddie saw the bright yellow flowers of the horned poppies that were growing in clumps on the edge of the shingle, and noticed the long seed pods that gave them their name. Horned poppies. She smiled at the *double entendre* of their name, and then wondered why it was that she was suddenly seeing dirty meanings everywhere. Something to do with the sultry heat and her constant awareness of sex, she thought. She wasn't usually this focused on it.

Ben and Maddie walked towards the Black Horse, the pub that stood a little way back from the beach. Maddie was surprised to see that, unlike the beach, the pub was fairly busy. They placed their order for food at the bar and, clutching their drinks, went back out into the sunshine. There was one last empty table in the garden, and they sat in the sun, drinking and chatting. Around them, children played in the adventure playground and adults chatted over their beers. At one nearby table a young couple in shorts and T-shirts were sitting side by side, so close that their thighs were touching. They were engrossed in

121

each other, whispering in each other's ears and acting as if the rest of the world did not exist; and as Maddie watched them, and saw the young man reach down and languidly caress the woman's thigh, she felt that, if she did not have sex soon, she would explode from frustration.

It seemed that Ben sensed this. He too had been watching the display of unabashed desire from the young lovers nearby. He leant over to Maddie and whispered to her, 'Looks like we're getting our own personal floorshow. Do you like it?'

Maddie did not take her eyes from the young couple as she answered him with a murmur of assent.

'I like to watch, too,' Ben whispered.

This was becoming too much for Maddie. She wanted some kind of sex, and she needed it now. She looked around the garden, to see if there were any secluded bushes that she could disappear into with Ben, but the flower beds were neatly filled with rows of low plants, offering no cover. There was nothing for it: she would have to give herself release, then. She stood up and quickly excused herself, and hurried to the ladies, which were situated in a low extension at the back of the pub. Ben silently watched her go, and Maddie felt a slight pang of guilt at her abrupt departure; but her driving desire for satiation governed all else right now. She had to relieve herself in the toilets, and not in the usual way in such a place.

She went into the loos through a wooden outer door with a FILLIES sign on it. She could guess that the gents would bear a matching sign saying STALLIONS, and she smiled to herself. She certainly knew a few stallions. It was a small room, with two basins set into a long plinth, and a large mirror along the wall above them. Under the window at the far end was a chintz-covered armchair. Opposite the basins were two lavatory cubicles. The doors to the cubicles were open, and she could see that the lavatories were spotlessly clean. The room smelt sweet, and Maddie smiled at the obvious pride the landlord or lady took in the presentation of the room. By the basins were two vases of cut flowers from the garden, and a large dish of sweetly perfumed pot pourri sat on a small table which also bore a small bowl containing spare bars of soap.

Maddie was about to enter one of the cubicles when the door opened and Ben came in.

'You can't come in here,' Maddie said, alarmed. 'What if someone else comes in?'

'They won't,' Ben replied. 'Look.' He opened the door and gestured at the piece of paper stuck to it: OUT OF ORDER. PLEASE USE OTHER LADIES TOILETS (INSIDE THE MAIN BUILDING, OFF THE LOUNGE BAR).

'But . . .' Maddie trailed. 'That wasn't there when I came in.'

'And I'll give you three guesses who put it there,' Ben said, closing the door, locking it, and advancing on her. Maddie battled briefly with the thought of insisting that Ben leave, but soon overcame it. After all, he could help her with what she needed.

'Christ,' he muttered, looking at her. 'You were going off to have a wank, weren't you? God, that's so filthy. Couldn't you have waited until we left the pub?'

Maddie shook her head.

'You had to have it, right here, without me. You dirty, dirty woman. You're like a bitch on heat. So go on, then.'

'What?' asked Maddie.

'Do it. Touch yourself. I've never seen a woman masturbate before. Do it for me.'

Maddie was taken aback by the strength of Ben's reaction, but it also aroused her. She loved it when desire was expressed so openly and directly. Even though she was unsure about doing something so intimate and revealing in front of Ben, she knew she would do it. He was hard to resist. Maddie kicked her sandals off and leant back against the plinth and, looking directly at Ben, started to pull her dress up. Her legs were bare. She was already wet, but Ben's presence and his desire made her stomach contract with another pulse of slickening lust.

She quickly pulled her dress right up over her head, and threw it on to the floor beside her feet. She stood before him in her panties and bra; her favourite white lacy summery set. The cups of her bra pushed her breasts up together, emphasising her cleavage. Her knickers were small, and she knew that the dark patch of her pubes could be seen behind the lacy panel. She was pleased by this, and it hadn't escaped Ben's notice. He eagerly scanned her body up and down, and Maddie remembered that he hadn't yet seen her fully naked.

She reached around behind her back and unclasped her bra, allowing the flimsy garment to fall down her arms and on to the floor. Her nipples were hard, bullet-like points, aching to be taken into Ben's mouth.

'Oh Jesus,' groaned Ben. Maddie could see that the front of his shorts had tented up. 'Go on, touch yourself,' he whispered.

Maddie slid both hands on to the front panel of her panties, feeling the soft lace and the springy hairs trapped beneath. She could feel the heat that was coming off her, too, even at this distance. She slid her right hand under the elastic, sliding it through her curls and lower into the warm damp cleft of her sex.

Ben stood riveted to the spot. 'Take them off,' he muttered. 'I need to see.'

In response, Maddie withdrew her fingers and, with a hand on the thin strips of material over her hips, she pushed them down. Once over her hips, they slithered down her legs and settled in a lacy pool round her feet. She was going to kick them free when Ben reached down and picked them up. He held them under his nose and breathed in deeply.

'God, you smell so good,' he said, his eyes closed. Maddie was a bit taken aback by this, but aroused too. Just when she was beginning to think she knew Ben, he would do something else that made her realise she still had a lot to learn about him. She wondered what she would learn when they made love fully, and knew that it might not be long before she found out.

Ben opened his eyes again and looked at Maddie, naked before him. 'You're so sexy,' he murmured. 'Touch yourself.'

Maddie leant back against the plinth and parted her legs slightly to allow herself better access. She brought her hands to her downy sex and began the movements she knew so well; movements which she had undertaken a thousand times before, but never with such a close and appreciative audience. She closed her eyes, concentrating on working her familiar pattern of tiny flicking touches, caresses, circling motions and dabs against her clitoris; occasionally dipping her fingers into her quim to gather her lubricating juices. She could feel her clitoris pushing its way from its hooded cover, hardening and throbbing.

'Jesus,' Ben muttered, his voice a strangled sound in the back of his throat. He couldn't take it any longer. In a flash he was with Maddie, his lips on hers and his hand reaching down to cover hers as they busily worked on her sex. Then Ben pushed her hands out of the way and took over, cupping her crotch and rubbing his palm back and forth over her. The sudden roughness after the gentleness of her own touch charged her, and Maddie moaned, biting Ben's neck as her head fell forward. Her senses were reaching overload. She could feel the sudden rush of her climax, arriving almost before she was ready for it. Her hands fluttered to his back, then his chest, before dropping uselessly by her side as she gave in to the overwhelming surges rushing through her body.

When the tremors had subsided, Maddie looked up at Ben, thinking how strange it was that he was still fully dressed while she was completely naked. She reached for the base of his T-shirt and started to pull it off over his head. Just then, someone outside tried the door handle, and then there was an angry knocking. 'This is the landlord. What's going on in there?'

'Shit!' Maddie whispered, pushing Ben away, reaching down for her dress and throwing it on. Ben gathered up her discarded underwear and shoved them into his pockets.

'Come on out. Come on.' The landlord sounded furious.

Ben opened the window and quickly climbed out, then reached in and gave Maddie a hand out. Once outside, Maddie paused briefly to put her sandals on, and then they ran back to the car park, giggling like naughty schoolchildren. In the distance, they could still hear the angry bellows of the landlord.

Chapter Six

It was the day that Maddie had been dreading. Hugh was coming down to check up on her progress, and she was required to spend the day taking him around Dorset and showing him the locations that she had organised. She had been hoping to have everything sorted by the time of his visit, but the furniture store was proving unexpectedly hard to arrange, and there were a couple of other locations that she had not been able to secure. She was still in the process of negotiating the contracts, and cursed that Hugh wasn't coming down just a couple of days later. She felt sure that she would have everything sorted by then.

Maddie decided to disarm Hugh with her good humour, and to refuse to allow his inevitable criticisms to crush her, and to be as co-operative and amenable as possible. She would check all her sarcasm and her biting comments this time. She hoped that they could get off to a good new start together. As she greeted him, Maddie was struck again, with a force almost akin to a body blow, by how handsome Hugh was. He shook her hand formally, and smiled; a surprising sudden smile that lit up his whole face and almost seemed to change his character. Maddie secretly crossed her fingers behind her back. Things were boding well.

But, by the end of the day, Maddie was almost in tears. Hugh had been even more critical than she had expected. Anything that she had organised was not enough for him: not good enough, not cheap enough, not organised quickly enough. She argued her side bravely, telling him that she had pared costs right down to the bone and worked much longer hours than normal, but Hugh still was not satisfied. He presented her with a list of things that he required to be remedied by the time shooting was due to start, and left her with a curt goodbye. Maddie saw him off and went into the bar to start work on her new orders, feeling utterly crushed.

Maddie was delighted when she saw Ben coming into the bar some time later. He saw her straightaway and came over to her, kissing her on the cheek. 'There'll be more of that later. Don't want all the gossips knowing about us, do we?' Ben whispered in her ear.

This comment pleased Maddie. Despite their closeness, they had still not fully consummated their relationship. Maddie was frustrated that they seemed to never quite get round to it – whether through lack of opportunity, given Maddie's hectic schedule, or interruptions when they did manage to steal some time together. Ben soon cheered Maddie up, and Hugh was quickly forgotten.

Maddie and Ben had been chatting for an hour or so when Callum came into the bar. Maddie was a little surprised to see him. He had been gone for so long that she had almost forgotten about him. Besides, she had a new distraction now ... She watched him as Callum walked to the bar without noticing them, which relieved Maddie. She didn't want to be put in the awkward situation of having to explain her obviously close friendship with Ben to him. A potentially embarrassing situation avoided was the best outcome, she reckoned. It would be fine as long as he didn't turn around.

She thought back to the last time she had seen Callum, and realised that it was the time he had fixed the MG and they had made love on the downs, and she was momentarily concerned that Callum would resent her talking to Ben; but then she reminded herself not to be so silly. She and Callum had enjoyed a brief fling, had made no demands of each other, and their relationship was nothing but casual, so what could he object to? Besides, she was only talking to Ben. It wasn't as if Callum knew what they had been up to over the past weeks. In fact, she thought with a wry smile, she wouldn't have minded too much if Callum *had* caught them fucking. At least then she'd have managed to achieve with Ben what so far had been frustratingly unattainable.

Grace greeted Callum warmly, rushing around the bar to give him a big hug. She was clearly glad to have her son home after his absence. Maddie watched as Callum chatted to Grace, and she reflected on what a handsome man he was. Maddie then saw Grace nodding in her direction. Maddie cursed under her breath. Callum turned and saw her, and grinned. He said something to Grace, took his pint off the bar and came over to join them.

'Hello, there,' he said, smiling.

Maddie shifted awkwardly on her seat. 'Um, hi there, Callum. Did you have a good time in Scotland?'

'Great, thanks.' Callum smiled, and Maddie felt uncomfortable under his piercing scrutiny. Any other time, she would have gazed quite happily into his large green eyes, but now she avoided making eye contact with him. It felt as if he were silently challenging her about what she was doing with Ben.

Maddie spoke to fill the awkward pause. 'Thanks for helping me out with the car the other week.'

Callum nodded, but said nothing. Maddie felt uncomfortable, and babbled on in an attempt to prevent any more painful lulls in the conversation.

'Where did you go in Scotland?' she asked. 'You're looking very tanned.' It was true. His face was much browner than when she had last seen him, and his hair had become a lighter, sandier colour, bleached by the sun.

'The Orkney Islands,' he said, followed by another silence. Callum was being frustratingly unforthcoming. Maddie wondered whether he was enjoying her obvious discomfort.

'Do anything nice up there?' she persevered.

'Visited the sights, swam with the seals.' This was proving to be an uphill struggle. Callum wasn't being Mr Monosyllabic, but he wasn't far off it, Maddie thought. She realised she hadn't made any reference to Ben, who had been sitting silently during this exchange.

'Have you met Ben Hudson?'

Callum and Ben looked at each other, and both laughed.

'Oh. Stupid of me. Of course you know each other,

living in the same village,' Maddie said lamely, cursing her unthinking comment.

'I should think so. How's it going, mate?' Callum asked, pulling up a chair without waiting to be asked, and chatting to Ben. Maddie was relieved. Callum seemed unconcerned about her being with Ben. He was easy with it, which boded well. Callum smiled at her and explained.

'Best mates, us two – we grew up together. We've known each other since primary school. Done just about everything together, haven't we?' he asked, turning to Ben.

Ben nodded. 'Yep, certainly have. We've shared quite a few experiences over the years, haven't we? Made home-made fireworks together and almost blew up the milking parlour on the farm . . .'

'Had our first cigarette together behind the bike shed at school,' Callum added, smiling nostalgically.

'Got pissed together for the first time on a bottle of whisky we nicked from behind the bar here. All sorts.'

'We share just about everything. Always have.' Callum looked at Maddie steadily, and took a long draught from his pint. She felt the twisting knot of lust forming in the pit of her stomach in the certainty that Callum was talking about sex. In his absence, and distracted by her dalliance with Ben, she had forgotten just how good-looking Callum was, and how attracted to him she was. She looked at Ben, then at Callum, then back at Ben. They were watching her, waiting for her response.

'Everything?' Maddie asked.

'Aha.' Ben nodded.

'Even women?' she asked.

'All the time,' Callum said. 'We've got very similar tastes.'

'Sometimes we share the same woman,' said Ben.

'And sometimes in the same place at the same time,' Callum added.

Maddie blushed and looked down at the table top. This was about as unambiguous as they could get.

Ben leant closer. 'What do you think about that?' he asked.

'I'd say that was very liberated and uninhibited of you,' she replied, looking shyly up at him. Ben's gaze was eager, his pupils wide open, as if he had just come in from a darkened place; and Maddie knew enough about human sexual responses to know that his eyes were signalling his arousal.

'How uninhibited are you?' asked Callum. Maddie caught her breath as she looked at him. His green eyes seemed even more piercing than before. They were brighter, sparkling, and smiling wickedly. She looked at Ben, and realised that she could read both men's intentions in their eyes. Ben leant across the table towards her.

'What we're asking you, Maddie, is this: is three a crowd?'

She looked at them again, then smiled and spoke. 'It's my lucky number.'

Callum grinned and jerked his head in the direction of his mother behind the bar. 'Let's go someplace else for a drink. My place or yours, Ben?'

'Maddie should choose. Where would you like to go?' Ben asked.

'Your place,' she said to Callum. She had already seen Ben's house, and was curious to know where Callum lived. She knew from Grace that it was somewhere in the village, but had not worked out exactly where. Maddie finished her drink quickly, and stood up. The two men seemed surprised by her decisiveness. They quickly gulped down the remains of their pints and stood up with her.

Callum led the way out of the bar. His cottage was a short way from the pub, up the main road and down a narrow lane. Maddie noticed that the front garden was neatly kept. Callum unlocked the door and switched on the light. Then he stood back and allowed Maddie to enter first. She walked into the living room and looked around.

'Do you live on your own, Callum?' she asked. He nodded. Maddie was pleasantly surprised, as it was far tidier than she had expected a bachelor's house to be. Ben followed Callum into the room, closing the door behind him gently. Callum went over to the CD player and put on some music, while Ben disappeared into the kitchen to fix them all some drinks. Maddie heard the clinking of bottles, glasses and ice cubes, and reflected that Ben was clearly at home here. She sat on the large sofa, wondering how this evening was going to pan out. It seemed an almost incredible position to find herself in; something she had often fantasised about but had never done. And here she was, having stumbled into a *ménage à trois* as easily as she might walk into a shop to buy a loaf of bread or into a post office to mail a letter. It seemed vaguely incredible. But it was happening, right now, to her.

'Do you want to dance?' Callum asked, standing over Maddie and extending his hand to her.

Why not? she thought and, smiling, she took his hand and allowed him to pull her gently up off the sofa. Maddie placed one hand on his shoulder, and the other around his waist. They danced to the soft music, their bodies separated by a tantalisingly small space. Maddie was keenly aware that she already knew this man, that she had been intimate with him. She was looking forward to repeating the experience.

Callum drew her closer towards him. She could feel his warmth and smell his particular smell. His body was pressed against hers up almost its entire length: their knees were touching, her thighs were rubbing against his, and his arm pulled her close against him at the waist. His other arm was against her back, the palm of his hand pushing her towards him, pressing her into him. Maddie looked up and they kissed. Callum grasped the back of her head with one hand and held her fast against him as they kissed, as if he didn't want to let her go.

Ben arrived with the drinks, and Maddie heard him put them down on the table. Then she became aware of another pressure against her back. Ben had placed his hands on her hips and was pressing himself against her from behind, swaying in time to the music. Pressed between the two men, Maddie felt almost drunk on the power of her own sexuality. They both wanted her, and she would give them what they wanted. Then Ben broke away from her and, as Maddie carried on dancing with Callum, she watched Ben take his drink, pull out one of the chairs round the dining table, and sit to watch them both. He had let her know that he was interested, but that he just wanted to watch for now.

The music continued, and Callum began to run his hands over her. Maddie could feel him slowly grazing over the curves of her waist, then her hips, then round to her buttocks. His hands rested over her bottom, each hand lightly grasping a buttock. He pressed against her as they swayed, and she could tell his arousal was well advanced. Gradually, Callum worked the material of her dress up over her thighs, then her behind, until he had pulled it right up round her waist. Maddie swung her hips, pressing herself into him, but also so that, behind her, Ben could see her pert arse moving seductively. Callum lowered his head and muttered thickly into her ear, 'Christ, you turn me on.' Maddie knew that Ben would be enjoying the view from where he was sitting, and this fired her on to greater acts of wantonness.

Maddie pulled away from Callum, breaking free so that she could slip the dress off over her head. Callum stood back a little way to watch, and then moved forwards to look closely and eagerly at her once she had cast her dress aside. She was wearing a red bra and matching panties, and she knew that they looked good against her dark skin. The cups of the bra were lacy, and her dark areolae showed through; her knickers were similarly transparent. She knew that, revealed and hidden at the same time, her body would drive the two men to distraction.

Callum reached out to touch her, pulling her close and bending to kiss her neck. Maddie threw her head back, as he kissed a path round from by her ear to the tender part of the front of her neck, and then downwards, burying his face between her breasts.

Maddie looked over to where Ben was sitting. She was startled to see that he was no longer an inert spectator: he had taken his cock out of his jeans. He was slowly massaging the huge rod which stood proudly in his lap. Transfixed, Maddie walked towards him. She had not seen his cock before, and she wanted a better view. She walked over and stood above him, looking intently down at the mesmerising sight before her. Ben smiled up at her.

'You like it?' he asked.

'I love it,' she replied truthfully, her eyes glazed with lust.

'It's all yours,' Ben whispered. 'If you want it.'

'I want it,' she murmured. She reached down and placed her hand above Ben's, encircling his rigid cock. He twitched under her touch, and she could feel him hardening yet more. He was circumcised, and very, very hard.

Maddie turned so that her back was to Ben. Callum had followed her across the room, and stood near her, watching intently. Holding Callum's gaze of rapt expectancy, Maddie shuffled backwards a little way, so that her legs were straddling Ben's legs as he sat in the chair. Reaching behind her, she felt for Ben's prick. She grasped it, and slowly lowered herself on to it, past the tiny thong of her knickers which she had pulled to one side. Ben groaned, realising what she was doing, and grasped her at the waist, helping her down. Before her, Callum moved forwards to watch, his eyes riveted to where Maddie's red lace-covered sex was slowly engulfing his best friend's cock.

Slowly, with his strong hands at her waist, Ben lifted her up again over his cock. Maddie was wet, and slid easily upwards, releasing him from her intimate grasp. She was taking some of her weight on her feet, and the stress transmitted up to her thighs, which were tensing under the strain. She knew her legs would give way under her before long; even sooner, if she came.

'Jesus,' muttered Callum. Maddie looked up at him and licked her lips. Callum needed no further invitation. Fumbling at his flies, he undid his buttons, pushed his jeans a little way down and pulled out his cock. It was as hard as Ben's, but not yet as moist. Maddie would remedy that. Callum held his cock and stepped forwards, pressing his hard prick against her lips. She shook her head gently from side to side, in a pretence of refusal, and then parted her lips very slightly, to accept his hardness. Behind her, Ben could sense what she was doing, and this drove him on.

'You greedy girl,' Ben whispered, his lips touching her back, his thrusts increasing. 'One cock not enough for you?'

Maddie closed her eyes, overwhelmed by sensation. She could smell Callum's arousal, taste his muskiness, feel him filling her mouth, hard and yet soft at the same time. Her lips slid over the tender skin, feeling the ridges of his veins and the ridge of his glans and, underneath it all, the pulsing hardness. She could feel his hands on her shoulders, as he fed himself into her; and further down she could feel Ben's hands, grasping her at the waist. Her centre was filled by Ben's massive cock, her wet quim sliding over him like a close-fitting glove. She felt that she was experiencing an intensity she had never known before. The abandon, the power of the urges that drove her on, the wanton carnality: all seemed so right, so natural.

Ben removed a hand from her waist and reached round, pushing his hand down the front of her panties and feeling for her clitoris. He started to caress her, but Maddie was impatient for release, greedy now, and his rhythm was all wrong. She pushed his hand out of the way and replaced it with both of her own, working busily inside her knickers.

She spread herself with one hand, flicking and teasing with the other, occasionally slipping down to feel the warm shaft where it was moving in and out of her, then back to her clitoris. Callum gazed down and saw what she was doing.

'You dirty tart. Can't get enough, can you?'

Maddie opened her eyes and smiled up at him, and then playfully pretended to bite his cock, clamping her teeth around him just hard enough to feel the resistance of his cock beneath her teeth. That would teach him to talk to her like that. Her action only seemed to spur Callum on.

'Eat me, Maddie. Eat me right up,' he said, putting his hand under her chin and feeling as he fed himself into her once more, all the way to the back of her throat. Then she felt him hardening and shudder, and the salty spurts of his come jetted into her mouth. He shook and groaned, falling forwards slightly, his grip increasing on her shoulders. Maddie could feel his fingers digging in, but she revelled in the pain.

Beneath her, Ben recognised what his friend had done, and thickened and thrust up into her, as if in competition. He groaned as Maddie reached down between her legs and cupped his balls in her hand. They were tight within their sac, drawn right up, and Maddie's touch seemed to act as the trigger for Ben's long-approaching orgasm. He roared, and thrust a final, lurching time into her, before falling back in the chair.

Now it was Maddie's turn. She didn't want to be left behind, unsatisfied. Her hands worked busily, bringing her up and onwards towards her orgasm. A blinding white light swept through her, dazzling her for a moment as she was electrified by her climax, bucking and shuddering under its intensity.

'Come with us,' Callum said, when she had recovered. He held out his hand, and led her through the dining room, up the stairs and into the bathroom. Ben followed, fondling her still-tender arse as he came up the stairs behind her. 'We need a shower,' Callum whispered.

Maddie was amazed to see that Callum's bathroom seemed to consist mainly of a massive shower. It was so big she thought it would be more in place in the changing room in a sports centre, rather than a private bathroom. Callum turned the shower on, while Ben removed her underwear. He then pulled Maddie in under the hot caressing blast. Ben moved in next to her, and soon the two men were busy with the soap and the shower gel, washing her gently. She stood still, flanked by the two men, and allowed them to cleanse her like two diligent servants bathing their mistress. Gently, they covered every inch of her body; sliding and slipping and soaping her down. She knew this was a mere preamble to more love, and she closed her eyes under the steady beat of the water, ready for what was to come.

The next morning Maddie woke very early, having had little sleep. It was light outside. She looked at the two still-sleeping men, one on either side of her in the bed, and smiled. If she had known a threesome could be this much fun, she would have tried it years ago. She looked across to the bedside clock, wondering exactly how much sleep she had had. The last time she had looked at it had been just after two, as they were finally settling down to rest after a long and torrid session of lovemaking, exhausted by their

140

lusts. The clock read twenty to four. Maddie guessed that Ben would be getting up soon to go to the farm to do the early-morning milking, and she wanted to be gone by the time that he or Callum awoke. She wasn't embarrassed by what had happened: far from it. She was looking forward to the next time. It was just that she wanted some time to herself, without having to explain herself or even to make conversation.

Maddie gently lifted Callum's hand from where it was resting over her breast, and untwined her leg from beneath Ben's, where he had thrown it over her in his sleep. Ben's head was resting on her other breast, having found a warm, fleshy pillow for the night, and she held her breath as she carefully moved his head away from her and back on to the bed. Rather than climb over either of the men and risk waking them, she crawled down to the foot of the bed and carefully lowered herself on to the floor. Maddie tiptoed into the bathroom and ran a tap, hoping that the plumbing wasn't as antiquated as the rest of the cottage and that her two lovers wouldn't be woken by the groaning of the water pipes. She was in luck: the water ran silently. She took a brisk shower, put on her undies and then tiptoed downstairs and gathered her crumpled and creased dress from where it had been discarded on the floor of the living room.

She let herself out of the cottage and walked back towards the pub. The dawn chorus was well under way. Maddie stopped to watch a male blackbird singing from the top of a tree. There was no one about, and there was the deserted stillness which only occurs in the very early hours of the morning, before anyone wakes. Maddie hoped that she could sneak back into the pub without waking Grace either. She was relieved that the key turned silently in the lock and that the stairs did not creak as she crept up them and, once in her room, she undressed and flopped on to the bed for another couple of hours' sleep. After all, she hadn't got much the previous night.

Maddie thought back to how the two men had taken it in turns to pleasure her further, and how they had caressed each other as well as her own supine and satiated body. She had achieved almost as much satisfaction from watching them together as she had from making love with them. She had always wanted to watch two men making love and, although Ben and Callum had only kissed and fondled each other, Maddie had found it intensely stimulating. She knew that the vivid vision of the two men would become a mainstay of her fantasising in the future. As she drifted off to sleep, Maddie was thinking that she couldn't recall the last time she had made love in a bed. As far as she was concerned, they were for sleeping in and that was it. And yet, last night had been pleasurable in the extreme. Maybe she might yet become a convert to sex in a bed.

The next thing she was aware of was a knock at the door. Grace called gently from the other side.

'Maddie, love, it's eight-thirty. I thought I ought to give you a shout.'

Maddie blearily looked around her, and then cursed when she realised that she had forgotten to set her alarm clock on getting in, earlier that morning. She shuffled off the bed, pulled her bathrobe around her and opened the door. Grace laughed when she saw her.

'My God, look what the cat dragged in,' Grace chortled. For one horrified moment, Maddie thought that Grace must know about her nocturnal escapade; but then Grace hastily added, 'Did you not sleep very well, last night?'and it became clear to Maddie from Grace's embarrassed reaction that her hostess was worried that Maddie might have misunderstood her gentle teasing and taken offence.

Maddie smiled, to show that no offence had been taken, and nodded. 'You could say that.'

Grace told her that her breakfast was prepared, and left her to get herself ready.

When Maddie turned and caught a glimpse of her own reflection in the mirror, she understood the reason for Grace's initial amusement. She looked terrible. Her long hair was messy and scarecrow-like, and she had big bags under her eyes. On closer inspection, she realised that most of this was the smudged remnants of her not-so-waterproof mascara, which she had managed to rub all over her face in the shower at Callum's house earlier that morning. She grabbed her wash bag and hurried into the bathroom to rectify matters. She took another quick shower, as much to wake herself up as to clean herself, and then she dressed in fresh clothes and went down to the kitchen, where Grace was standing ready with a coffee pot and cup.

'Damn, I'm really late. Thanks for getting me up, Grace,' said Maddie.

'No point in busting a gut to get on,' said Grace. 'You should take a tip from us here in Dorset. Slow down. Change the pace. You'll get it done, you'll see.'

'I wish I had your confidence,' said Maddie, slurping the hot coffee quickly. Then she grabbed an apple and an orange from the fruit bowl. 'Can't stop for breakfast. See you.'

Grace handed her a lunchbox and a flask. 'Thought you might need some more coffee,' she said.

'You're an angel, Grace,' Maddie said, kissing her on the cheek and then hurrying outside to her car. She had work to do.

Time passed all too quickly. It was nearing the end of Maddie's allocated three weeks, and she was trying not to panic. She still had several locations to organise, including the elusive furniture store. The manager of the store in Bournemouth was due back from her holiday on a Friday evening, and Maddie had made a nine o'clock appointment with her the very next morning. Filming on *Beneath the Hillfort* started on the following Thursday and, although the furniture-store scenes were not the first to be shot, Maddie wanted the location to be securely organised at least.

Grace had been a calming influence on her, telling her not to worry. Maddie was not so easily assured, however. She felt that she was very likely staring failure in the face – something that had never happened to her before. She had never yet failed to complete her work on schedule. Her anxiety was causing her to fret even more than she normally would be.

It was while Maddie was eating her breakfast on the day of her appointment at the furniture store that Grace appeared at the kitchen door.

'You've got a visitor, Maddie, dear,' she said, and then stood aside to let Greg enter the kitchen.

'Bloody hell, Greg!' said Maddie in surprise, with a spoonful of cereal halfway to her mouth.

'And a very good morning to you too,' said Greg, parking himself on a seat next to Maddie. 'Mind if I join you?' he asked, reaching across for a plate and helping himself to some toast. Despite her abrupt greeting, Maddie was pleased to see a familiar face. It almost felt as if the cavalry had arrived. She watched in a still-stunned silence as her unexpected guest spread the toast with butter and then a thick dollop of marmalade. He demolished the slice in three mouthfuls. He reached for another slice, and then another, and then another. When he had finished, he wiped his mouth on the back of his hand and smiled at her.

'That's better. I was getting pretty hungry.'

'It's lovely to see you, Greg. I take it you didn't come from Cambridge to Dorset just to have breakfast with me?' Maddie asked. 'Is there a problem in the office?'

'Nope,' Greg replied. 'Everything's fine. I didn't have anything to do this weekend, so I thought I'd come and offer you a hand. I heard that Hugh had been a snot, the other day.'

'Oh. Good news travels fast,' said Maddie flatly.

'Well, you know how Polly listens in to Freya's calls. She overheard you telling Freya how shitty Hugh had been. He sounds a real prick.'

Maddie nodded solemnly.

'Anyway, Freya mentioned to me that you were pretty busy and hadn't had a day off yet, so I thought I'd offer a hand. You never know when I might come in useful.'

'That's really sweet of you, Greg,' Maddie said with feeling. Once again, she was reminded of what a kind and thoughtful man Greg was. 'You must have set off from Cambridge in the middle of the night to get here at this hour.' She checked her watch. It was seven-thirty.

'Yeah, well, the roads are empty in the wee small hours, so it was an easy drive. Also, I'm in something a little faster and a little more reliable than Freya's MG.' He grinned and winked at Maddie.

'Oh, so you heard about that, too? I was bloody annoyed: when I told Freya about the problems with the MG, she just laughed. Oh, well. I guess I should have expected that the car was going to be temperamental, if it's anything like its owner. So, what's the hot gossip from the office?' Maddie asked. 'How is our beloved leader?'

'As loopy as ever. Doing her nut with Miles. He's being a real prima donna, now he's on the Pascali film.' Greg caught himself. 'Oops. Sorry, you probably don't want to hear about that.'

Maddie smiled thinly. 'No, it's OK,' she said unconvincingly. 'How's he getting on with it?'

'He hasn't actually started work on it, yet. They've put the shoot dates back, so that's put all the pre-production dates back, too. Everything's on hold for the mo.'

Maddie smiled. 'I can't say I'm too sorry to hear that.'

'But the way Miles is carrying on, you'd think he's already some Hollywood big shot. He's demanding that Freya keep his schedule clear so he can be free to start, the moment the word comes through from Sam Pascali. As you can imagine, Freya was so unimpressed by this that she told him that if he wanted a free schedule, he'd have to take unpaid leave. That shut him up a bit, and now he's working on a car commercial, searching for a suitable slate quarry in a remote part of Wales. Apparently, it's

146

been pissing down with rain there and he thinks he's caught pneumonia. Not quite as glamorous as working on a Hollywood movie.'

Maddie was heartened by the news that the location scouting hadn't yet started on *D-Day Dawn*.

'So. Found any nice willow trees recently?' Greg asked with a grin.

Maddie laughed. 'No. But there's plenty of places I've got my eye on round here,' she said, watching for his reaction.

'Any chance that we might have to go and see any of them today?' Greg asked, reaching under the table and stroking her thigh.

'There might be,' she replied, pretending not to notice his hand. She knew that feigning disinterest would only spur him on. 'But first, I have an appointment with the manager of Spencer and Staples in Bournemouth. Fancy coming along?'

'Try to stop me. I didn't drive all the way down here this morning to stand on the doorstep and wave you off to the office.'

They drove to Bournemouth in Greg's car, and Maddie was pleased to sit back and be driven for a change. It also gave her a better opportunity to look around her and make some notes.

'Do you want me to come in, or shall I meet you in a while?' Greg asked as he parked in a metered bay outside the store.

'Come on in, Greg,' Maddie said. 'The manager's a woman, so maybe you'll be able to charm her, if I can't get what I want from her.' These words weren't spoken idly. Greg was a very charming man and Maddie had seen in the past how easily he could negotiate a deal with women. They seemed to acquiesce without demur to anything he wanted.

They walked into the busy furniture store. 'Let's just have a shufti around, first,' Maddie said. 'I've already checked it out, but I'd be interested in your opinion.'

They wandered through the show kitchens, past the rows of three-piece suites, and around mocked-up bathrooms. Maddie led Greg into one of the show bedrooms. It was bounded on three sides by flimsy partition walls some eight feet high, against which were set a dressing table, a chest of drawers and wardrobes, all part of a fitted bedroom suite.

'This is the one I had my eye on,' Maddie said.

They looked at the script, checking the shooting requirements against the layout of the room. In the film, two of the characters would be caught by a member of the staff as they were getting amorous on the bed, and a short fight would ensue before they were then ejected by security guards. The room seemed perfect, and was also large enough to allow the film crew plenty of space.

'Imagine that. Getting down to it in somewhere as public as this!' said Greg, a twinkle in his eyes.

'Terrible, isn't it?' asked Maddie. 'Whoever would do such a thing?'

'Let's have a look in here,' said Greg, pulling Maddie across the room to one of the large mirrored wardrobes. Maddie watched with curiosity as he opened the door and detached the clothes rail hanging across the top. He threw it on the bed and then pulled her in to the wardrobe with him. Maddie giggled as he shut the door on them both. In the dark, Maddie couldn't see a thing, but she could feel Greg next to her, and hear his heavy fast breathing.

'God, I've missed you,' he muttered with feeling, reaching for her and pulling her to him. Maddie searched for his face with her hands, and then cupped it as she brought her lips up to meet his. Greg's hands played lightly over her body, teasing her nipples through the thin material of her dress and then cupping her breasts. He pushed her neckline down and buried his head in her cleavage, kissing the tender skin. Maddie felt downwards, and was rewarded by the satisfying feel of a large hardon beneath Greg's trousers. She unzipped his flies, and pushed down his pants, releasing his cock.

It then happened very quickly. Greg turned her and pressed her against the back wall of the wardrobe, scrabbling to lift her dress. Maddie jumped up and wrapped her legs around his waist, and he held her under her buttocks, using one hand to pull her knickers to the side. It didn't matter that neither of them could see what they were doing; they were guided by touch. Greg found her already wet centre with his fingers, and then replaced them with his prick. Bending at the knees, he fucked her urgently, his hands cupping her buttocks. The wardrobe was none-too-solidly built, and it rattled and shook with Greg's thrusts, but Maddie couldn't have cared less. The urgency was what drove her on, and she delighted in the impropriety of what they were doing. Soon Greg's guttural grunts warned that he was going to come.

'Come on baby, give it to me,' Maddie whispered in his ear. 'Let me have all that lovely, thick spunk.'

Greg groaned, and shuddered as he pumped deep into her. He collapsed forward, pressing Maddie even harder into the back of the wardrobe, and moaned.

'Jesus, that was intense,' he whispered. He stood still for a while longer, and then lifted Maddie off his still-hard prick. Maddie groped blindly on the floor for her knickers, and used them to clean herself up. She felt for Greg.

'You OK?' she asked.

'Mm,' he said. 'Just a bit knocked for six, right now. Jesus, I'm almost seeing stars!'

After waiting a while to allow him to recover, she asked, 'Ready?'

'As I'll ever be,' he laughed, and Maddie cautiously opened the wardrobe door, squinting into the harsh artificial lighting of the store. There was no one about. 'Quick,' she hissed, and pulled Greg out of the cupboard behind her. Greg reinstalled the rail, and Maddie picked up her notes where she had left them on the floor by the bed. She replaced them, and her knickers, in her shoulder bag.

'So, are you going to add this to your list of secret places?' Greg asked with a smile.

'I might do,' Maddie smirked, and stepped up to him and gave him a long, lingering kiss.

'Haven't you got a manager to meet?' Greg asked.

'Oops. Almost forgot about that.' Maddie grinned. 'I had other, more pressing things on my mind.' With that, she reached down and gave Greg's groin a gentle squeeze through his trousers. 'Come on then!'

'Where? To the manager or back in to the wardrobe?' he laughed, and Maddie swatted him playfully on his arm as she dragged him away to find the manager's office.

Chapter Seven

*M*addie was working as usual at her table in the bar when Grace came over to her.

'You've got a phone call,' Grace said. 'Wouldn't give his name.'

This immediately told Maddie that it wasn't Hugh: reticence was not one of his characteristics. She went up to the bar and picked up the phone.

'Hi, Maddie, it's Harry.'

Maddie paused as she tried to recall a Harry. She met so many people in her job and wasn't always successful in remembering them all.

Harry prompted her. 'Remember me? Badly parked balloon pilot in Weymouth?'

'Oh, Harry; yes, of course. I'm sorry. How are you?'

'Fine, thanks. Look, I was ringing to see if I could persuade you to come on a flight with me.'

'Um, that's very kind,' said Maddie. She didn't think she could spare the time.

'Shall I tell you what I think?' Harry asked, then

continued without a pause for Maddie to answer. 'I think you need a day off. I'm sure you've been working too hard and, despite the MG, I think your boss is taking you for granted.'

Maddie smiled at Harry's mistaken and yet correct idea about her boss. After all, what was Hugh to her right now, if not her boss? He certainly did take her for granted, and she had to do everything he said. She was little more than a hired hand to him, he had made that abundantly clear. And she was feeling very tired after almost three weeks of non-stop work without a day off.

'Do you know, Harry, I think I might just say yes,' Maddie said suddenly and emphatically. Sod Hugh and his film. She deserved a day off and, if nothing else, it might help to clear her mind, relax her and so enable her to work better. Maddie could justify most things to herself if she needed to.

'Great,' said Harry. 'How about tomorrow?'

Maddie knew she had no appointments then, and so agreed. Harry arranged to pick her up from outside the pub.

And so, at just before eight on the next morning, Maddie put her camera, purse and notebook into her small bag, which she then slipped over her shoulder, and she stepped out into the bright sunlight. It was another hot, clear day, and there was a slight breeze; perfect for ballooning, she imagined. Right on time, Harry drove up in his car. Maddie had expected there to be a large trailer hitched to the back.

'Morning, Maddie,' beamed Harry as he opened the passenger door for her.

'Hi there, Harry. Lovely to see you again. Where's the balloon?'

'Today is your treat, remember? You don't think

152

I'd ask you to give me a hand getting it all set up? It's quite a fiddly job, not to mention time-consuming. My assistant has set it up at the launching place. All we have to do is get there. I've chosen somewhere quite special.'

Some time later, Harry parked the car in the car park at Lulworth Cove. Maddie had not found time to visit this famous Dorset beauty spot before, and was very pleased to have the chance. She told Harry as much, saying that she had a jigsaw of Lulworth Cove as a child. The scene before her was so familiar that it almost felt like meeting an old friend.

'You'll get to see it from the air too, a double bonus,' Harry told her. He led her a little way to a grassy area close to the high cliffs. There the balloon was laid out on the grass, with the basket attached to it, lying on its side. Maddie noticed the sandbags hanging on the outside of the wicker basket. A series of guy ropes was strung from the basket to the ground to anchor the balloon. It had attracted a lot of attention, and groups of people were standing around, watching the proceedings with interest. Harry had a few words with the man who was checking the ropes, and then went over to the basket. He reached in his pocket, got out a packet of matches and lit the burner. The flame roared fiercely, and Maddie took an instinctive step or two back. There was a ripple of appreciative comments from the onlookers.

Harry held out his hand to Maddie. 'It's OK. Don't be afraid.'

He still had the matches in his hand, and Maddie recognised them as the box he had just bought from the shop when she met him in Weymouth. Maddie smiled to herself, remembering their meeting, and took his hand. She watched as the balloon gradually filled with hot air, puffing and plumping up before collapsing down on to the ground again under the strength of the breeze. The balloon slowly filled with hot air as Harry oversaw the burner, and soon it held enough to lift itself off the ground. The balloon gradually rose upward, gently pulling the basket over on to its base. Slowly, it lifted higher and higher over their heads until, looking up, Maddie could see that the fabric was taut and the balloon was fully inflated. The guy ropes were creaking under the strain of holding the basket down. Maddie was struck by the sheer scale of the balloon. Standing under it, she felt dwarfed.

'In you get,' Harry said, helping her into the basket. She was surprised at the size of the basket, and Harry explained that it could hold eight people easily. Maddie noticed a matching wicker hamper strapped into one corner, and the two folding director's chairs tied against one side of the basket.

'There's a good breeze blowing from the east-south-east. It'll push us inlands slightly, and we'll drift more or less westward. Should be a lovely day,' Harry said.

Maddie had never been in a balloon before, but was surprised that she wasn't too nervous. Looking at what would be holding her up, hundreds of feet above the earth, it all seemed very insubstantial; but she had complete trust in Harry. And the prospect of seeing Dorset from the air was too exciting for her to feel much fear.

Harry climbed in next to her, and adjusted the burner so that it burnt even more fiercely. The noise was terrific, a loud roaring sound, and for a while

Maddie couldn't talk to Harry as it was so loud. She put her hands to her ears, flinching at the volume.

The creaking from the guy ropes was becoming louder, signalling the increasing strain they were under, and Harry signalled to the man to release them. With a slight lurch, the basket left the ground. Maddie grabbed the side of the basket for support, stricken by a sudden moment of panic. It was too late to turn back now.

'Do you have any parachutes?' she asked nervously. 'You know, in case anything goes wrong?'

Harry smiled reassuringly. 'Nothing will go wrong, Maddie. Believe me. I wouldn't do this job if I didn't believe it was perfectly safe – I'm too much of a coward. And I certainly wouldn't bring you along if there was any risk. So you can put your complete faith in my equipment: a basket made of a few twigs woven together, some string, some silk and a load of hot air.'

'Don't tease, please,' she begged. 'I'm not too sure about this.'

Harry realised that his flippancy might have been misjudged, and he hastily apologised and tried to reassure her. Maddie looked over the side of the basket, secretly relieved that the sides of the basket were fairly high. She watched the ground receding below her, and the people and the cars in the car park gradually shrinking until they seemed like toy figures from some child's game. The perfect notch-shaped bay of Lulworth Cove lay beneath her; and next to it Stair Hole, a smaller scoop in the coastline, rimmed with crazily folded layers of rock; and a little further to the west she could see the rock arch of Durdle Door stepping out into the sea. She had expected to feel queasy, but the flight was so calm and steady it almost felt as if they were still on terra firma. Harry kept the burner going until they had achieved a fair altitude, and then turned it off. Maddie didn't dare ask how high they were. She decided that, in this case, ignorance was bliss.

The silence was almost complete. All Maddie could hear was the ruffling noise of the balloon silk, the creaking of the wicker basket and the breeze in her ears. No traffic noise, no excited children's screams, no barking dogs. The rapture and wonderment on Maddie's face must have been apparent, as Harry grinned at her and said, 'It's fantastic, isn't it? On days like this, I think I've got the best job in the world.'

As they had gained height, the panoramic views increased, with the horizon receding further and yet further. To one side of the basket was the sea, azure blue by the shore then receding to a deeper, darker blue further out, its surface glittering with the reflected sunlight; and to the other was the green, lush farmland. Until that moment, Maddie didn't feel that she had ever appreciated just how many different shades of green were possible.

'It feels like we're on the top of the world,' Maddie murmured. Below her, the Dorset countryside looked pristine in its tiny perfection, and sailboats on the sea looked like toys. Above her, puffy white clouds slowly moved across the sky. Maddie knew that they were way below the level of the clouds, but it felt as if they were close enough to reach out and brush them.

'Hope you're not in a hurry to get anywhere,' Harry said. 'Our progress will be stately, to say the least.'

Maddie turned a full 360 degrees in the basket,

looking around her. 'I don't care if we stay up here forever. This is perfect. Thank you so much.'

Harry smiled. 'My pleasure.'

Maddie was fascinated by the view below her. Gradually, they drifted westward. Maddie yelped with delight when she saw the figure of a man astride a white horse on a hillside. She hadn't come across it in her research about Dorset. 'Good grief, it must be massive, to be so clearly visible from up here,' she said. Harry nodded, and explained how it had been formed by cutting into the white chalk hillside, the turf and soil removed to reach the pure white chalk bedrock a few inches below.

Some time later, they passed near Dorchester, and what Maddie knew as a busy, bustling market town was reduced to a neat map-like arrangement of roads, houses and parks; a perfect toytown that she felt she could reach down and rearrange if she wanted. But Maddie's biggest thrill was when the balloon drifted over Maiden Castle. She had visited it when she had scouted the hillforts for the shoot; but only now, with the tiny figures below who were waving at the balloon acting as a scale, could she fully appreciate its size and the complexity of its earthworks. She went up on tiptoe, leaning so far over the side of the basket, and craning at the wonderful sight below her, that Harry put his hands around her waist to hold her. When she straightened up again, he left his hands there, and leant forwards and whispered into her ear.

'Do you know what I really love about being up here?' he asked.

Maddie turned to him and grinned. 'No,' she said. 'Tell me.' Harry was very close, and she could see the questioning look in his eyes.

'You can do and say absolutely anything. You can make love, or scream obscenities at the top of your voice, or take all your clothes off, or even take a piss over the edge of the basket, and no one knows. It's the ultimate secret place. And even if someone does see – maybe a passing helicopter pilot, say – they can't do anything about it. We're in our own little world, here.'

'A secret place,' Maddie murmured. She smiled at Harry, thinking that here was someone else who might like their loving *al fresco*. How had he guessed? But they had all day in the balloon, and these things could wait. 'Do you know, I have never thought of the possibilities of ballooning in those terms before? I always thought it was to do with sightseeing and experiencing nature's beauty in an environmentally friendly way,' Maddie teased gently.

'That only goes to show how wrong you've got it,' Harry replied. 'You should try it.'

'Try what?'

'Being disreputable in a balloon.'

'What did you have in mind?' she asked, thinking that showing an interest wouldn't do any harm, either.

'This and that,' he replied, smiling.

'And maybe a bit of the other?' Maddie laughed, amused by the vagueness of his comment when they both knew what it was that he was referring to. Maddie held his gaze for a few moments, communicating her complicity, and then turned and peered over the edge again, delighting in the views that were slowly unfurling beneath her. Harry gave the burner another blast, and the balloon gently rose higher. For a while they drifted in a happy, companionable silence. Harry seemed content to wait.

A little while later, alerted by his movements, Maddie watched as Harry knelt by the hamper and released it from where it was fastened against the side of the basket. He undid it, and inside Maddie could see a set of porcelain plates, some silver cutlery and two crystal champagne flutes fastened to the underside of the lid by leather straps. The basket was filled with various containers of food, and at one side was a champagne bottle. Harry had thought to make sure it stayed chilled by wrapping a freezer blanket around it. Maddie was impressed.

'I think we should celebrate,' Harry said, lifting the bottle out.

'Anything in particular?' Maddie asked.

'How about you losing your virginity?' he said with a smile.

'I'm afraid we're a bit late for that particular celebration,' she laughed.

'No, your ballooning virginity. You did say this was your first time?'

Maddie laughed, and nodded.

Harry undid the wire cage and gently eased the champagne cork out of the bottle, placing it in the hamper. Maddie sensed that he was trying to impress her, and yet he had resisted the grand gesture of firing the cork over the side of the basket and out into the Dorset countryside. She knew enough about speed and velocity to know that a cork falling from a great height could be dangerous to those below, and she admired his thoughtfulness. Harry poured out two glasses of champagne, and handed one to Maddie. She raised her glass to him.

'Cheers. To new experiences.'

'I'll drink to that,' Harry replied, grinning.

The gentle creaking of the basket accompanied

their silent enjoyment as they drifted westward. Disguising her scrutiny as interest in the scenery behind him, Maddie watched Harry closely. He gazed up, checking the balloon and looking to see if he needed more hot air. She could see the pulse beating in his throat, and his Adam's apple bobbed up and then down again as he took another sip of champagne. He was a big hulking man, but had a gentleness about him too. He was dressed in a rugby shirt and jeans, and Maddie felt that he must be hot in the thick, closely woven shirt.

'Why don't you take your shirt off?' she asked him. 'It's so hot, especially with the burner going.'

He looked at her and smiled. 'Only if you'll take yours off,' he said.

Maddie laughed. 'Deal,' and, before Harry had a chance to do anything, she pulled her own shirt off over her head and then advanced on him. Mock-alarmed, he shrank back against the wall of the basket.

'That's coming off,' she said, undoing the buttons on his shirt. She noticed with pleasure that Harry was gazing down at her breasts, nestled in the lacy cups of her bra. She helped him out of his shirt, and then pressed him back against the basket edge. He seemed surprised by her ardour and her directness, and she guessed that maybe Harry wasn't used to a woman being the dominant partner in his relationships.

'I'm going to ravish you,' she whispered, going up on tiptoe and murmuring in his ear.

'I don't think so,' Harry replied, grabbing her by the waist and throwing her down on to the floor of the basket. Maddie could feel his excitement growing against her. 'No, I think you've got it quite wrong.

I'm going to ravish you,' Harry muttered, deftly rolling Maddie over on to her back, and fumbling with the clasp at the front of her bra. They tussled some more, in a pretence of opposition, on the floor of the basket, and Maddie could feel herself becoming turned on by the struggle. Harry finally succeeded in unhooking Maddie's bra, and her breasts fell free. They were already pointed by her hard aroused nipples, and he bent and took one and then the other in his mouth, kneading them in his hands. Maddie moaned softly. She revelled in the sensation of bare flesh against bare flesh, but she wanted to be fully naked with Harry.

Maddie reached down and undid the waistband of his jeans, and then unzipped the flies. Harry's cock sprang out at her almost instantaneously, unfettered by underwear. He was circumcised and thick. She shivered inwardly, wondering if she could take him. Harry had followed her lead, and was undoing her shorts. As he unzipped her flies, he slipped his hand down under her panties, as if he couldn't wait to get her clothes off before touching her. She was wet and ready for him, and felt him slip down her furrow with ease and disappear inside her. He took her breast in his mouth as he slowly began to bring her to orgasm on the floor of the basket.

Maddie reached out for his cock, and began to manipulate him too, spitting on the palm of her hand to lubricate his cock against her hand. She had to let go as she came, fearful that her uncontrollable jerks as she lashed about and the automatic clenching and unclenching of her fists might hurt him. She cried out, bucked and arched, and then fell limply under Harry.

Harry lay back, regarding her. 'I want to see you

naked,' he said, so Maddie slipped her shorts and knickers right off. Then she stood before him, turning round fully so that he could view her from every angle. He clearly liked what he saw, as he took his thick prick in his hand and started to play it back and forth. She stood with her back against the edge of the basket, and Harry came to her, reaching down with one hand while he pleasured himself with the other. Then he moved his hand to her waist and turned her around, so that she was facing outward.

'Hold the side,' he whispered to her, and Maddie gasped as she felt him close behind her, pressing his great cock against her sex. He was bending his knees to bring his prick level with her, and she went up on to tiptoe to try to make it easier for him. The height difference was too great, and Harry pushed the hamper over to her. She stepped on to it, and Harry entered her almost immediately, and began a languorous pumping rhythm. She screwed her eyes shut, ignoring the beautiful countryside, as Harry thrust into her; and her grip on the edge of the basket tightened as she felt another orgasm welling within her. As Maddie's climax came, so did Harry's, and they called out in abandon as the urgency of their passions melded and merged. They fell back on to the floor and lay there, still locked, and slept.

Later, they woke and dressed each other, sleepily sated by sex. The wind changed direction, pushing them towards the coast.

'We'll have to land soon, else we'll be out over the sea,' Harry said. He reached over the side of the basket, untied a sandbag and let the contents fall in a fine spray. 'You let some out as well,' he said, and Maddie obeyed quickly. She did not relish the idea of a ditched landing in the sea, strong swimmer though she was. She didn't feel a lurch as they dropped, but could tell from the way their horizon was decreasing that they must be descending at quite a rate. As they neared the ground, Harry regulated the descent by alternating the emptying of the sand-bags with short bursts of the burner; and Maddie could tell how skilled he was when they landed in a field with nothing more than a soft bump. Harry turned off the burner. The slowly deflating balloon fell and settled on the grass next to the basket, and Harry helped Maddie out. He consulted a map, and made a call on his mobile, telling his assistant where they were.

'He won't be here with the trailer for another half hour,' said Harry with a twinkle in his eyes. 'Got any ideas how we might kill the time?'

It was early in the morning of the first day of filming. Maddie had not yet finalised all the locations, but that could not be helped now. Filming was going ahead regardless. She would have to try to finish the negotiations in the evenings and over the phone while undertaking her filming duties – whatever they might be. Despite having had a wonderful time, she felt guilty for having allowed Harry to persuade her to take a day off. Something had nagged in her subconscious then about it not being a good idea, and she had ignored her instinct – always a bad move. Now she was rushed for time, and would have to double up her work. That'll teach me for bunking off, she thought ruefully.

Maddie set off from the New Inn, having packed all her things, eaten a large breakfast and said good-bye to Grace, reminding her sad-faced hostess that she'd be back before too long with the rest of the film crew. Over the previous three weeks, the two women had become very close, Grace becoming something of a confidante-cum-surrogate-mother to Maddie.

'I feel like I'm losing all my babies,' said Grace miserably. 'First Callum goes off, and now you're leaving too.'

'I'll see you soon, I promise,' Maddie said, kissing Grace on the cheek. Grace sniffed in reply.

'Don't be a stranger,' Grace said as Maddie got in the MG and started up the engine. As she drove past, Maddie gave a big wave to The Watchers on the Green. Despite the early hour, they were sitting at their usual observation post; and the two women pretended not to have noticed Maddie's greeting. They had steadfastly ignored her since Callum's shocking revelation about the nature of her business in Winterborne St Giles.

Maddie drove over to Dorchester, and got there just before seven thirty. She was going to meet up with the other members of the production at the Haddon Grange Hotel on the High Street. When she enquired, she was informed at the reception desk that the group had been staying there since the previous evening, and had already departed for the location shoot that morning. The receptionist also told her that she had been expected the previous night. Maddie's heart sank.

'Mr Shepherd said to give you this,' said the receptionist, handing over an envelope.

Maddie opened it and read the unsigned note in the familiar crabby handwriting: 'Glad you have deigned to join us. We are at the maze. Get there *now*.'

Maddie cursed. This was not a good start to the

filming. Hugh had said nothing about expecting her to join the cast and crew at the hotel the previous evening. She wasn't a mind-reader – how could she possibly have guessed that this was what he wanted? And he was going to be even more displeased with her when he found out that she still hadn't managed to complete on a couple of the contracts. She gritted her teeth and drove out to Brigham House.

Maddie had visited plenty of film shoots before, although she had never worked on one. Normally her work was done long before the first scenes were filmed, and any location problems during filming that the unit manager couldn't fix were normally solvable by a few phone calls from her desk in Cambridge. She knew what to expect: the mass of lights and reflectors, cameras on large unwieldy-looking bases, tracks laid across the ground for the cameras to move on; boom microphones dangling so low that they must surely be in shot, and the miles of electrical wiring. She also knew all about the behind-the-scenes activity: the hairdressing and make-up artists; the continuity people; the props and wardrobe staff; and the cohorts of technicians over-seeing the setting up, moving and maintenance of all the equipment. Then there were the lesser-known but just as essential members of the crew: the cater-ers, the chaperones when children were involved, the assistants and the runners who did any odd job needed.

What greeted Maddie at Brigham House was not what she was prepared for. She wandered round to the maze, where rehearsals of a scene were taking place. There were perhaps eight or nine crew mem-bers, no more. There was a single camera and cameraman, a lone sound man, and Hugh directing from next to the camera. Maddie knew that the film was low-budget, but wasn't expecting it to be quite as low-budget as this. She had seen larger crews for the filming of a television series.

Hugh was talking to the cameraman as Maddie walked up to them. Hugh turned from his conversation and stood silently watching her as she drew near, making his disapproval clear. His face was set in a stern expression.

'Maddie. You're late.'

Maddie began to explain, but Hugh silenced her with an imperious wave of his hand.

'I'll hear your excuse later. See over there, on the floor next to my chair?' Hugh gestured to a single folding chair. It seemed that the others would have to stand in his presence. 'That's your continuity notepad.'

So that was what Hugh had planned for her. Continuity.

'You've got your polaroid camera with you?'

Yes, no thanks to you, Maddie thought. He hadn't told her she would need one for this part of the job; luckily she used one for her scouting. She nodded.

'You know what to do?'

'Not really,' said Maddie sourly. 'I know what continuity is, I just don't know how to achieve it. I'm a locations manager, not a bloody continuity woman.'

'While you're working for me, you'll be whatever I say you are,' Hugh snapped. Then he began to speedily rattle off the requirements of her job. 'You have to be on the ball, as the scenes aren't going to be shot in sequence. Check that there is continuity between elements that stretch over several scenes – clothes are a prime example. In connected scenes, make sure the characters are wearing the same clothes, hairstyles, make-up and jewellery; that objects stay in the same position unless a character has moved them. Example: you will ensure that once an earring is taken off in one shot, it remains off in the shots that follow chronologically in the film, and does not magically reappear again on the actress unless we see her put it on in the action. Make notes, take photos, whatever it takes. You have to be accurate. I'm relying on you. Got it?'

Maddie wasn't sure she liked being spoken to like this, but Hugh had already turned from her and was shouting orders at two men and two women. Maddie judged from their costumes that they must be some of the actors. One of the men was dressed in mud-splattered overalls and wellington boots, and the other three in everyday clothes.

The cameraman came up to her and grinned, holding out his hand in greeting. Maddie warmed to him immediately – he was the first person to have sought her out to greet her. He had a thin angular face and Maddie could tell that he had a similarly lean body under his jeans and striped T-shirt. His hair was cropped very short, but his slightly alarming appearance was diffused by the warmth of his smile. Maddie liked what she saw.

'Hi, I'm Finlay. Don't mind Hugh. Have you met everyone?'

Maddie shook her head. 'No one, actually.'

'Come with me. There's time.' Finlay took her by the hand and led her around the group of people, introducing them and giving her a brief explanation of what their role in the production was. Maddie made a big effort to remember everyone's names – something she wasn't always too good at. She was touched by Finlay's thoughtfulness. Hugh couldn't care less if she went unintroduced. Everyone greeted her warmly, and it struck her that this disparate group of people seemed to have already gelled into a friendly, bantering tribe, only one day in to shooting. She wondered if many of them had worked together before.

'Now, have you got an up-to-date copy of the shooting script?' Finlay asked when all the introductions had been made.

'No, 'fraid not.' Maddie replied.

'Have mine. I know what's happening for this shot, and I'll get one off Melinda later on. No time now. We're on page fifty-six, the scene where they meet by the maze.'

Maddie didn't have time to thank Finlay properly, as Hugh had turned from a heated debate with Jeff, the lighting man and shouted at Finlay to get behind the camera. The other cast and crew members exchanged glances, clearly unimpressed by Hugh's directorial style.

The first day's shooting was something of a baptism by fire for Maddie. Through necessity, she learnt the job as she went along, making notes on who was standing where, who was wearing what, who was holding what. She recorded anything that might need replicating in another shot from a different angle within the same scene; anything that carried over several scenes, like the overalls and wellies that one of the actors wore in five consecutive scenes; and anything that had to be present in every scene, like the wedding ring on one of the actresses. It was nerve-wracking, and Maddie was sure she wasn't doing it properly. Had she recorded enough? Still, she reckoned, if Hugh didn't want to employ a professional continuity person, that was his concern. The old adage was true, she thought: you get what you pay for.

Maddie had quickly become fully *au fait* with how things went on the shoot: first there would be the camera rehearsal, where the actors went through their scene and Finlay checked his camera angles, moves and focusing; and then filming would take place. By midday, she was getting thirsty. As she had expected, there had been no breaks, but she wondered where the catering trailer was so that she could get some coffee to drink as she worked. She looked round, but couldn't see it, so she asked Finlay. He laughed.

'You've got a bit to learn! Don't forget that this is the lowest of all low-budget movies. Hugh's arranged for a lady with a sandwich van to come round at lunchtime. You've got to pay for the food, mind.'

Maddie shook her head in disbelief. She knew that catering was always provided and paid for by the production. It wasn't a perk of the job, it was a necessity, given the long hours and arduous work undertaken on a shoot. Besides, it seemed commonsensical that a well-fed crew would be a happy crew, and a happy crew would be a hard-working one.

That evening, filming finally finished at seven o'clock. Hugh left first, leaving the others to clear up for the evening. Equipment was packed away into a couple of lock-ups which had been messily dumped on the beautiful lawns of the house. The lock-ups were old lorry containers, and were very capacious. Despite the quantity of equipment to be stored, the work was achieved quickly by the group, working as a single efficient body. No orders were needed:

169

they all knew intuitively what to do. As the last pieces were being stowed, a tatty old minibus drove up the driveway of Brigham House and parked by the lock-ups. The actors and crew piled in, apart from Finlay, who had his own vehicle. Maddie walked to her MG, and followed the bus back to Dorchester, feeling an uncomfortable pall of doom settling over her. She was trapped, for the next five weeks.

At the hotel, Maddie was shown to her room, and was pleasantly surprised. She had thought that, given Hugh's obsessive economy drive, she would be sharing a room; but she had a room all to herself. From the way the skirting boards, the picture rail and the old Victorian plaster mouldings ended abruptly at one of the walls, she could tell that it had originally been a much larger room, now partitioned into two. Despite this, there was an en-suite bathroom in her room, albeit a very compact one. There was a television, a phone by the bed and attractive views over the hotel garden from the window. Maddie ordered a sandwich from room service, unpacked and took a quick shower.

As she changed into fresh clothes, Maddie sighed. She still had a lot of work to do, the penalty of her double job with Hugh. There were locations to finalise. Just as all the others would be eating, drinking and relaxing, she would be setting off again to try to sweet-talk the last recalcitrant landowners into signing the contracts. On her way out, she met Juliet, one of the actresses, coming out of the next-door room.

Maddie couldn't place Juliet's age. She looked as if she were in her early twenties. She had a sweet, doll-like face framed by neatly cut brown hair, big brown eyes and a look of surprised innocence about her; but this was at odds with her personality, which suggested she was much older and far more wordly than someone in her early twenties. From the way she talked, Maddie could tell that Juliet had been around a bit, and she had one of the filthiest senses of humour Maddie had ever come across, either in a man or a woman.

'How are you holding up?' Juliet asked. 'I heard Hugh giving you a hard time. He's got big problems, that man.'

Maddie was touched by Juliet's concern. 'Fine, thanks. I'm kind of resigned to it, by now.'

Juliet touched her arm and smiled sympathetically. 'Keep your pecker up,' she said. 'See you in the bar later?'

Maddie nodded. 'I hope so.'

Maddie got back to the hotel at half past ten, relieved that she had managed to finalise the last locations. She felt she wanted to celebrate her small achievement and, as she could hear laughter in the bar, she poked her head around the door to see if any of the film crew wanted a drink with her. She was pleased to see that nearly all the cast and crew were there, and was equally pleased to see that Hugh was not.

Finlay looked up and greeted her. 'Hi, Maddie. Come and join us.'

Chairs were shunted up to make room, and George, the sound man, pulled a chair over from another table. Maddie sat down gratefully, and soon was chatting away as easily as if she had known these people all her life. She watched the way the group interacted together, trying to work out the relationships between the various people in this disparate group. She noticed that there was playful

171

sparring rivalry between Finlay and George; that Melinda, the production assistant, was being gently teased by Turner, one of the actors; and that Rob, the electrician, seemed very keen on Annie, one of the other actresses. Doubtless she would get to know them all well over the following few weeks.

Maddie said her goodnights at midnight, realising that these people were hardened party animals, and she would find it impossible to keep up with them. There were attempts to delay her departure, but she was quietly insistent, and made her way to her room.

She was woken some hours later by a woman's soft moans. The sound was so clear that at first Maddie thought that someone was in her room, but then she realised that the noises were coming through the wall behind her bedhead, from Juliet's room. The plasterboard partition ensured that she could hear everything as clearly as if the two rooms were still one. She listened as the moans continued, and then Juliet spoke in a low, urgent voice.

'That's good, just there. Not so fast. Mm, that's it.'

Maddie could feel her face and ears and neck burning with embarrassment at this unintentional eavesdropping. What was going on next door was unmistakable: perhaps not the precise nature of it, but the generalities at least. Maddie buried her head in her pillow, trying to block out the noises of the lovemaking from the adjoining room, but it was ineffectual. She would have to listen, whether she wanted to or not.

Gradually, Maddie's annoyance at her interrupted sleep turned to interest. Juliet's low, demanding commentary continued, and then Maddie heard a man's voice, but didn't recognise it. 'You like that, don't you?' the man asked. Maddie sat up in bed, placing her head close to the partition, and listened with gathering desire.

'Don't stop, please,' Juliet begged quietly from through the wall. 'Oh God, I'm almost there. Don't stop.' Juliet gasped sharply a couple of times, and then cried out. Maddie smiled, wondering who Juliet's lover was. There was silence for a while, and Maddie was frustrated that it all seemed to be over. But then, the distinctive rhythmic sound of fucking, with mattress springs being depressed and a headboard banging against the wall, confirmed that there had merely been a lull rather than a halt. Juliet and the man were soon gasping and groaning almost in unison, urging each other on to greater and yet greater things with their cries.

Maddie sat bolt upright. She was sure she had heard a third voice. She listened, straining to hear. The noise of the frantic coupling continued, and then another man said, 'Yeah, keep going. Oh, that's great.' Maddie's eyes opened wide with surprised shock, and then she smiled and shook her head, thinking that it just went to show how deceptive appearances could be. Juliet looked so demure; and yet, along with her earthy sense of humour, she clearly had the appetites of a man-eater. Appetites to rival my own, thought Maddie, remembering her own recent introduction to the pleasures of threesomes. The banging of the headboard against the wall reached a crescendo, and then the noises next door died down. Maddie strained to hear, but heard no more voices. She could picture the three of them, falling asleep in a tangle of arms and legs, much as she had with Ben and Callum.

Still stimulated, Maddie lay back in her bed and closed her eyes, thinking again about what she had just overheard. As she did so, she gently brushed her hand down over her naked flesh, seeking and finding her sex and the tiny fiery point which held the key to her release. She knew that she would only be able to relax once she had achieved that release, and so began the slight, gentle movements that would bring her exquisite pleasure, and then sleep.

Chapter Eight

*T*he shoot had moved to Home Farm. Maddie was amazed by how compliant Ben had been. He had accepted the invasion of his home, and the inevitable disruption to his work without a word of dissent. Patty, one of whose many jobs was set dresser, had decided that Ben's combined kitchen and living room was too dingy; and so the whole room had been emptied of his furniture, the walls repainted in a pale yellow colour, and new smarter furniture moved back in. The same had happened in the bedroom chosen for filming.

Meanwhile, all Ben's furniture from the house was stacked in the Dutch barn. Maddie noticed that, as the barn had no side walls, his belongings were poorly protected from the weather, and the roof didn't look too watertight, either. Mercifully the weather had been perfect for the entire period that she had been in Dorset, but she didn't think it wise to tempt fate; and so she took it on herself to ask Danny, the production jack-of-all-trades, to go and buy a big sheet of polythene to cover up all Ben's things. Maddie warned Danny to keep it quiet from Hugh, who doubtless would baulk at the extra cost of a single sheet of polythene. It was, after all, part of her location manager duties to keep the property owner happy, Maddie figured. Then she became annoyed that she was even having to think about justifying what would be the norm on any other film.

Having sorted out Ben's belongings, Maddie wandered back to where Hugh and Finlay were discussing the setting up of the first scene to be filmed at the farm. It was going to start in the old stone barn, and then would become a tracking shot as it followed the two characters as they left the barn and walked through the farmyard. Hugh was clearly annoyed about something, and was talking very aggressively to Finlay, who seemed to be taking it all in his stride. Around them, the crew members were scurrying to lay the track on which the camera would travel. Maddie walked past Hugh, hoping that he wouldn't notice her. She prepared the clapper board, one of her several other duties apart from continuity. Unlike a decently budgeted film, where electronic clapperboards were the norm, Maddie was using the old-fashioned wooden board, with the scene details and date chalked on to it.

Maddie had forgotten from her previous visits to shoots just what a slow, painstaking business filmmaking was, and how much time a large proportion of the cast and crew would be standing around doing nothing. Ben had found a few chairs for the actors to sit on while they waited for the technical aspects to be sorted out, but there were not enough to provide something similar for everyone. Maddie leant against the wall of the barn and looked over to where Juliet and Sean were sitting. Sean was doing the crossword in a newspaper and Juliet was knitting an enormous red sweater out of fluffy mohair wool. Juliet looked up and saw that Maddie was watching her, and beckoned her over.

'God, this is boring, isn't it?' she asked as Maddie approached. 'Isn't Hugh odd?'

'Yes, and yes,' Maddie said, grinning.

'Have you worked with him before?' Juliet asked.

Maddie snorted. 'No, and I honestly hope that I'll never work with him again,' she said with feeling. 'Have you?'

'Only on a television advertisement that he directed for a building society. It was a couple of years ago. I was "Woman wanting mortgage advice" for a day and a half's filming. It paid well, though; much better than this. Well, actually, it couldn't be much worse than this, seeing as I'm doing this for free. I didn't have anything else lined up, so it was either this and the dole, or back to night shifts at the crisp factory. I reckon that the exposure will do me good. Still, mustn't grumble. There are some perks to this job.'

'Such as? I can't say I've found any,' Maddie said with a forlorn smile.

'Take a look around you,' said Juliet, jerking her head in the direction of the double barn doors. Maddie looked over to where Juliet was indicating, and there was Ben, watching the proceedings – or, rather, the lack of proceedings – with amused interest.

'Not bad, is he?' Juliet whispered, even though Ben was too far away to hear. 'Fair sets my ovaries a-rattling, he does. I've always fancied a bit of country rough. Touch of the old Cold Comfort

Farms. And I bet he's bound to be called Seth or Reuben, isn't he, looking like that?'

Maddie laughed. 'His name is Ben.'

'Ben, is it? Ooh, I like that. Not quite a biblical name, but it's got a good, solid, rustic air to it. Have you seen the younger brother yet?' Juliet asked. This was news to Maddie. Ben hadn't told her that his brother was back from agricultural college, and she was surprised that she hadn't seen him around the farm. She looked over towards Ben again, but he had gone.

Juliet carried on, clearly warming to her theme. 'Yes, the younger brother. Not to be sniffed at. He was in the tractor earlier on, shirt off and straw in his hair. Very tasty. I wouldn't kick him out of bed for farting, know what I mean?' Juliet laughed like a drain. 'I like 'em young. More corruptible.' She smirked.

'I thought you and Sean were an item,' Maddie whispered.

'Nah. That's a casual thing – we fall back on each other when we haven't got anyone else. It's pretty convenient that way, and it doesn't get messy. There's no emotional turmoil because we both know the score.'

Maddie wondered if it had been Sean in Juliet's bedroom the other night, but she was still no nearer guessing who the third man had been. Since that night, Maddie had been carefully listening to her male colleagues, trying to match voices with the ones she had heard through the bedroom wall in the hotel, but she hadn't succeeded. Looking round, Maddie felt that there were plenty of possibles to choose from on the production. The male crew members were mainly in their twenties and thirties; most were unattached, fun-loving and, from the amount of sometimes crude bantering between the men and the women on set, clearly interested in sex. It had already crossed Maddie's mind that if she were to want a casual fuck, it would be pretty simple to find one here. Juliet had certainly found it easy enough. Maddie looked over at Sean, who was chewing the end of his biro. He had sensed her attention, as he looked up and smiled at her. Embarrassed, Maddie looked down hastily.

'Maddie. Over here,' Hugh's voice barked out over the babble of the technicians.

Maddie caught Juliet's eye, and shrugged. She went over to where Hugh was regarding a pile of straw and manure. Earlier that morning, Ben had shovelled it out of the stable where he kept Minto, his horse, but had not yet cleared away the resulting mess. It was piled in a heap by the stable door, next to a wheelbarrow and a shovel.

Hugh gestured at the heap. 'Move this, Maddie. I don't want it in shot.'

Maddie looked at Hugh. It seemed strange to her that, with all the strong young men in the crew, he should call on her to perform this arduous and rather unpleasant task. She sensed that he was making a point. 'Why me?' she asked.

'Just do what you are asked,' Hugh snapped, walking away.

Maddie considered walking away as well, but she didn't want the crew to think she was a prima donna. After all, the others weren't really aware of the history of antagonism between herself and Hugh. They wouldn't realise that this was to humiliate her, a little gesture to remind her of his professional power over her. Maddie reluctantly took up the shovel and started to shift the steaming pile into the barrow. Then she pushed the barrow over to the large heap of manure in another part of the farmyard and upturned the barrow, adding the load to the heap.

When she returned to her position, she saw that Hugh was watching her, the slightest smile playing about his mouth. She ignored him, deciding not to let him know that he was getting to her.

'OK, to your marks, Juliet and Sean,' Hugh called out. The technical problems had been sorted out and he was ready to film.

Ben reappeared, watching with interest, and Maddie sneaked up to him while Finlay quickly took a final measurement between the actors and the camera with his tape, in order to check focal length needed for the shot.

'I didn't know your brother was here. Are you going to introduce me to him?'

Ben smiled, and shook his head. 'He only got here last night, and he's left already. He never tells me where he's going, or how long for. He just ups and offs, and that's it.' Ben laughed ruefully. 'God, I sound more like his mother than his brother. Sometimes he goes to stay with his mates in the village; other times he buggers off abroad. I don't know when he'll be back, so I can't promise you'll meet him. Sorry.'

'Maddie!' Hugh barked. 'We're waiting.'

Maddie scooted back to her position and took up the clapper board.

'Right. Roll camera!' Hugh called out. The camera whirred into life, and Maddie quickly darted into shot. She announced the title of the film, the scene and the take numbers, clapped the stick on the board, and bobbed out of the frame again. She then got her continuity gear together and started to make notes.

The good weather had to break: it was inevitable. The days of airless, humid heat and a muggy oppressiveness had to end. It was affecting the crew, making them tetchy and irritable. Tempers were stretched and fraying.

On the shoot, Juliet's elaborate hairdo had collapsed limply in the sultry heat, and everything was on hold for the few minutes it would take Gillie, the hairdresser, to repair the damage. Ben came up to Maddie as she was waiting with the others, fanning herself with her copy of the script. She was hot and uncomfortable. Beads of sweat were trickling down between her breasts.

'There's going to be an almighty thunderstorm,' Ben said, sniffing the air. 'It's too still. Something's got to give.'

Maddie kept her eye on the sky as she prepared for the next scene. It was an exterior scene, in the farmyard, and if it rained this would have disastrous ramifications for all sorts of reasons. Continuity would be much more difficult if she had to cope with some scenes filmed in the wet and others in the dry; and if the rain was prolonged, it could set the shoot back, with all the resultant financial implications.

Sure enough, Ben's prediction came true. At about half past five, a ruffling breeze blew up. There was a collective sigh of relief from the crew – the stillness had made the sticky heat all the more unbearable. The sky had gradually darkened at the horizon, the clouds a lowering, bruised blue, occasionally lit from the inside as lightning discharged within them. Maddie counted the seconds out between the flashes and the low rumbling of the thunder. The gap diminished with every count, signalling the approach of the storm. Everyone looked up, waiting for the inevitable.

As the storm crept nearer, great crackling flashes of lightning ripped across the sky and down to the earth. There was an appreciative murmur from the crew at the grandeur of this natural light show. The clouds slowly spread over them; the low rumbles of thunder gradually increased in force and volume, becoming loud, brutal crashes; and then the rain came. First there were a few fat drops, splattering heavily on to the dry ground, leaving dark circles in the dust; and then came a sudden, torrential downpour, so heavy it seemed to Maddie more a tropical monsoon than an English summer shower.

The entire crew ran for cover – into the Dutch barn, into outbuildings, back into the farmhouse or into the make-up and wardrobe trailers and the lock-ups. Within seconds, the scene was deserted. The last in to cover was Finlay, who was delayed by stopping to place the heavyweight covers on his camera. He picked up the small lightweight video camera and walked slowly towards the farmhouse, as if he barely noticed the rain.

'Come on, Finlay, you'll get soaked,' Juliet called from within the doorway of the farmhouse. She stood looking out into the rain.

'It's all right. I'm Scottish: I'm used to this kind of weather,' he shouted back at her.

Maddie and Ben both ended up in the great barn. Laughing, they wiped the drips of water from their faces, and looked down at their bedraggled clothes.

In the short time that it had taken them to run to the barn, they had become drenched through. Maddie could feel the cotton of her shirt clinging wetly to her, and its damp contact had caused her nipples to pucker and darken. She knew that Ben couldn't help but notice, and this pleased her. He, in turn, was looking charmingly dishevelled, his curly hair clinging to his scalp, and his long dark lashes seeming even longer and darker, now they were wet. His shirt was plastered to his chest, and Maddie could clearly see the definition of his pectoral muscles, and even the tiny points of his nipples.

Maddie looked around. The barn had been filled with bales of straw from the previous harvest, but over the winter months Ben had gradually used the straw for bedding for his stock. The removal of some of the bales left a kind of natural arena in the middle of the barn, with a thin skin of loose straw remaining on top of the last layer of bales. The hayloft over one end of the barn was filled with more bales, together with piles of junk that Ben had stored up there and never got round to getting rid of.

They were surprised to find themselves on their own. No one else had sought out the barn for shelter. Maddie looked out of the double doors. The rain was pouring down outside, almost like a solid sheet of water, and above her she could hear it hammering fiercely on the tiled roof. A few drips of water inside showed where the rain was finding its way in.

'This is a lovely building,' Maddie said, looking up at the massive beams that supported the roof. 'How old is it?'

'Haven't a clue,' said Ben. 'Old. Three, four hundred years?'

'I hadn't fully appreciated what a beautiful building it is,' Maddie said. 'So old, too – just think of the tales it could tell!'

'You're a bit of a romantic at heart, aren't you?' laughed Ben. 'The only thing I think when I look at it is "How much could I get for selling it off as a barn conversion to some rich townies?" I could get a lot of money for it, I know that for sure. Barn conversions are very desirable, so the estate agents tell me.'

'But could you really bear to part with it? Don't you have any sentimental attachment to it?' Maddie asked.

'Nope,' said Ben. 'But then again, maybe I'm not sure I want close neighbours. Might cramp my style.' Ben looked at Maddie and grinned; then he paused, thinking. 'No, that's not quite true about not having a sentimental attachment. I did lose my virginity in here, come to think of it.'

'There you are!' said Maddie. 'So it is special. What a nice place to lose your virginity – a bit more romantic than in the back of a Morris Minor.'

'A Morris Minor?' Ben asked in amazement. 'What are you? A contortionist?'

Maddie laughed, and then stopped abruptly. Suddenly, it was as if they both had exactly the same idea at exactly the same time. They stepped towards each other. Ben lifted his hand and gently brushed Maddie's wet hair back from her face, and they kissed. Maddie ran her fingers over him, feeling him through his wet clothes. He had a marvellous body, honed by the hard physical work on the farm, and she thought she would never get bored of exploring it. She shivered, overtaken by a wrench of want for him. Ben mistook it for something else.

'You'll catch your death in those wet clothes. Let

me help you out of them. There's some old dunga-rees and a shirt hanging on a hook over there.'

Maddie stood, still and compliant, as she allowed Ben to undress her. He slowly undid the buttons of her shirt, his hands brushing against her breasts. She caught her breath as she felt him part the shirt and peel the wet material off her skin. Her nipples were so hard now they almost ached, and Ben reached to cup her breasts in his hands, gently stroking her soft skin and teasing her nipples through his fingers. Then he bent to kiss them, taking one nipple and then the other between his lips, sucking and rolling them, before becoming more rapacious and taking more of her breast into his mouth.

Maddie reached to undo Ben's shirt and then pushed it off over his shoulders, and he broke away from her breasts and hurriedly shrugged off the shirt and shuffled out of his trousers. Maddie marvelled at the sight of his broad, tanned chest and his firm, muscular legs, and stepped close again to rub his bulging prick through the material of his pants. Eagerly, he pulled them down, and his cock reared out at Maddie. Naked before her, Ben undid Maddie's shorts and pushed them down over her hips. He stood back and excitedly exclaimed, 'You've got no knickers on, you bitch!'

Maddie smiled at him, both surprised and pleased by the strength of his reaction. 'It was too hot for undies,' she explained simply, and only part-truthfully.

'Oh God, you mean you were walking around out there with nothing on underneath? Those shorts aren't very long – anyone could have seen!'

'I know,' Maddie smiled. 'That was the idea.'

'You filthy, dirty girl. You like to show men what

you've got, don't you?' Ben was clearly aroused by the idea. 'Tell me about it,' he whispered. He took her by the hand and led her over to the loose straw. He reached behind one of the bales and took out a cotton throw and spread it over the straw. Maddie smiled.

'Were you ever a boy scout?' she asked.

'Uh?' Ben replied, confused by the strange tack of her question.

Maddie gestured at the throw. 'You know, "Be prepared"? You've done this before, haven't you?'

Ben smiled a wicked smile. 'I've done most things before, Maddie. You should know that by now. But I want you to tell me what *you've* done.' He pulled her down on to the throw, and on to him. She lay against him, feeling his hot flesh against hers, his muscular hardness and the urgent pressure of his prick against her stomach. 'Tell me,' he whispered again. She slid off him and settled by his side, pressed close against him. Reaching round with her left hand, she grasped his cock in her hand. Ben moaned and closed his eyes, as she began to slide her hand over him.

Maddie moved close to his ear, so close that the fine downy hairs on his lobe tickled her lips.

'What do you want to know?' she asked, gently caressing him.

Ben turned his head so that their lips were almost touching. 'How you've shown yourself to other men. Tell me everything: where, when, how, what you were wearing. I need all the details.'

Maddie smiled. She was intrigued by Ben's interest in her past love life. She had found that a lot of her lovers had been jealous of what had gone before, but he seemed to be interested in it; truly turned on by the idea of her with other men. Working him slowly, she began her story.

'The last time was only a few weeks ago. I was doing a recce of some army barracks in Yorkshire, looking for a suitable location for a television advertisement I was working on. I got clearance from security to look around, although I had to have a chaperone with me, to check that I didn't go anywhere that was out of bounds. I needed to see the assault course, and this guy – a cute corporal – showed me around.

'When we got to the course, there was a group of about fifteen squaddies going over it; climbing ropes and coming down nets, crawling under low barbed wire, scrambling up high brick walls. They had obviously been at it for a while, as they were muddy and sweaty, and some of them were visibly tiring. The sergeant major was bawling at them to get on, using some pretty ripe language, and they were struggling to complete it. It was a really tough course.

'The sergeant major saw me there, and shocked me by shouting, "If you poxy lot finish this course, this beautiful young lady here will show you her underwear."'

Ben moaned, and buried his face in Maddie's neck. Maddie felt him stiffening in her hand, and she continued her story.

'I almost choked, hardly believing what I'd just heard. The corporal laughed, and told me not to pay any attention. Anyhow, the sergeant major's words had a noticeable effect on the squaddies, because they all perked up and rushed to finish the course. Then they waited there, sweaty and panting and knackered, some bent double by their exertions, but they were all looking at me expectantly.

'I was feeling rather frisky that day: I hadn't had sex for a while and the sight of all those horny young men set me off. I thought what the hell, got up on to the platform next to the sergeant major, and started to lift my skirt, very slowly. The soldiers started cheering, egging me on. I lifted the hem higher and higher, past my knees, slowly inching it upwards. I knew they were in for a bigger surprise than they were expecting. When I lifted the skirt right up, a massive cheer went up, and lots of crude comments. Like today, I wasn't wearing any knickers. I like to think that there were a lot of sweaty, sleepless young men in the barracks that night, each and every one wanking furiously while they remembered my little display.'

Ben's eyes were screwed tight shut. He groaned again. 'Jesus, you filthy bitch.' Not a word of the story was true, but Maddie found that the thrill of voicing her own fantasy, and of telling Ben, was overpowering. It had as much of an effect on her as it had on him. Suddenly energised, she whispered to Ben, 'Fuck me now.'

She got on to her hands and knees, presenting herself wantonly to him. He needed no further bidding, entering her quickly and thrusting rapidly, clearly aroused by what she had just been telling him. Maddie was equally rapacious, thrusting back to meet him, and Ben pushed her down, driving into her with long, slow strokes. He slapped her buttocks as he moved within her, and bent down to bite the back of her neck, his chest pressed against her back.

'You like people to look, don't you? All those

squaddies, all looking at you, all wanting you,' he whispered.

Ben felt so deep within her, Maddie could not contain her cries. She was so aroused that she thought little about her colleagues overhearing, calling out in her frenzy like a demented being. She had never known such physical, almost brutal love-making, on her own part as well as Ben's. It was as if the extremity of their passion was met in the tumultuous weather outside; the flashes of lightning and rumbles of thunder, and the torrential down-pouring of rain a foil for their own inner tempests.

Another day's shooting had ended. It was past eight in the evening when Hugh had declared himself finally satisfied with a scene. It had taken poor Sean and Annie some thirty-odd takes to get there. Hugh's criticisms were for the smallest things: he didn't like the intonation or stress placed on a certain word, Annie's make-up didn't satisfy him, or he wanted a prop in the background of the shot moved. Maddie could also see how tense the actors were becoming, and their frustration and nervousness about getting it right was causing them to make silly mistakes. The more they had to work at the scene, the staler it became.

Then there were aborted takes for other reasons: the scream of a low-flying military jet drowned out the dialogue; the sun went in behind a cloud, posing continuity problems with the following scene, which had already been filmed in bright sunlight; a crew member wandered into shot or the overhead boom dipped too low into the frame. Maddie reckoned that Hugh's near-crazed emphasis on perfectionism was out of kilter with the tight budget. The more takes

Hugh took, the higher the costs. She and the cast listened mutely as he ranted on, saying that he felt that the 'true essence' of the screenplay had not been correctly portrayed by the actors, that they were all amateurs, that he had never worked with such a collection of incompetents.

Everyone heaved a massive sigh of relief when Hugh finally called, 'Print it!', indicating his satisfaction with the last take. But they knew how capricious Hugh was, and that he might easily order the crew to set up for another scene, even at this late stage of the day with the poor light. Everyone waited with baited breath for his orders.

'That's it for the day,' Hugh said, handing his script to Maddie and walking over to his car. There was no expression of gratitude for the cast and crew's hard work; no suggestion that he might help with putting the equipment away for the night; no offer to give anyone a lift back to the hotel in his car. Maddie watched him drive away, shaking her head. That man was unbelievable. She had a good mind to toss his script on to the dung heap, but resisted it.

Maddie helped to pack some of the equipment into the trailers and the lock-ups, laughing and chatting with the others about Hugh's inadequacies. Criticism of their director gave the cast and crew a strong and common bond. Not one member of the production had expressed anything but dislike for him: and dislike was just about the mildest opinion expressed.

As she was about to walk to the minibus with the others, Maddie saw Ben driving in to the farmyard in his tractor. He jumped down and came over to her.

'Hi. How's things?' he asked, wiping the back of a

dusty hand over his face. Maddie thought how attractive he looked; hot and sweaty and messy.

'All the better for seeing you. It's been a pig of a day. Several of us came very close to strangling Hugh.'

'Only some of you?' Ben laughed.

The minibus engine started up, and the horn sounded. Maddie looked up, and saw the others gesturing at her. She was the last to get on board.

'Hell, I've got to go. See you tomorrow, maybe?' she said.

Ben held her gently by the arm, staying her departure. 'Look, I've got a suggestion. Why not stay here? It seems stupid you going back and forth to Dorchester every day. You're filming here for – what is it? – another couple of weeks or so? Why not stay?' Ben spoke persuasively, and Maddie smiled. She knew that Hugh would be angry, but she didn't care. In fact, she rather relished the idea of annoying him, and she hadn't much enjoyed living and working with Hugh, seeing him at breakfast, lunch and supper. This would give her a welcome break from her despotic director.

'OK. You've convinced me. I'll just run and tell the others.'

She hurried over to the minibus, and explained to Juliet what she was planning, and asked her to bring her gear from her hotel room with her the next day.

'Are you sure?' asked Juliet. 'God, I wouldn't want to be in your shoes tomorrow. Hugh isn't going to like it one little bit.'

'Well, that's just tough. If he doesn't like it, I'd be more than happy for him to fire me.'

Everyone cheered. A shout of, 'Up the revolution,' came from the back of the bus, and left Maddie smiling as the minibus drove away. She walked back to Ben, who put his arm around her waist and gave her a comforting squeeze.

'Having persuaded you to stay, I'm going to have to leave you briefly. I've got some harrows to pick up from the top field. Won't be more than half an hour. Why don't you go inside and make yourself a drink or have a bath?'

'OK,' Maddie replied happily. She watched as Ben climbed back into the tractor and drove off. Now that everyone had gone, the farm was returning to its normal sleepy state. The chickens were warily returning to the yard, and the only sounds were their contented clucking as they searched for scraps, and the gentle lowing of the cows in the fields beyond.

Maddie noticed that Finlay's car was still parked in the lane leading to the farmyard, half-hidden behind one of the ramshackle sheds. She wondered why he hadn't yet left. Maddie decided to wander down through the wildflower meadow to the river for a paddle. The calming sound of the low murmuring burble of the shallow water, and the cooling effect on her feet would help to ease away the stress and tension of the day. As she walked, she wondered if Hugh had ever bothered to stop and think that he would get much more out of his cast and crew if he was more supportive, and less critical. No, somehow she doubted it. Hugh would never question that what he was doing was anything but absolutely right.

The wildflower meadow was one of Maddie's favourite places on the farm, and she was secretly glad that it wasn't being used as a location for filming: all the moving about of the people and equipment would have flattened the fragile grasses and flowers. The meadow was a riot of colour: brilliant red poppies, pale-blue field scabious and bright-yellow buttercups jostled for space with the large white flowers of the ox-eye daisies. Feathery grass heads swayed among the flowers. Maddie moved slowly through the meadow, frequently stopping to look at a flower, or a butterfly that had momentarily settled; or her attention was captured by the greeny-black metallic sheen of a beetle crawling up a grass stem. Unseen crickets beat out their scything rhythm, and swallows swooped low to catch the insects drawn to the flowers.

It was as she looked up from the close inspection of a spider on its web wrapping a hapless fly in silk that Maddie noticed Finlay over on the far side of the meadow, not far from the river. He was standing still, his head and shoulders hunched. Maddie held her hand over her eyes to shield out the glare of the low sunlight and squinted into the distance, and then could see that he was holding a video camera and was filming something. She wondered if he was taking some shots of the scenery as a personal memento of his time in this idyllic part of the world; but, as she drew nearer, she could see from the angle of the camera that he was filming something quite close to him on the ground, rather than taking panoramic shots. Perhaps he had spotted some interesting wildlife. Ben had told her that there were otters living near the river, but Maddie hadn't yet seen any. Excited, she crept closer, as silently as possible, not wanting to disturb them.

What she saw as she drew up behind and slightly to one side of Finlay made her draw up straight with shock. In a nest in the grasses and the flowers were two people, naked: a man and a woman. Maddie bit her lip to silence herself. She recognised the woman: it was Melinda. She was lying beneath the man, her legs spread on either side of him, her arms grasped tight around his back and her head thrown back in rapture. The man was tall and muscular, and Maddie could see his buttocks flexing and quivering as he thrust into Melinda. His toes were digging into the soft earth, and he was bearing his weight on his knees and forearms. Melinda was groaning, and as Maddie watched, Melinda dug her nails in to the man's back, scratching him. Maddie watched as the red weals slowly formed, but the man didn't appear to notice.

Neither had Finlay. He was so intent on capturing the action that he had not sensed Maddie's approach. He altered the focus, and called out in a low voice.

'That's great. Looking good. Yeah.'

Maddie was thunderstruck. Was Finlay some kind of kinky voyeur who got his thrills from watching other people fuck? How had he persuaded Melinda and the man to let him film them? Maddie dragged her eyes away from the lurid scene beneath her and looked at Finlay. She realised with another shock that he was using the production video camera. She couldn't begin to think what Hugh would say if he knew his equipment was being used in this way.

Melinda's moans drew Maddie's attention again. Still undetected, she stood and watched silently, and could feel herself reacting to this display of wanton carnality. She had not witnessed other people having full, penetrative sex like this before, and she was fascinated and turned on in equal measures.

Then the man disengaged himself from Melinda and slid down her body, kissing her breasts, her stomach and then the downy curls of her pubic hair.

Melinda's legs were still thrown wide apart, but she drew her knees up instinctively, bringing her swollen redness into easier reach.

Maddie swallowed hard. She loved receiving oral sex, and seeing it happen to another woman was doubly stimulating. She could see the pleasure that Melinda was receiving and could imagine that it was her own cunt that was receiving the gentle licks and nibbles. Maddie watched with a strange combination of familiarity and strangeness. She had received cunnilingus plenty of times but had never seen it, not even in a mirror. In Melinda's reactions she recognised her own. She recognised the way Melinda moved her hips, swivelling and rotating them in an attempt to precisely locate the man's mouth where she wanted it. She could see Melinda's breathing quicken, and the nervous darts of her tongue over her lips as her pleasure mounted. She watched as Melinda brought her hands to her breasts and played with them, grasping them and then playing her nipples between her fingers to further harden them. Then, as Melinda's orgasm approached, Maddie saw her put her hands on the man's head and try to force him yet further into her.

'Deeper, faster,' Melinda called out. The man complied, burying his face right into her, and Melinda arched back off the ground as her climax rocketed through her. She pushed the man away roughly, and Maddie recognised that too: the almost unbearable tenderness of her clitoris after an orgasm, when any touch came perilously close to pain.

'OK, now change positions,' Finlay commanded, breaking into Maddie's reverie. The man sat back on his knees, and wiped his mouth with the back of his hand. Maddie noticed that he did it slowly, breathing deeply and taking in Melinda's smell. Maddie watched as Melinda rolled over on to her hands and knees and presented her rump to the man. He moved forward, and took one of her buttocks in each hand and massaged them, before taking his hard, glistening cock in one hand and slowly guiding it into her.

Finlay moved forwards and crouched, zooming in on the action.

'That's it, right in to her. Give her a really good fucking.'

The crudity of Finlay's language shocked Maddie far more than what she was witnessing. She suddenly realised why this all seemed so familiar. Finlay was directing Melinda and the man just as Hugh directed the actors and crew on the film set. He wasn't a by-stander, a passive onlooker. Finlay was orchestrating this.

The man's grunts were becoming louder and more frequent, and it was clear that he wasn't far from his climax. Finlay clearly knew this.

'I need to see you come. We need the pop shot. Pull out and come on her back.'

The man didn't need any further bidding. He quickly withdrew his cock and bent forwards, laying it over the crack of Melinda's buttocks. Maddie watched, hypnotised, as the man's rigid prick twitched a couple of times and then a thick jet of come arced forwards and landed at the nape of Melinda's neck. It was followed by another and another of decreasing force. The man's hands gripped Melinda's hips tightly, and juddered, his head flopped forward so that his chin rested on his chest. His mouth was open and he was gasping for air like a landed fish. When he finally released his grip, Maddie could see the white finger-shaped

196

indentations in Melinda's flesh, gradually colouring as the blood returned.

Maddie turned and crept away as quickly as she could, suddenly embarrassed. It was not so much embarrassment at what she had witnessed – she experienced arousal, far more than any other reaction; but by the thought that the others might be uncomfortable knowing that their private business had been snooped on without their knowledge. As she tiptoed down the grassy bank to the river, she heard Finlay commenting.

'Good work, Melinda. Nice one, Paul. That was hot.'

She wondered who Paul was. He was not one of the cast or crew. And how had Finlay recruited his two compliant actors? It seemed vaguely unreal – accidentally stumbling across the making of a blue movie like that.

What she had just seen would come back to her frequently, both in the hot sweaty nights to come, and in moments of day-dreaming, when she would wonder who would watch the film, and how Finlay had become involved, and why, and with who else?

When Maddie got back to the farmhouse, Ben had already returned from his work. Maddie deliberated about telling him about what she had witnessed in his meadow, but decided against it. She didn't want Finlay to accuse her of stirring things.

He greeted her with a long kiss. 'I guess I should ask you this out of politeness. Where do you want to sleep? Do you want your own room, or . . .?'

'I'd like to have my own room, if that's OK with you. Then we can go with the flow,' Maddie replied. 'I don't want to cramp your style.'

'And vice versa,' replied Ben, grinning. 'With the emphasis on "vice"!'

Chapter Nine

*I*t was a rare day free from filming, and Maddie was determined to enjoy a precious lie-in. Ben, however, had different ideas. He came into her room at eight o'clock, and drew back her curtains. Maddie squinted into the light, and couldn't stay annoyed with Ben when she saw that he had prepared her some breakfast and brought it up on a tray.

'I'm taking you sight-seeing today,' he explained. 'Pack your swimmies and a towel, grab your camera and be by the Range Rover in an hour!' With that, he left a bemused Maddie to eat her breakfast in peace.

By the end of the day, Maddie was exhausted. They had driven all over Dorset, visiting familiar places, as well as other places that Maddie had no idea existed, despite all her research. Conscious of this failing, she was foresighted enough to make some rough notes in case she was ever called on to find locations in Dorset again.

First they had driven westward, and visited the pretty harbour town of Lyme Regis. Maddie did her impersonation of Meryl Streep in *The French Lieutenant's Woman* on the stone wall of the Cobb, the rough harbour wall curving out into the sea; and they had hunted for fossils on the undercliff above the beach, finding tiny ammonites that looked like gold-leafed snail shells. Then they headed eastward. As they drove by, Ben had pointed out the bakery in More-combelake that made biscuits called 'Dorset Knobs', and they had giggled like smutty-minded school-children at the name. They went on to Abbotsbury, and visited the swannery and the sub-tropical gardens, and then they drove further east and visited the tiny cottage where Lawrence of Arabia had spent his last years. They visited hillforts and stately homes, swam in the sea and ate too much ice cream. Maddie hadn't had so much fun for a long time.

It was late when they finally headed for home. It had been a wonderful day.

'There's one more thing I have to show you,' Ben said. Maddie looked about her. They were in the heart of the countryside: no hillforts, no grand and imposing houses, no historic towns. 'Where are we?' she asked.

'A little way north of Dorchester,' Ben said, as he parked the car in a small car park and helped Maddie out of the car and led her towards a fence.

'What do you think?' Ben asked, smiling.

'About what?' Maddie asked, mystified. She didn't know what she was supposed to be looking at.

'Over there,' said Ben, pointing to the hillside.

'Oh, my God!' exclaimed Maddie, when she recognised what it was exactly. Carved into the hillside, much like the white horse she had seen from the balloon, was a gigantic figure of a man, his body outlined by the white chalk where the overlying grass and soil had been cut away. One hand was outstretched, and in the other he was carrying a club. His ribs were marked, as were his nipples; but the most extraordinary thing, and the thing that had caused Maddie to cry out, was his massive, erect penis. It lay up his stomach, and the attention to anatomical detail was such that his creators had even remembered to give him his two balls beneath.

'I don't believe it. That's ... obscene!' Maddie laughed.

'Maddie, meet the Cerne Abbas Giant. It's not quite what you expect to find in the English country-side, is it? A 180-foot-high man with a 30-foot-long hard-on!' chuckled Ben. 'Want a closer look?'

'Why not?' Maddie laughed, and together they started the long walk across the fields and then up the grassed hillside to reach the figure. He was surrounded by a low fence to keep the grazing sheep off, and Maddie and Ben climbed over the fence for a closer look.

The outline of the figure was formed by a shallow trench. They stepped over it, so close now that it was hard to orientate themselves on his body. The slope of the hill added to the foreshortening effect. But there was one part of his body that Maddie had no difficulty in identifying when she saw it. She walked over to the giant's scrotum, and then up the shaft of his penis until she reached the very tip. Ben joined her.

'Talk about Dorset knobs!' she exclaimed. 'This has got to be the biggest of them all.'

They walked over the figure for another half-hour or so, pausing to look at the view from the hillside and then bobbing low to inspect the wildflowers that grew on the giant. Ben impressed Maddie with his knowledge of the flora of the area, and he reminded her that he had kept the wildflower meadow as just that because of his interest in wildlife.

'Hard as you'll find it to believe this, but I don't make any money out of that field. I keep it like that for the love of it. I could get massive subsidies if I planted it up with flax or put it to set-aside. I'm not completely driven by the desire to make money, despite what you might think.'

Maddie laughed. 'I know you're not completely driven by it, because I can name at least one other desire that drives you. Sex.'

'Oh. Am I that transparent?' Ben look crest-fallen, but Maddie knew it was an act for her benefit.

'Completely, Mr Hudson,' she grinned.

The light was starting to fail, and so they decided to make their way back down the hillside and head on home.

'How old is he?' Maddie asked, as they walked away from the massive body of the giant.

'No one's quite sure, but they think he might date from Roman times, some two thousand years ago. He's supposed to represent the god Hercules with his club; but all the locals reckon he's an old pagan fertility figure. There's a tradition that if a couple want to conceive, they come up here and make love on his dick.'

Maddie laughed. 'Good thing we didn't get fruity up there. I'm not ready for motherhood just yet!'

As they descended, they passed a young couple trudging hand-in-hand up the hill.

'So they're off to . . .?' asked Maddie.

Ben nodded, and laughed. 'Some nights there's a queue, I hear!'

When they got back to the farmhouse, Maddie didn't follow Ben straight into the house. She stood outside for a bit, watching the bats flitting about in the dark. She heard the low hooting of an owl in the distance. There was no moon, which meant that the stars were particularly bright. Maddie looked up, making out the familiar constellations: the Plough, the large 'W' of Cassiopeia, and the Northern Cross. The street lights of Cambridge ensured that she could rarely see the night skies so clearly there. She caught the sudden flash of a shooting star arcing across the sky, and made a silent wish on it.

Maddie finally decided to go in when she felt a slight chill from the dew settling on her face and arms. As she turned to walk back to the house, Maddie got a shock as a white shape swept silently in front of her. She almost cried out in alarm, and then realised that it was one of the barn owls that were nesting at the farm. She thought it was probably taking some food to its young, who were calling noisily from somewhere in the roof of the barn.

'Maddie. Come on in.' Ben met Maddie at the front door and pulled her hurriedly into the kitchen. 'I want you to meet someone.'

Maddie looked at him quizzically, then at the man standing by the range.

'Maddie, this is my brother, Paul.'

Maddie drew in a sharp breath of surprise, and then shook the hand of the man she had last seen engaged in some energetic sex with Melinda in the wildflower meadow.

'Nice to finally meet you,' said Paul. 'I've heard all about you.'

Maddie blushed furiously and shot an accusing look at Ben. Had he been discussing all their intimate

202

secrets with his brother? But Ben just looked blank at this comment and shrugged at Maddie, indicating that he didn't know what Paul was on about; and she could tell that Ben's response was an honest one.

As the two brothers chatted on, Maddie regarded Paul with interest. She wasn't surprised she hadn't guessed who he was when she had first seen him – he looked nothing like Ben. He was handsome, but in a very different way from his older brother, and Maddie couldn't work out if his youth was a large part of the attraction. He could only be twenty or so, she guessed. She wondered if she would get to know him as well as she knew his brother.

Filming had finished for the evening, and Maddie was busy cooking supper at the farmhouse for Ben and Paul. She had taken to a housewifely role with gusto, enjoying looking after the two strapping men of the house. She heard the front door open, and called out, 'Food'll be ready in about an hour.' There was no reply, and she was surprised when Hugh strode into the kitchen unannounced.

'Quite the picture of domestic bliss,' he said dryly, looking at her.

Maddie wondered what this late visit was about. It couldn't involve her, as Hugh would surely have said something during the day. Ben and Paul were out, still working on the farm, and Maddie curtly informed Hugh of this. She also reminded him about the mutual agreement between the film crew and Ben that, outside filming hours, the parts of the farm used as locations were strictly out of bounds. This was to ensure that Ben and Paul got some privacy.

'But you're a crew member, Maddie,' Hugh snapped back.

Maddie was pleased. Her lack of respect clearly annoyed him. 'And I'm here by invitation. You, on the other hand, are not. Not after eight o'clock.'

'This brings us neatly to the reason for my visit. You must move back to the hotel in Dorchester.'

'Why?' Maddie asked, with as much insolence as she could summon.

'Several reasons. One: it's not good for cast and crew morale if they think one member is getting special treatment.'

Maddie snorted. What would Hugh know about special treatment? He treated everyone like dogs, period.

Hugh continued. 'Two: I need you to be there, in case there are any problems with the locations or if I need any late night or last minute discussions with you.'

'So ring me. There's a telephone here,' Maddie said.

'I might need to consult paperwork or maps,' Hugh countered.

'Unlikely. You haven't needed to, so far on the shoot.'

'I have to provide for the possibility, Maddie. You understand about forward planning, surely.'

Maddie was not impressed. So far, his reasons had been paper-thin. 'Why don't you just admit it, Hugh? You don't like me here because you can't keep an eye on me and you can't control me so easily when I'm away from you. And it's all about control with you, isn't it?'

'Not at all. It's about practicalities.'

'It's not in my contract that I stay in the hotel. I don't want to, so I shan't.'

'Maddie, you might not have a contractual obligation to stay in the hotel, but I remind you that there are other ways in which I can exert pressure on you. Sam Pascali won't be too pleased to hear that you've been giving me problems. He certainly wouldn't want to employ a troublemaker on any of his productions, I'm sure.'

Maddie knew that Hugh had her trapped. He knew how desperately she wanted to work with Sam Pascali, and that gave him all the leverage he needed. In exasperation, Maddie threw down the knife with which she had been preparing the vegetables. It clattered harmlessly along the table top past Hugh. He regarded it for a moment.

'You'll have to do better than that if you want to do me some damage,' he smiled. 'Now run upstairs and pack your bags.'

Hugh further humiliated Maddie by driving behind her all the way back to Dorchester. 'This is bloody ridiculous,' she thought to herself. 'Where does he get off being so obnoxious?'

Back in the hotel, Hugh stood over her as she re-registered. He watched as she picked up her suitcase and struggled with it towards the lift. He made no attempt to help, but came and stood next to her in the lift.

'For God's sake, Hugh. You're not accompanying me up to my room, are you? Don't you trust me?' It seemed he was determined to make her humiliation complete.

Hugh looked at her and smiled thinly. 'Not at all, Maddie. My room is on the same floor.'

As she let herself into her new room, Maddie glanced up the corridor and saw that Hugh was standing at his own door, watching her. She pushed her suitcase through the door, went in and slammed the door shut after her. She hoped he had heard. She knew it was an ineffectual protest, but it was protest nonetheless.

'Pillock,' she muttered angrily. Her new room was larger than the other one she had been in, and she was pleased to see that this time there were no plasterboard partition walls. She looked out of the window, which overlooked the High Street. She could see Finlay, Turner, Danny and Juliet walking down the street and then entering one of the pubs. She left her suitcase where it had toppled, and hurried out to join them.

Maddie had had a bad day on set, worse than usual. The production had been filming at the hillfort, and Hugh had been impossible. He had seemed to fly into a rage at the smallest things, and had generally been behaving like a spoilt child. Maddie could understand that his behaviour was fired by his quest for perfectionism and his need to fulfil his vision but, for a film of such transparently poor quality, it hardly seemed worth the bother. The technicians and actors were all doing their best, but they were facing an uphill battle in the face of the atrocious script and the miserly production values. Hugh's behaviour had been inexcusable. He had reduced Melinda to tears, and had surprised even some of the more foul-mouthed members of the crew with his noxious invective.

Maddie had tried to keep a low profile, reckoning that it was best to keep out of Hugh's way when he was in such a mood. However, he called her over at one point in the day to where he was standing next to the pile of manure. Maddie reflected that here he was in his element, perfectly located. Hugh demanded to see her continuity notes. She handed them over unwillingly, and he flicked through them like some impatient, irate schoolmaster.

'There's not enough detail in your notes,' he snapped. 'Good God, am I employing imbeciles around here?' The cast and crew had gone silent, everyone frozen by the vitriol in his voice.

Maddie decided silence was the best tactic. Her jibes in the past had tended to rebound on her, calling down the full wrath of the director on her, and so she bit her tongue.

Hugh hissed at her. 'Start doing a better job. You know what will happen if you don't buck your ideas up.' He thrust the notepad back at her, but let go of it before she had grasped it. The pad fell to the ground, landing in a pile of muck. Humiliated, Maddie had to bob down at his feet to pick it up. The blatant insult of Hugh's action was noticed by everyone present, as he had intended. As Maddie rose again, she looked at him, angered by the way he kept deliberately and publically baiting her. He was a hateful man.

'Oops, sorry; my hand slipped,' he said with a smile, and walked off.

When, at the end of the day, the bus dropped the weary and exasperated cast and crew off at the hotel, Maddie didn't follow the others inside. She went straight round to the car park, got in her MG and drove the ten miles or so to Weymouth. She needed relaxation, and during that stressful afternoon it had suddenly occurred to her to visit the baths. The filming had not yet been undertaken there and, on her first scouting visit, she had promised herself that, if she got the chance, she would visit as a customer, rather than as an employee on a fourth-rate film production.

Maddie felt the calm and relief wash over her the minute she walked in through the door. She collected her towels and quickly changed, before moving into the relaxation room. She was surprised that the place wasn't busier – she had expected it to be full of businesswomen winding down after the stress of a working day; girlfriends chatting bawdily away from the inhibiting presence of men, and mothers relaxing in the peace and quiet, enjoying a brief period of self-indulgent respite away from their clamouring children. Apart from herself, there was only one other woman in the room, an elderly lady who was wrapped in a white towel and reading a copy of *For Women*. Maddie smiled, wondering if that was part of the provided literature at the baths, or if the woman had brought it in herself. Maddie rather hoped it was the latter: she liked this woman's open affirmation that there was life in the old girl yet.

Maddie lay on one of the benches and took a magazine from the pile on the small table next to it. She flicked through it briefly, before deciding it was time to go through to the warm room. Maddie could hear the light murmur of women's voices coming from the other side of the door, punctuated by laughter. She opened the door, and saw that the women in this room were all naked. Maddie stepped in and nodded a greeting to the other women, before removing her towel and sitting on one of the long benches. She didn't feel at all self-conscious. She had no reason to, as she knew she had a good body and that a few of the other women would be looking on her with some small degree of envy.

Soon Maddie was chatting across the small room

to the other women. After about ten minutes, she could feel that she was sweating, and thought that she was ready to move into the hot room. She picked up her towel but didn't put it on. There didn't seem much point. The women here were all at ease with their nudity, and there was no hint of the prurient glances that might be expected if men were present. Maddie thought how refreshing it was to be naked without having to be concerned about who might see and who might be offended. It felt so natural to be without clothes, and she wished that she could go naked outdoors more easily. As she padded past the basins, she filled a brass bowl with water and poured it over herself. It was blissfully cooling.

Maddie was only able to spend a very short period in the hot room. The dry heat was so extreme that she had to sit on her towel to prevent her buttocks from burning on the tiled bench seats, and soon she felt that her lungs were near-searing in the heat. There were a couple of other women in the room who were struggling similarly with the conditions, and for a while all three of them bore the blistering heat with a look of resigned fortitude on their faces. Although the last in, Maddie was the first to crack. She got up and moved through to the relief of the steam room. She could just see through the billowing clouds of steam that it was empty.

She closed the door behind her and sat back against the wall, feeling the droplets that had condensed there running down her back, wondering how she had managed to look around when she had been on her scouting visit. The thought now of being clothed anywhere in the baths was an uncomfortable one. As she sat back with her eyes closed, she recalled the extraordinary scenes she had witnessed near the plunge pool. As if with a will of its own, her hand moved to rest over her crotch. She could feel the soft curls of her pubic hairs and the firmness of the mound beneath them, and she was becoming aroused.

The two other women from the hot room came in, and the three of them sat there, feeling the sweat starting to pour off them. Maddie finally got up when the sweat had gathered so much on her brow that it had dripped in to her eyes, stinging slightly. She walked through to the plunge pool room, hung her towel on a peg and stepped down the ladder into the water, before launching herself out and swimming the four strokes it took to reach the other end of the pool. Then she dived under the water, to remove the sweat that was prickling her scalp. Maddie loved swimming underwater. She could feel her long tresses trailing behind her, like some freshwater mermaid. Emerging from the pool, she felt wonderfully invigorated. As she walked back to the steam room for a second session, the two women passed her on their way to the pool, and said their goodbyes.

'We've had enough,' one of them said. 'It's blissful torture, isn't it?'

Maddie laughed and reflected on the truth of the woman's words. Discomfort and pleasure came perilously close here.

Sitting alone in the steam room, Maddie drifted into a daydream again, thinking of the two men she had seen by the pool. Turkish baths seemed a perfect place for lovemaking; the heat and moisture in the atmosphere masking that which was generated during the act itself. And then there was the pool, perfect for a refreshing post-coital dip.

The door opened, and Maddie looked up. A tall

dark-haired young woman entered. It struck Maddie that she was almost a mirror-image of herself, with long, curling dark hair and olive skin. She too was naked, and Maddie noted her stunning body, and then adjusted her mirror-image assessment. This woman was younger and far sexier than she was. The woman smiled at Maddie and came to sit right by her, which surprised her. It was very unlike the normal British reserve, trying to avoid close physical contact with strangers at all costs.

'Hi. I'm Maia,' said the woman. 'Who are you?'

Maddie smiled at the sudden explanation for this forthrightness. She could tell from Maia's accent that she was American.

'Maddie. Pleased to meet you.'

They chatted on, and Maddie learnt that Maia was travelling around Europe for a year, and had settled in Weymouth for a while. 'Bumming around,' Maia said. 'Doing odd jobs, y'know.'

Maia had an easy, bright confidence, and she spoke quickly, and without censoring her thoughts first. She also had a sharp sense of humour, which Maddie found very attractive. Maddie already felt as if she had known Maia for years. She found herself looking at the woman, her eyes drawn to the beautiful lithe brown body so close to her. Maddie was reminded of her brief view of Kate and her lover in the shower back home, and once again she was surprised that she could find a woman so arousing. She was undeniably attracted to Maia.

After a while, Maia sighed. 'Gotta go. It was nice talking to you. See you around.'

'I hope so,' said Maddie with feeling. She felt a keen disappointment that Maia was leaving, and it shocked Maddie slightly when she realised that what she had been doing was flirting with Maia. It was true. She had been using all the techniques she usually used on men: listening to Maia with an exaggerated attentiveness, laughing at things she said that perhaps weren't that funny, being flattering and making a lot of eye contact. She couldn't tell whether Maia's response was a return of that flirtation, or simply her natural friendliness. Maia sighed again, and gathered up her towel. Maddie watched her leave the room, and felt a sharp pang of what she couldn't deny was lust. Maia's behind swung bewitchingly, her rounded buttocks full beneath her slender waist, her long, elegant back and her equally long, shapely legs drawing Maddie's eye irresistibly.

After Maia had left the steam room, Maddie felt a keen disappointment. She shook her head, filled with confusion. First Kate, now Maia: she had experienced that same reaction twice now. Perhaps there was something to it, after all. She had always considered herself heterosexual, but maybe this new facet of her sexuality had always been lurking beneath the surface, waiting for the right woman to unleash it. Maddie sat in the steam room for some ten minutes more, before going for another cooling plunge in the icy water. This time, she really needed cooling off.

After a dip in the pool and a quick blasting shower in the wonderfully antiquated brass contraption, Maddie padded back to the relaxation room. It was time for a massage. She was surprised to see that the room was empty, but a glance at the clock on the wall showed her that it was nearly ten o'clock. She reckoned that most of the clients would have gone home by now. She walked over to the massage table. There was a pile of fresh towels on a low table next to it, and a small bell. A sign next to the bell read: MASSAGE. RING FOR SERVICE.

Maddie rang the bell, spread a fresh towel over the table, and climbed up on to it. She lay down on her front, crossed her hands and lay her chin on them, and then closed her eyes. She lost track of time, unsure how long she had been lying waiting. Then she felt a pair of warm, slippery hands on her back.

'Mm. Full massage, please,' said Maddie. Then, as an afterthought, she added, 'but not too rough.'

'OK,' a female voice acknowledged her request, and Maddie felt the oiled hands start to slip over her back, working first her shoulders and upper arms, then her back, and then lower, to just above her buttocks. Then the attention switched to her legs, and the masseuse worked from the ankle upwards, on one leg and then the other. Soon Maddie's skin was covered in slippery, sandalwood-scented oil.

The masseuse certainly knew what she was doing. She worked deftly and firmly but, as Maddie had requested, she was gentle, too. Maddie could feel complete relaxation spreading over her. Her limbs felt almost as if they were floating away from her; and if the touch on her skin weren't quite so tantalising, she knew that she could easily be lulled into sleep. Maddie gradually became aware that the masseuse's touch had changed. From being deftly professional, it had become more like a caress, swirling over Maddie's body like a lover's trace on her skin. Maddie tried not to let it show that she was aroused by this, hoping that the masseuse wouldn't sense her quickening breathing and feel her involuntary quakes as she touched her skin.

The caresses moved to her back again; and with

slow sweeping movements, the warm oiled hands slid over her back and grazed over her flanks, brushing against the sides of Maddie's breasts. Maddie drew in a sharp intake of breath. It felt too deliberate, too slow and lingering to be accidental. Then, never breaking contact with her skin, the hands slid over Maddie's back again and down on to her buttocks. Here the movement changed from a gentle caress to a different motion. Maddie could feel the two hands holding her buttocks and kneading them. Maddie could feel her cheeks being gently pulled apart and then brought together again, and she knew that, when they were spread, the masseuse would be able to see down to her sex. Maddie lowered her head and bit the back of her hand, wondering if this was the purpose of this particular movement.

Then the hands moved again, back to her thighs. One hand moved to her inner thigh and pushed the other one away, forcing Maddie's legs apart. Then the hands slid down and began moving upwards from her knees, gently working their way back towards her thighs. Maddie could sense the trace of the fingers on her skin, which was so over-sensitised that she was beginning to get goosepimples. The hands seemed to tease, brushing perilously close to Maddie's sex before fluttering away again, back down her thighs. Then, inevitably, they would begin to travel upwards once more. Maddie knew she was wet and open, and wondered whether the masseuse could see her response to the skilled ministrations. Maddie screwed her eyes tightly shut, willing the hands to travel further, higher, but they remained on the periphery, gently brushing against the edge of her pubic hair, and going no closer.

Maddie groaned. She could take the tension no longer.

'Too much for you, babe?' a familiar voice asked. Maddie pushed herself up off the table and turned to see. Maia was standing at her side, her hands still on Maddie's upper thighs. She was naked, as before, and Maddie noticed that her nipples, which before had been slight points, were now hard and erect. Maia winked at Maddie. 'Surprised?'

'Yes . . .'

'I work here, hon. Masseuse to all you good lady folk. I was taking a quick break back there in the steam room.'

Maddie was overtaken by feelings of consternation, embarrassment and the strong thrill of arousal.

'Want me to finish you off?' Maia asked. The question was loaded, and Maddie lay back down on the table as before, closed her eyes and murmured, 'Please.'

'Turn over, get rid of the towel,' Maia whispered. Maddie obeyed and felt Maia pushing her legs further apart, so that Maddie was completely open and exposed, with her legs dangling over the side of the table. Then Maia placed her hands on Maddie's hips and dragged her forward on the table so that her buttocks were right by the edge. Lubricated by the massage oil, Maddie slipped effortlessly on the surface of the table.

Maddie hoped that what she wanted to happen next would. She waited, holding her breath, for Maia's next touch. Nothing happened. She opened her eyes, and craned her neck to look down between her legs. Maia had bobbed down, so that her face was level with the table – and Maddie's sex. She was looking intently at Maddie, studying her.

'Maia?' Maddie asked quietly.

Maia looked up at Maddie. 'Oh, God, I'm sorry. I couldn't help myself. I just love cunts – love the look of them, the smell of them, the feel of them, the taste of them. Don't you?'

Maddie smiled. She pushed herself up on the table, and sat looking down at Maia. 'I've only known my own,' she said.

Maia looked up, startled. 'You mean you're not a dyke? The way you were looking at me in the steam room, I would have sworn you were.'

Maddie flushed. 'Perhaps I've never tried making love to a woman because of the lack of opportunity.'

'Hon, if you want the opportunity, I'm giving it to you. Right now,' said Maia, standing up. 'You wanna?' She held her hand out to Maddie.

Maddie dithered for a second, no longer, before taking Maia's hand and hopping off the table. Maia wrapped a towel round Maddie, and then another round herself. She led Maddie through the baths, back to the changing room, and into the offices. She opened the door to the office vestibule where Maddie had waited to meet Jack. Maia went over to the door of Jack's office, opened it, and beckoned Maddie in. Maddie paused, uncertain.

'C'mon, it's OK. He went home hours ago.'

Maddie nervously entered Jack's office, thinking how she was abusing the hospitality of the man who had given her free membership to the baths – in this very office. Maia pulled her in and shut the door behind her.

Maia stepped up to Maddie, and stroked her hair away from her face. So slowly that it seemed to

Maddie to be in slow motion, she leant forward and kissed Maddie lightly. Maia's lips were plump, and tasted of something unrecognisably sweet. Maddie lifted her hands to Maia's face, stroking her cheek and neck. Maddie couldn't believe how incredibly tender this moment was. Maia was gentle, her body all silkiness and soft curves, her smells sweet.

Then their passion took over and their kisses became greedier, more exploratory and more urgent. Maia's hands started to sweep over Maddie's body, and Maddie responded with equal ardour. She put her hand to Maia's breast, marvelling at its fleshy softness and the hardness of the dark puckered nipple. She caressed it, then bent to take it into her mouth, and knew instantly why it was that all her male lovers did this same thing to her.

Maia broke free. Her eyes were wide, her lips parted and moist with their intermingled juices. 'Come,' Maia whispered, leading Maddie to the long leather sofa. She gently laid Maddie down, and lay between her legs. Breast to breast, the women caressed each other, before Maia slid herself gently down Maddie's stomach, covering her path with tiny, tender kisses. Maddie could feel her stomach contracting and cinching with desire. Maia's head hovered over her sex for what seemed an excruciating moment, but which was probably only a second or so, before she lowered her face. Maia breathed in deeply, and then kissed her way around and in, along and up the contours of Maddie's quim. She licked slowly, teasing Maddie to distraction, and then used her tongue to probe and taste her innermost parts. Maddie threw her head back, delirious with desire. She had never known cunnilingus like this before. It was so skilled, alternately rough and tender, teasing and playing her out, gauging her excitement and accordingly delaying and then bringing on the pleasure again. Maddie only had to imagine Maia's mouth on her, and she came. She jerked with the force of her spasms, and grasped Maia's head as she spent out her last shuddering moments of her orgasm. Maia sat back, smiling contentedly.

'Now it's my turn,' Maddie whispered.

Maia was an able tutor and, under her guidance, Maddie learnt many secrets about how to pleasure another woman. The two women delighted in each other's bodies all night, heading down to the plunge pool when their bodies became too feverish with love; and Maddie finally crept from the building just before dawn, half an hour before the cleaners arrived.

A few days later, shooting had moved to the pub at Winterborne St Giles, and Maddie was glad to be back on familiar, friendly territory. She had driven out from the hotel much earlier in the morning than the others were due to leave, and Grace had greeted her like a long-lost daughter. Maddie had filled her in on the progress of the shoot, and Grace listened in enthralled rapture. Maddie had forgotten that Grace was a big film fan, still star-struck by the process of movie-making. Grace was disappointed to learn that Maddie would be staying at the hotel in Dorchester.

'If it gets too much for you, the bed in your old room is made up. Here's a key,' said Grace, slipping the key to the back door into Maddie's hand. This reminded Maddie of the last time she had used the key to sneak back into the pub.

'Is Callum about?' Maddie asked, trying not to

betray any particular interest in his whereabouts. 'I didn't see his car by the garage.'

'That boy will be the death of me. He's only gone and taken himself off to do some rallying in Wales, at some sort of special driving school, I believe. It's so dangerous, I don't even want to think about it.' Grace shuddered, expressing her feelings.

Maddie didn't enquire further. She would have liked to have seen Callum again, but there were plenty of other opportunities to keep herself amused.

Throughout the day, Grace spoilt Maddie during filming by bringing out cups of coffee and snacks. Maddie felt that she ought to introduce Grace to Hugh, out of politeness, as his production was going to be disrupting life at the New Inn for a few days. Despite having heard from Maddie about Hugh's unpleasant mode of doing business and his unappealing character, Grace was excited by the prospect, saying that she had never met a real live film director before. She was almost child-like in her excited anticipation of the meeting, and Maddie wondered whether she should tell Grace a little more about exactly what Hugh was like. After all, when she had been staying with Grace, she had only told her about some of Hugh's milder character defects and shortcomings. Hugh solved Maddie's dilemma by shaking Grace's hand, saying, 'How do you do?' and walking off again.

'He's not a very polite man, is he?' said Grace.

'You can say that again,' Maddie said with feeling.

After filming finished that evening, Maddie decided to stay on in the pub for a chat with the regulars, to catch up on the news in the village. She would drive back to Dorchester later on. One of the locals, Bert Rawson, approached her. Maddie remembered that he was married to one of the two old ladies Maddie had first encountered on her arrival at the village.

'I see they're making a film about it now,' Bert said.

'About what?' Maddie asked. As far as she knew, the subject of the film had not been publicised, and Hugh had given strict instructions that the cast and crew were not to discuss it with anyone apart from the other production team members.

Bert looked annoyed at what he perceived as her obtuseness. 'You know,' he reminded her, 'that thing you were working on when you stayed here before.' Maddie still looked blank. He lowered his voice and hissed at her. 'The Dorset Pensioners' Sex Ring Scandal.'

Maddie gazed at him, bemused, but didn't say anything. She had almost forgotten about that little joke of Callum's.

'I gather they're filming in one of the bedrooms here tomorrow. I was wondering whether they, you know, need any help?' Bert muttered conspiratorially, looking around him to see if anyone else was eavesdropping on the conversation. Then, in case he wasn't making his meaning clear enough, he winked at Maddie. 'Extras, you know. Or action shots. I'm a pensioner, I'm over sixty-five,' he added, in case she might doubt his qualifications.

'I think we might be requiring some body doubles,' Maddie said, desperately trying to keep a straight face. 'Do you know what they are?'

Bert shook his head.

'They're the actors called in for the shots that the principal actors refuse to do. These shots are usually sexually explicit and involve nudity. Would you be happy with that?'

Bert nodded his head vigorously, and licked his lips, clearly relishing the thought.

'You should go and speak to the director, Hugh Shepherd. He'll be here tomorrow morning. I'm sure he'll be more than happy to oblige.'

'Right ho then,' said Bert, leaving happily, and Maddie couldn't help but start laughing once he had gone back into the other bar. She knew it was slightly unkind to make fun at Bert's expense. She simply hadn't been able to resist it. Like a lot of things, she reflected with a grin.

Maddie could keep her curiosity to herself no longer. The scenes she had witnessed in the wildflower meadow had been haunting her for days, now, and the more she thought about what she had seen, the more she wanted to know about it. During a brief break in filming at the pub, when Finlay was snatching a quick sandwich and a drink from a flask, she approached him.

'Finlay, can I ask you a question?'

'Fire away,' said Finlay, his mouth full of food, and crumbs falling down his chin.

'What were you doing in the wildflower meadow the other evening?'

Maddie was glad that Finlay paused to finish his mouthful and swallow before answering, but she wondered if this was a ploy to gain himself time to think of an excuse.

'Pretty much what it looked like: making a porno movie,' he said, unabashed.

'Oh,' said Maddie. 'So you saw me.'

Finlay nodded. 'It's a shame you sloped off. I was

going to ask you to join in. You certainly seemed to be enjoying it.'

'I was only curious to see what you were doing,' Maddie said defensively, immediately aware of how weak her excuse sounded.

Finlay roared with laughter. 'Yeah, right. And it took you half an hour to figure it out?'

'Well, I was . . .' Maddie trailed off, unable to think of a convincing excuse and not wanting to admit to the truth.

Finlay finished her sentence for her. 'Turned on? It's OK to admit it, you know. I'd be more surprised if you weren't, not to mention disappointed – that would mean that it wasn't going to be a very good porno movie, wouldn't it?'

Maddie nodded. 'But,' she floundered, trying to think how to phrase her questions. 'But how? I mean, why . . .'

'I'd have thought the "why" is pretty obvious. Why do people do most things? For the money. And as for the "how" – well, you just take two people, put them together and let them get on with it.' Finlay laughed, a deep, rude chuckle. He was clearly enjoying Maddie's struggle to express herself.

'No, I mean – how did you get into this? How did you persuade Melinda and Paul to take part?'

'How long have you been working in the film industry?' Finlay asked. Maddie thought it strange to answer her question with another, seemingly unconnected one; but she answered, wondering where this line of questioning would lead.

'Well, then,' said Finlay, 'surely you've been around long enough to know about the porno scam?'

Maddie shook her head.

'Ah, an innocent,' Finlay said, his voice heavy with

irony. 'Not many of those around here. How on earth have you managed to stay unsullied?'

'This is the first shoot I've actually worked on. Normally I just do the pre-production scouting and managing. Once the shoot is under way, I've always handed over to the unit manager in the past as my job is pretty much finished.'

'I'll enlighten you, then. It's a perk of the job. It's quite common for the technicians and actors to film a porno movie in tandem with a "proper" feature. It's invariably done without the director's knowledge, and we do the filming mainly in the evenings, once work on the proper film has finished for the day. That way, we get to use everything for free: lighting, cameras, sets – even the film, if we're lucky. We do it all without any of the bigwigs and money men realising – there's no way it would be allowed – and the film is released direct to video and sold through sex shops and adult magazines. Ninety-nine times out of a hundred, the production company and all the people involved in the financing of the main film never know a thing about it.'

Maddie listened with mounting incredulity. 'The technicians and actors are in on it? You mean, there's more than you three involved?'

Finlay nodded and smiled. 'I'm the only one on the filming side; after all, have video camera, will travel. Don't need lights, don't need a sound man, just me and my camcorder. Some of the crew are acting in it, not that acting's really the word. As you saw, it's all for real. But I can't tell you who they are. Too dangerous. Careless talk costs jobs.' He tapped the side of his nose conspiratorially, then brushed the crumbs off his shirt and screwed the top back on his flask. 'And now, back to work.'

Maddie looked at her watch, and followed him. She looked around the group of cast and crew, wondering who else was in the film. She was intrigued.

Maddie had not heard from Freya for a while. She wanted to know what the situation would be with *D-Day Dawn* once she had finished her time on Hugh's production. During a lull in filming one afternoon, she took the opportunity to ring her Cambridge office on her mobile.

Polly answered, and squealed down the line.

'Oh, my God, Maddie, we've missed you! You won't believe what's been going on around here.'

Maddie had a feeling that Polly was going to tell her anyhow.

'Freya's been sick, poor love, for the last couple of weeks, and so she hasn't been in the office. Miles has sort of taken over in her absence and he's being impossible. Greg and I call him "El Presidente", behind his back. Talk about a jumped-up little dictator!'

Maddie was about to ask Polly about Sam Pascali's film when she heard the sound of one of the other office lines being picked up.

'Maddie, it's Miles. If you're ringing to find out when you join me as my assistant on *D-Day Dawn*, forget it. I don't need one.'

Maddie guessed that this was bluster. She had been Sam's first choice, after all. 'Have you started scouting yet?' she asked.

'No. There's been another delay. The shoot date has been set back, and so all the start dates on pre-production have been delayed correspondingly.'

'When do you start?'

There was a pause on the other end, and then Miles reiterated, 'I don't need an assistant.'

Maddie sensed that Miles was being less than truthful. 'Miles. You'd better tell me now or I'm getting in the car and driving straight up to Cambridge to find out. When do you start?'

'Two weeks,' Miles replied quietly.

'I'll be finished here in a week and a half. That means I can come back on to *D-Day Dawn*, just as Sam originally wanted.'

'No. He doesn't want you any more,' Miles said. 'You're off the project.' The phone went dead, leaving Maddie in a fuddle of blank incomprehension. Sam surely wouldn't want her off the production, when he had been so enthusiastic about her involvement earlier on. She couldn't believe it.

Chapter Ten

Over the following few days, Maddie had forced herself to put thoughts of Sam's movie out of her mind. She had work to do. Early one morning, before filming started, she drove over to Home Farm to find Ben and explain to him what it was that his field was wanted for. He'd been pestering her for weeks, wanting to know, and now she could finally tell him.

'So, are you going to tell me what you're proposing to do to my field of lovely ripe wheat?' asked Ben.

'We want to flatten part of it to make a crop circle. Not one of those elaborate fractal ones, just a plain old circle.'

'Great!' said Ben.

Maddie laughed. 'That's not the reaction I was expecting. You're being surprisingly accommodating. May I ask why?'

'The way I see it, crop circles are good for business. If the circle doesn't get too messed up during filming, I'll get lots of grockles coming out for a look.'

'Grockles?' asked Maddie.

'Tourists. I can charge them a couple of quid each to go into the field and wander round in it and, if I get the right publicity, that could add up to a fair amount. I can see the headlines now: "Mystery from the skies: farmer stunned by unexplained overnight appearance of a crop circle". No need to spread it about that the circle wasn't made by little green men, is there?'

'I see,' said Maddie, grinning. Ben's keen business sense was manifesting itself once more.

'Are you sure you only want to make a plain circle?' Ben asked. 'The bigger and more complicated the design, the more I can charge the gawpers.'

'Just a plain circle, Ben. Anyhow, you can't charge them for looking from the road,' said Maddie.

'But I can stop them,' Ben replied, with a wicked twinkle. 'My land runs right up to the road. I'll put up a high stack of straw bales to block their view.'

Maddie shook her head in good-humoured disbelief. She had only just told Ben and already he had every angle covered, every eventuality worked out.

Ben was on a roll. 'Yeah, I can see it now. Together with the compensation included in the location fee from your lot, I could be on to a nice little earner. I'll certainly make a lot more than if I simply harvested the crop.'

Maddie regarded him with amusement.

'In fact, maybe I could put a proposition to you,' said Ben, clearly formulating another plan. 'This one would have to be between just you and me, though. Suppose the crop circle simply appears one night, and I don't know anything about it, and you don't know anything about it. It would be a lovely coincidence, wouldn't it, considering you need to use a crop circle for filming the next day? We just wake up on the morning of the shoot and bingo! There it is. Then I could claim for the damage to my crops on my business insurance as well; category, "damage to crops by persons (or aliens) unknown". That way I make it pay for itself not once, not twice, but three times over. Location fee and compensation from you lot; money from the insurance company, and tourists. Only thing is, we'd have to make it "appear" without anyone else knowing. Some of my neighbours would be more than happy to squeal to my insurance company.'

'You realise that what you're proposing is not strictly legal?' said Maddie.

'Once a wide boy, always a wide boy,' grinned Ben. 'So, who were you planning on doing this with?'

'I was going to get some of the crew to come out and give me a hand to make it,' Maddie said. 'But I guess you won't want me to ask them now. Would I be right?'

'Spot on. We'll do it, just you and me, the night before you need it for filming.'

'And would I be right in thinking that you've done this before?' Maddie asked, suddenly sensing that she was on to something.

'You might be,' Ben said non-committally. 'Or you might not. I'm not saying. Let's just say that I don't believe in aliens.'

'So what's your theory, then? You're not telling me that they're all made by farmers on the scam, like you?'

'I'm not on the scam,' said Ben in cod-hurt tones.

'Let's just call it creative accountancy. And I don't think they're made by farmers, on the scam or otherwise. Think about the distribution of crop circles. They're concentrated in Wiltshire and Dorset, right? What else is concentrated there?'

Maddie looked at Ben, struggling vainly to follow his drift.

'The army,' Ben said, as if it was self-sufficient explanation. Seeing Maddie's continuing blank look, he elaborated. 'Just think. It's perfect training: get in there under the cover of darkness, execute an incredibly intricate and precise design which involves complicated surveying and the accurate deployment of a lot of men, do it all in a few hours without detection, and get out without leaving any traces behind. It's got to be. I've got a good mind to ring up the local garrison and tell them any time they want to do some night exercises, they can feel free to use my fields.'

When he eventually enquired about it, Maddie blithely told Hugh that the crop circle was already prepared. She knew he was too busy to insist on coming out to look at it. And so, long after everyone had gone to bed but only hours before the crop circle scene was due to be shot, Maddie sneaked out of the hotel in to the darkness of the night, and drove off to meet with Ben at the farmhouse.

Maddie had certainly entered into the spirit of the exercise. She was dressed, as Ben had instructed, in camouflage. She had felt foolish buying a black woollen balaclava from an army surplus store in the middle of one of the hottest summers on record, but Ben had been insistent that they had to avoid detection at all costs. She wore black jeans and a black shirt, and had even smeared some dirt into the small strip of her face that was visible beneath the balaclava. The subterfuge and risk of discovery added to the thrill. Maddie hadn't felt so deliciously naughty since she had climbed over her neighbour's fence one night to steal some of his raspberries when she was a girl.

'Let's check we've got everything, before we go,' said Ben. He looked over into the back of his pickup, pulled out a rucksack and checked off the inventory of its contents. 'Rope, rag, wooden mallet, peg: yep, all there; plus the plank and the pole in the back. I think we're ready for the off.'

'What about torches?' Maddie asked.

'We can't use torches. Remember, we don't anyone to see. There's a bit of moonlight, but we'll have to do it mainly by feel. That shouldn't be too hard,' he winked at her.

Ben parked the pick-up on a lane near the field, rather than driving right up to it. They had to carry the equipment in the darkness, and Maddie was stumbling and falling about so much that she got an attack of the giggles. Ben shushed her.

'Noise travels much further at night. We have to whisper.'

They finally got to the edge of the wheat field. Maddie hadn't seen it since her first visit to the farm, but the dry papery rustling told her that it had grown considerably and now must be golden ripe. The heads of the wheat brushed lightly against her thigh in the gentle breeze.

'We'll walk along one of the tractor tramlines; that way, we won't leave any tracks in the crop,' Ben whispered. 'I'll go first, and you follow. We'll have to carry the pole and plank between us.'

He hitched the rucksack on to his back and they

slowly made their way into the field, walking along the narrow gap in the crop where one set of tractor wheels had travelled, first during sowing and then during later spraying. The night air was refreshingly cool after the heat of the day, and Maddie could feel the moisture in the air that was already settling as dew.

They reached the spot right in the middle of the field that Maddie had indicated all those weeks previously. They put the plank down on the bare earth of the tramline.

'I'm intrigued to see how we're going to do this,' Maddie whispered.

'How big do you want it?' Ben asked.

'It'll need to be big enough for Juliet, Sean and Turner to walk around inside it; and, as we'll be shooting part of the scene as a long shot from across the valley, it's got to be fairly imposing. Let's say ten metres.'

'Sounds good. But didn't you say the damage would be about a hectare's worth? This isn't going to damage a hundredth of that.'

'Ah. Some of the other shots are going to be taken from an overhead crane right by the circle.'

'Driving it along the tramlines isn't going to damage them.'

'We're going to shoot from all angles around the circle, not just from on the tramlines. You've seen all the equipment, and how many technicians will be attending – plus there'll be all the bored actors not involved in that particular scene, but coming along to watch for something to do. They'll all be milling about, crushing the wheat.'

'Point taken,' said Ben, clearly impressed. 'You're good at your job. You think things through.'

'Got to,' Maddie said simply. 'Thanks for the compliment, though. It's about the only one I've had about my work, all the time I've been here.'

'So, ten metres it is, then.' Ben took out the rope from the rucksack and measured out two arms' lengths of string, and then another half arm's length. Maddie watched as he walked a little way further up the tramline, then tied one end of the rope round the peg, placed the folded-up rag over the looped head of the peg and then hammered it most of the way into the ground.

'Why the rag?' Maddie asked, mystified. She couldn't see what purpose it served.

'Dulls the sound,' explained Ben. 'Don't want the whole valley hearing, do we?'

Maddie watched as Ben tied the other end of the rope around the base of the pole.

'Now for the fun bit,' he said. He walked out into the wheat with the pole held upright, until the rope pulled taut. Then he turned so that his back was to the peg and his legs were straddling the rope, and started to shuffle in a wide circle around the peg. Maddie could see Ben's arms and back straining as he kept the tension on the rope, which was only about three inches above the ground. Slowly, the rope pushed over the wheat at the base. Ben held the pole out in front of him so that the edge of the circle was demarcated by the pole; a crisp edge unspoilt by his footprints. Maddie knew that such careful attention to detail meant that Ben must have done this before. When he had finished a complete circuit he stopped and surveyed his handiwork. Some of the wheat was already starting to spring back up. He walked out over the crushed wheat and back along the tramline to where Maddie was standing.

'Now for the plank,' he said. 'I need you to help me with this, please.'

Together, they carried the plank along the tramline and into the circle. They placed it on the ground, so that it radiated out like a spoke from the central peg, and walked up and down it a few times to press the wheat right down beneath it. They gradually moved the plank round the circle in this manner, methodically pressing down the stems of the crop. Crushed for this second time, the wheat stayed flattened. It took a long while, but Maddie wasn't sure quite how long as she hadn't worn her watch.

'Superb,' said Ben, when they had finally finished. 'Just the job. One crop circle, ten metres diameter, as per order.'

Maddie was very pleased with their handiwork, and couldn't wait to see it the next day in the daylight.

Ben spoke quietly to her. 'You know, of course, that these things are endowed with magical and spiritual powers. I had a woman tell me that in one of the circles I made last year. I didn't have the heart to tell her the truth. Let her carry on believing it, if it makes her happy.'

'So you *have* made these before then. I thought so,' said Maddie. 'You seemed a bit too organised for this to be your first time.'

'Is it your first time?' Ben asked.

'Well actually, yes. There aren't that many calls for crop circles in my job, I can tell you.'

Ben stepped closer to her. In the monochrome dimness, she could make out that he was smiling.

'I like you, Maddie Campion,' he said.

'You're not so bad, yourself,' she replied, stepping closer to graze his lips with a light kiss.

233

'Hey, not here,' Ben grinned. 'Might damage our creation. Fancy making a crushed patch in the wild-flower meadow instead?' He laughed and winked at her, and they gathered up their equipment and walked quickly back to the pick-up, eager to hurry to the wildflower meadow, to make love in among the lady's bedstraw and yellow archangel, the corn cockle and the musk mallow; beneath the honey-suckle and sweet briar and the sliver of silvery moon.

The following evening, there was a knock at Mad-die's bedroom door. She looked up from the sea of papers and notes that were spread over the coverlet and resting on her knees as she sat cross-legged and barefoot on the bed.

'Come on in,' Maddie called out. She thought it was probably Annie or Melinda, wanting to borrow some toiletries or make-up, or to have a gossip. The door opened, and Hugh came in.

'Oh, you're working,' said Hugh.

'There's no need to sound so surprised,' Maddie replied with scarcely concealed irritation. How the hell did he think she could get everything done unless she worked late into the night? She had her rough continuity notes to write up, all the paperwork concerning the use of the various locations to keep up-to-date, and location payments to authorise.

'Sorry to bother you,' Hugh continued. 'I won-dered if we could have a chat?'

'Be my guest,' she said, gesturing at the bed. The single armchair was covered with a pile of her dirty washing, ready for a trip to the launderette, and she certainly didn't want Hugh seeing what lay within it. Typically, Hugh had told his crew that they could not use the hotel laundry service as it was too expensive.

Hugh looked down at the pile of papers on the bed, wondering where he could perch. Maddie solved his dilemma by reaching forwards and sweeping some of them on to the floor. She picked the notes up off her knee and deposited them with the others.

'It's OK. They were in no particular order, anyhow,' she said. 'Besides, I'm fed up with the sight of them, right now. So, what do you want to have a chat about? Got another job you're going to second me on to?'

Hugh smiled patiently. He was clearly inured to Maddie's jibing. 'No. I just wanted to thank you for all your hard work. Everything on the locations front has gone terrifically well.'

'But of course,' said Maddie tersely. 'That's my job. You wouldn't expect anything other from me.'

'Yes, of course,' Hugh said hastily. 'I was especially impressed by the crop circle today – you did a magnificent job. And your work on the shoot has been invaluable. Thank you. I know how hectic the last few days of a shoot can be, so I wanted to find a quiet time to thank you properly.'

Maddie was a little taken aback by this. Hugh's behaviour was distinctly out of character. 'Well, considering I wasn't given any option about working on this production, I've been surprised by how much I've enjoyed it.' No thanks to you, she thought. If it hadn't been for the rest of the crew, I'd have gone insane.

'Good,' said Hugh. 'I hope you would consider working with me again?'

'You mean I'd have a choice in the matter next time?' Maddie asked sarcastically.

Hugh laughed. 'There were special circumstances that led you to be working here, remember? My location manager dropping out and Sam offering your services. It won't happen again.'

Maddie snorted. Just the mention of Sam Pascali's name was a bitter reminder of what she was missing out on.

'Look. It's not so late that the pubs have shut. Let me take you out for a drink, to show there's no hard feelings,' said Hugh.

'No, thanks,' Maddie answered. She was suspicious of his motives, as his behaviour now was strikingly at odds with that during all the previous weeks, when he had acted so badly towards her; and she wasn't sure she wanted to be seen around and about with Hugh. Dorchester wasn't a big town and she knew how tongues would wag amongst the cast and crew if it was known that she had been having a closeted *tête-à-tête* with him. He wasn't best known for his socialising skills with the others, after all.

Maddie was surprised to see that Hugh looked downcast at her reply, and she felt that the abruptness of her refusal might have seemed a bit rude. Even after all that he had put her through, she felt a twinge of pity for him.

'How about I order something from room service?' she said, to make amends. 'It's not so bad in here, is it?' And it was screened from prying eyes and tattling tongues too, she thought, a little uncharitably. Maddie only hoped that no one had seen Hugh going into her room. She reached for the phone and placed an order for a bottle of red wine.

'Make that champagne,' said Hugh. 'My shout.'

This, too, was out of character, after the parsimony of the shoot.

'Right, then. You said it,' Maddie grinned, and took great pleasure in ordering the most expensive champagne that the hotel stocked and asking for it to be charged to Mr Hugh Shepherd's bill. She watched for Hugh's reaction as she did so, and was perplexed when he didn't react at all. This was not what she had expected from the meanest man in moviedom. In a few minutes, there was a knock at the door and one of the hotel staff brought in a silver tray, bearing some champagne in an ice-packed glass cooler, and two cut-glass champagne flutes. Maddie cleared a space on the bedside table and he set them down. Maddie was sure that she could see him grinning as he left the room, and felt the urge to run up to him and explain, 'It's not what you think.'

Hugh got up and went over to the champagne. Maddie watched as he undid the wire cage around the cork and eased it out of the neck of the bottle with his thumbs. It left the bottle with a satisfying pop, and Hugh filled the two glasses.

'Here's to the success of the film,' he said, raising his glass. 'Thanks for all your hard work.'

'So what was it that you had on him?' Maddie asked instead of replying to his toast. She knew it was churlish, but she couldn't help herself. Hugh was so pleased that his work had gone well, that he had got what he wanted. She wanted to prick his little bubble of self-satisfaction, and let him know that she wasn't nearly so pleased with the proceedings.

'I'm sorry?' Hugh replied, clearly confused.

'What made Sam lend me to you, at such short

notice and when he really wanted to work with me? What did you blackmail him with?'

Hugh looked at Maddie with amusement. 'You're a very cynical person. Why does it have to be blackmail? Is it so hard to believe that Sam made that gesture of his own free will? That he wanted to help me?'

'Why should he want to help you?' asked Maddie. 'You said that he owed you a favour and it was time to call that favour in. What was it? Drugs? Financial misdealings? Some sort of sex scandal? Did you catch him in bed with someone who wasn't his wife? Or is it homosexual blackmail?'

Hugh laughed. 'Good grief, Maddie. If I'd known that you had such a lurid imagination, I'd have got you to write the screenplay of *Beneath the Hillfort* for me! The truth is far more prosaic. His aunt was holidaying on her own in Britain a few years ago, and she collapsed in the petrol station where I was working at the time – I was working nights to pay my way through film school in London. I took her to hospital and looked after her for a time after that, while she recovered; contacting her relatives in the States and popping in to see her, things like that. Sam flew over to take her back home, and told me that whenever I needed a favour, to get in touch. He promised to help me, whatever it was I needed.'

'Oh,' said Maddie, deflated and with all her righteous indignation suddenly evaporating. Much as she hated to admit it, Hugh had done a kind, altruistic thing. He wasn't so bad, after all. Maddie found this disclosure slightly annoying, as it was so much easier for her to paint Hugh as an ogre rather than to admit that he was an ordinary human being with a good side to counter his failings.

238

'I didn't want to take up his offer, but the situation with my location manager dropping out so near to the start of shooting was such a massive problem that asking for Sam's help seemed the only solution. Sam said he could fix me up with whoever I wanted, and I knew and liked your work, so I said you. He hesitated at first, but then said he was a man of his word, and so you it would be. I didn't know at the time that you were lined up to work with him.'

'But when you did know I was working for him, you still insisted.'

Hugh looked down at his feet. He was clearly embarrassed; another novel emotion for him to be displaying, Maddie thought. This little chat was turning into quite a revelation.

'That was because, when I met you, I was all the more determined to work with you.'

'Oh.' Maddie was lost for words. Was this an admission that he liked her? It seemed too bizarre to be true.

'So, why are you a director? Because you like to control people?' she asked, after a few moments of silence.

'You could say that,' Hugh admitted. 'I find it difficult being told what to do. I'm not very good at taking orders. I want to be the one dishing them out instead. I guess I must be some kind of egotist, but I always want to do it my way or not at all.'

There was another long silence. Maddie couldn't think what to say.

'I'm very attracted to you, Maddie.'

Maddie was unprepared for this sudden admission. She looked down at the bed, her ears and cheeks burning. Their conversation was taking an unexpectedly intimate turn, and she wasn't sure she could cope.

'You hadn't guessed?'

Maddie laughed bitterly, and couldn't resist the urge to spar with Hugh, to needle him. Weeks of his bad behaviour towards her made her act like that, almost automatically. 'I can't say I had. Being shitty to someone seems an odd way of showing them you like them, wouldn't you say?'

'I'm sorry,' Hugh apologised. 'It's just the way it came out. I was, well, almost trying to deny it to myself.'

There was a pause as Maddie took in the implications of what Hugh had just told her. She was confused, but flattered. She looked at him closely. His face was tilted downwards, as he regarded the coverlet. It was as if he was too embarrassed to hold her gaze. She looked at his hair, his dark eyelashes, his long straight nose, his lips. She couldn't prevent the direction her thoughts were taking.

Maddie remembered her reaction on first seeing Hugh. That morning in Freya's office, she had been mentally undressing him and bedding him even as she was being introduced to him. But then she had learnt the reason for his visit, and her antipathy towards him had grown. Now, two months later, she was starting to reassess her attitude towards him. The shoot was almost over and her strained relationship with him was nearing an end; and a more endearing side of him that had previously been well hidden was now revealing itself. And he was a very handsome man. As he sat on her bed, so close to her, he was affecting her with an almost visceral knot of lust in her stomach. She wondered whether he had to be in control in his personal life too; if he had one, that was.

Hugh sat silently, as if content with their mute proximity. Maddie could sense that he was watching her as she battled with her conflicting inner emotions. She knew that she desired Hugh more intently than she had ever desired anyone before in her life, and yet she was appalled by that desire. Her overwhelming urge was to make love to him, and to be made love to by him. But she knew what he was like. Her head messaged a warning, but she already knew her heart – or more accurately, another, lower set of organs – would ignore it. It was almost inevitable. Maddie looked at the man sitting on her bed, and was swept away with lust. She had to have him, regardless of the consequences, regardless of how she would feel with herself in the morning, regardless of how badly he would inevitably continue to behave towards her afterward. She felt like a moth being drawn towards a flame; the hypnotic, powerful pull of this man could not be resisted. She knew he was trouble, she knew it was a foolish thing to contemplate, but she was moving beyond the realms of reason. Her baser instincts had taken over.

Hugh shocked Maddie by gently reaching out and touching the clasp of one of the straps of her dungaree shorts. 'I like these,' he said. 'They suit you.' She felt a jolt at the contact. Underneath the dungarees, Maddie was wearing a tight cropped T-shirt. The ribbed material of the T-shirt caused it to cling closely to her contours, emphasising her breasts. Maddie knew she was looking good, and that Hugh couldn't have failed to notice, too. She was breathing rapidly now, her breasts surging up and down as she felt the featherlight touch of Hugh's fingers on

241

the metal clasp over her breast. So close, only milli-metres from being a caress. Her eyes met his. She struggled with herself. This was unthinkable, and yet it was about to happen.

Hugh's hand drifted down, and was now playing with one of the pockets on the bib of her dungarees, pulling at its mouth and then slipping his fingers inside. Maddie could feel him brushing against her breast through the material. She gulped back her rising want. Hugh leant closer, so that his face was only a fraction away from her own. Maddie looked into his dark, dark brown eyes, and knew that she was lost.

Their lips now only a hair's breadth apart, Maddie held his gaze as Hugh started to undo the clasps of her dungarees. He threw the straps back over her shoulders, and the bib flopped forward into her lap. Then Hugh's fingers were at work at her waist, undoing the buttons on either side, all the time holding her gaze. Now Maddie moved for the first time since Hugh had entered her room. For all that time, she had been sitting cross-legged on the bed, but now she got up and pushed the dungarees down over her hips. Hugh sat back on the bad, staring at her.

'God, you're gorgeous,' he muttered.

Suddenly, something of her old antagonism towards Hugh bubbled up again. How dare he be such a pig to her if he liked her? Maddie approached him, and grabbing his shirt by the front flaps, she ripped it open, sending the buttons flying across the room. She pulled the shirt off him, and then pushed him back so that he was lying on the bed. She undid the belt around his waist, unzipped his flies and roughly tugged his trousers off. Hugh tried to sit up, but she pushed him back on to the bed. Maddie stood back, viewing his bulging underpants with satisfaction. His erection was so strong that he was pushing up and out beyond the waistband. She returned, and pulled his pants down his legs and tossed them away.

Maddie decided to act on impulse. She reached over to the chair with her dirty washing and grabbed a pair of stockings. She then leant close over Hugh, so that the tips of her breasts were brushing against his chest, and whispered in his ear.

'I'm going to do to you what you've done to me for the past couple of months,' she murmured.

'And just what is it that I've done to you?' Hugh asked with a quiet intensity.

'You tied me up against my will. You did it metaphorically. I'm going to do it literally.'

'Who says it'll be against my will?' he asked.

Maddie grimaced. Negating her pleasure in his discomfort was a subtle move. He still had the upper hand. But she doubted that someone as keen on control as Hugh would like to be without it for long. She moved quickly, pulling his arms above his head, crossing his hands at the wrist and fastening them with one of the stockings. Then she crossed his ankles, and tied his feet together. Hugh made no attempt at resistance. Maddie checked that the silk wasn't too tight around his skin, and then tested the knots. She was pleased that they held firm, and thought to herself with wry amusement that those years spent in the Girl Guides had paid off at last.

'What are you doing?' Hugh asked, opening his eyes and looking down at her handiwork. 'You should have tied me to the bed. I can move around, see.' Hugh demonstrated by shifting on the bed. 'If you're going to do a job, do it properly. Immobilise me.'

'For God's sake, can you just stop being the director for once?' Maddie snapped. Then she bent low and murmured in Hugh's ear once more, 'I've done exactly what I intended to do, and I'll show you why.'

With that, she threw one leg over Hugh and knelt above him. His eyes were fixed where she knew that inevitably they would be. Slowly, she lowered herself, so that first the curls of her pubic hair brushed against Hugh's lower stomach, and then the moist warmth of her sex dabbed against his skin. He shifted his hips, trying to push his cock towards her. Each time he thrust towards her, she moved forwards and out of his reach.

'Not so easy to guide him in without your hands, is it?' Maddie asked. She slid back down his stomach, and then lifted herself slightly and repositioned herself, so that she was now kneeling with her sex resting lightly over his cock. She slid herself slowly up and down his length, feeling his hard ridge sliding between her lips and experiencing the delicious sensation of total control. She was going to drive him wild.

'You can look but you can't touch,' she said. She pressed harder against him so that, as she moved herself back and forwards along his cock, she gently pulled his foreskin back too, exposing the vibrant purple dome of his glans. She licked a finger and reached down between her legs.

'That's it. Touch my prick,' Hugh said, his teeth gritted with desire.

'Who's in charge now?' Maddie asked coquettishly. 'Not you, I think. I'll do what I want.' She had been about to caress the sticky dome of Hugh's cock with her spittle-covered finger, but his order made her change her mind. He didn't deserve it. Instead, she slipped her finger over her own engorged clitoris and down into the welcoming wetness of her own sweet sex.

'You're just going to have to watch, Mr Shepherd,' she murmured, building up the slow rhythm that she loved so well. She could feel Hugh's cock pulsing under her, slick with her juices. She slid herself up him so that her very centre was positioned right over the tip of his rigid manhood.

'That's where he wants to go, isn't it? Such a shame that he can't,' she said teasingly.

Then she bent forward from the waist so that her whole body was resting against Hugh's. He would be able to feel her: her breasts pressing against his chest, her quim pressing down on his cock, her mouth tickling his ear as she murmured her triumphal words: 'I'm in control. And you can't do anything about it.'

Hugh moaned, and looked up at her. 'You prick-tease. You know exactly what you're doing, don't you?'

Maddie looked at him. His eyes were wide and his lips were parted. His nostrils were flared, but whether this was with outrage at what was happening to him or with pure lust, she couldn't tell. She kissed his lips, tasting the salt from the tiny pricks of sweat gathering above his upper lip.

Everything happened very suddenly after that. With one smooth movement, Hugh swung his arms down from above his head and pinioned Maddie to him, trapping her arms by her side. She jerked up in surprise, but he was strong and held her down effortlessly, his tied wrists digging into the small of her back. She tried to wriggle free, but it was no use. Hugh was too strong for her. Maddie was shocked by how quickly the balance of control had changed. One minute he was helpless beneath her, now she was under his command.

Hugh saw her discomfort and laughed. 'What was that you were saying about being in charge? I don't think so.'

The more Maddie struggled, the closer Hugh held her to him. She felt his cock jerking and jabbing against her again and, this time, she realised with appalled certainty that he could easily have her. This time she could not move out of his reach. But she was also so aroused that perhaps she wanted to be unable to resist. He pressed against her, and she could feel the dome of his cock against her, slowly pressing and insinuating until, with one great thrust, Hugh entered her.

He was big, and Maddie gasped, her eyes widening. She felt herself being stretched as he started to thrust in a lazy, irregular rhythm.

'Don't pretend to me that this isn't what you want,' he murmured into her ear. 'You like it, don't you Maddie? You love the feeling of a big cock inside you, don't you?'

Maddie gasped as he drove deeper into her with each statement. He was right. Damn him, he was right. She had wanted him right from the start, their mutual antipathy a disguise for a deeper desire. She bent down to kiss him, tasting again the salty sweetness of his lips. Hugh continued his slow movement beneath her, holding her tight as he plunged into her, and she began to move with him.

Hugh groaned; and mirroring his increasing

arousal, his rhythm within her speeded up, becoming more urgent. Maddie felt Hugh building inside her, and then he came with a shuddering groan. He collapsed back into the pillows, his ardour spent, and lay, his chest heaving and his eyes closed. Despite the enervating effect of his orgasm, he was still pinioning Maddie hard against him, with her arms locked uselessly by her sides. Maddie didn't mind. She rested her head against his chest, listening to his heart hammering. Maddie closed her eyes in contentment, wishing all this could have happened long ago. Then she lifted her head again, gazed down at Hugh, and kissed him once more, this time lightly on his closed eyelids.

Hugh moaned, and whispered, so softly that Maddie had to strain to hear his words. 'I knew you'd be good.'

'How was that?' Maddie whispered back, flattered.

'I know all about you. I've heard you fucking like some wild animal, and I've seen you in action in your little movie.'

Maddie froze, and then she jerked her head and shoulders back from Hugh, the only parts of her body that she could move away from him.

'What did you say?' she said, shocked. 'When did you hear me? What movie?'

Hugh opened his eyes, and looked at her, and smiled. 'In the barn during the thunderstorm. You weren't exactly subtle or circumspect about it, were you? I think the whole crew could hear. Probably the village, too. And as for the movie, I'm referring to Finlay's sordid little opus.'

Chapter Eleven

Maddie was speechless. She felt a lurching sick sensation deep in the pit of her stomach. 'I'm in Finlay's movie?' she finally mumbled.

Hugh smiled up at her. 'Star of the show, my dear. You steal all the acting honours, I must say. Such naturalness, such unbridled passion.' Maddie struggled against him, trying to get free, but she couldn't break away. Hugh laughed, clearly enjoying her confusion and embarrassment, and the futility of her struggle; and finally he loosened his pincer-like grip. He raised his arms above his head, releasing her. He looked up at her knowingly, almost triumphantly.

Maddie scrabbled off him and sat back, still stunned. Her mind was racing. Finlay had filmed her making love? When? And, more to the point, with whom? She tried to cover up her horrified alarm with a question. 'You've seen Finlay's film? But how?' Maddie was flummoxed. 'When did you find out?'

'Only a few days ago. I caught him giving some of the others a sneak preview. They were watching your scene, in fact. They all seemed to be enjoying it greatly.'

Maddie was appalled. 'Who's "they"?' she asked quietly, not wanting to hear the answer.

'Just about all the male cast and crew members. They'd had a lads' night out in Dorchester. They went on a pub crawl and then on to a nightclub, and they didn't get back to the hotel 'til gone three in the morning. They were being very rowdy – the sitting room is right below my bedroom – so I went downstairs to give them all a bollocking. They were watching a video: and there you were. You were the subject of quite a few crudely appreciative comments, I can tell you.'

Maddie was aghast. She wondered how she would be able to face all those men, now she knew what they had seen. How could Finlay have done this to her? She had thought that he was her friend. Maddie jumped off the bed and threw on her bathrobe. She stormed out of the room, leaving Hugh lying on her bed wearing a self-satisfied smile. She marched along the corridor, up a flight of stairs and along to Finlay's room. She hammered on the door and opened it without waiting for a reply.

Finlay was not in his room, but the splashing sounds coming from the bathroom told Maddie where she would find him. She threw open the door. Finlay was in the bath, lying back in the soapy water with his eyes closed. He looked up at her and, seeing the anger flashing in her eyes, he smiled.

'Coming to join me?' he asked, shifting up in the bath and gesturing at the space he had made.

'You shit!' Maddie hissed at him.

'Ah. I've been expecting this visit,' Finlay said, unconcerned. 'Who told you?'

'What does it matter? You filmed me, you bastard! When? Where?'

'Oh, so there's been more than one chance for me to film you? That was very careless of me to miss such an opportunity. Or should I say, opportunities?' Finlay laughed.

Maddie was furious. She felt angry and impotent, and she lashed out without thinking, catching Finlay a sharp blow on the cheek. Infuriatingly, Finlay merely laughed some more.

'Would you like to see?' he asked. 'You're very good. You could turn professional, you know.'

Maddie hissed at him. 'Get out of the bath.'

'Turn your back, then,' said Finlay, mock-modestly. 'I don't want you seeing.' She knew he was taunting her. He, after all, had undoubtedly seen her naked. She stood, facing him, hands on hips. She would allow him no dignity, as he had robbed her of her own. She glared at him angrily, staring him down.

'Very well, then,' Finlay said. 'Don't say I didn't ask.' He put a hand on either side of the bath and pushed himself up out of the water. Maddie's eyes were still fixed on his, but she could not prevent her gaze from darting downwards. It was an almost instinctive reaction, and she was impressed by what she saw. Finlay saw where her eyes had momentarily settled, and grinned at her. He walked towards her, and his sudden approach made her dart out of the way. She felt foolish when she realised that he was merely reaching for the towel hanging on the heated towel rail behind her.

'Come on, then. I expect you want to see it,' he

said, walking through to the bedroom. Maddie noticed that a tape was sitting on top of the video player by the television, and she knew without being told that it was the porn video – her porn video. She wondered whether Finlay had been watching it on his own, late at night. Her anger was mellowing, transforming into something else.

As Finlay bent over the video player and inserted the tape, Maddie could see the contours of his buttocks through the short cotton towel which he had wrapped tightly about his waist. She could even see the slight hollows on either haunch and, below the towel, she could see the dark damp hairs of his legs, thicker and darker on the inner, upper parts of his thighs, just below the hem of the towel. His back was muscular, and Maddie had the momentary urge to go over to him and pull off the towel to see him fully naked.

Finlay switched on the television, and lay back on the bed, propping himself up on his elbows. Lying down caused the towel to drape over his groin more closely, and Maddie could clearly see the rise of his genitals. She couldn't help noticing that it made an impressive bulge. She was still moist, and could feel herself becoming aroused once more. She was greedy for it.

Finlay pointed the remote control at the video player, and began rewinding the tape. This pleased Maddie. It meant he *had* been watching it. She wondered which part he had been watching; and a tiny bit of her hoped, against her outrage at his duplicity, that he had been watching her, that he had become turned on by her, that maybe he had even masturbated to her image.

Finlay looked up at her and grinned. 'You might

as well get comfy,' he said, patting the bed next to him. 'It's four hours long but, when I get round to editing it, I'll cut it down to about an hour and a half.'

Maddie perched on the side of the bed. Finlay looked up at her, and patted the bed next to him again. 'Don't be shy. Remember, there's few secrets between us. I've seen plenty.'

Her anger dissipated, Maddie did as Finlay suggested. After all, he had a point. And it would be foolish to waste the opportunity to get so close to a handsome and near-naked man, just as he was about to watch a pornographic movie with her. Who knew where it might lead? Maddie didn't want to seem too keen, though, and so she lay on her stomach, her head next to his feet, and propped her chin on her hands to watch the show. Playing hard to get never hurt, she thought, and this position would also give Finlay an excellent view of her arse, just in case he hadn't fully appreciated it before. The tape whirred to a halt.

'Shall we?' asked Finlay. Maddie couldn't see his face, but she knew that he was smirking.

'Just run it,' she said, wondering what she would see.

The blank screen on the television flickered into life. Maddie watched in fascination. She had no idea that so many of her colleagues were involved. Jeff and Patty, Annie and George, and more. It seemed wrong to be watching them in such intimate activities, but they, after all and unlike her, had participated through choice.

One of the earlier scenes was strangely familiar. Juliet was lying on a bed, with Rob positioned between her spread legs, his head buried between them as she writhed in ecstasy. Shocked at seeing her friends in such a position, Maddie looked away. Finlay chuckled a dirty laugh of amusement when she looked back at the screen again, unable to resist watching.

'You dirty cow, you're just as bad as the rest of us! What's all that crap I hear about women not enjoying pornography?'

Maddie ignored Finlay. She suddenly realised why she had had a sense of recognition at the scene, when she heard Juliet say, in that low urgent voice Maddie had heard before, 'That's good, just there. Mm, that's the spot.' Maddie knew then that what she was watching was what she had heard through the wall in her hotel room, some weeks ago. And the third man's voice that she had heard that night must have been Finlay's, as he directed the action. So it *had* been a threesome, only not quite the kind she had imagined.

Maddie was finding the scenes before her extremely arousing, but didn't want Finlay to know. She had never watched a dirty movie with a man before, let alone while lying on a bed with a nearly naked man; and it was an enormously stimulating situation to be in. 'There's not much in the way of plot, is there?' Maddie commented, her flippancy a mechanism for covering up her arousal.

'Maddie, this is a fuck movie, not War and Bloody Peace. What do you expect? If I put some plot development in, the punters would only fast forward through it to get to the next dirty bit, so why bother? Besides,' Finlay added, almost defensively, 'don't forget I haven't edited it yet.'

'Oh right, so the finished version's going to be so much more polished and professional, so much more profound than this,' Maddie said sarcastically, looking over her shoulder at him with a smile.

They watched on in silence. As the scenes unfurled in front of her, Maddie could feel the growing, throbbing sensation within her: the need for release. She wanted to slip her hand under herself surreptitiously as she lay on the bed, and touch herself; but Finlay was too close, too watchful. She couldn't see him, but she was sure he was watching her reactions rather than the film itself. She could almost feel his eyes boring into the back of her head.

She smiled to herself when she felt his hand lightly stroking the back of her knee, under the hem of her bathrobe. He had held out longer than she had given him credit for. She had been expecting him to pounce on her within a few minutes of the film starting.

'Do you like it?' Finlay asked.

'What? The movie or you groping me?'

'I'm not groping you. I'm caressing you,' Finlay said. He surprised Maddie by leaning across her prone body and nuzzling the back of her neck. 'Mmm. You smell good. Sexy.'

You mean I smell of sex, she thought. The scents of her encounter with Hugh were still fresh on her; smeared on her skin and over her lips, and concentrated at her groin. She licked her lips, thinking suddenly of Hugh, and tasting him on her mouth. She wondered if Finlay could recognise the smell; if it was some primal, instinctive reaction that had caused him to comment on it.

She could feel Finlay's hands on either side of her body, and depressions in the mattress by her feet where his own feet were pushing into the bed; and she knew that he was hovering only inches above her, as if doing a press-up. She thought again of the bulge under his towel, and was sure it would be much larger by now.

'Your bit's coming up next,' Finlay whispered into her ear.

Maddie watched, too aroused now to be appalled. The scene changed abruptly, from Gillie and Turner in a bedroom, to inside the barn. The camera-work was shaky, as the camera climbed into the hayloft of the barn and crawled towards the edge, overlooking the main floor of the barn. To one side, Maddie could see the open double doors of the barn and the rain pouring down outside, and there, in the centre of the screen where she knew inevitably that they would be, were Ben and herself.

'But how did you get in?' asked Maddie. 'I didn't see you come in to the barn.'

'Have you ever seen a barn with only one set of doors?' Finlay asked. 'And even if I had come in through those double doors and stood right in front of you, I don't think you would have noticed. You were rather preoccupied, weren't you?'

The view zoomed in until their images filled the screen, and Maddie watched in fascination, remembering the sensations she had experienced as she and Ben had fucked that afternoon. She was intrigued to see how she looked on screen. She was certainly putting on a wanton display, her head thrown back and her loud, urgent calls ringing out over the rain. No wonder Hugh had heard it from outside.

'What do you think? Be truthful, now,' Finlay asked, still leaning over her.

'I like it,' Maddie whispered.

Finlay lifted one hand from the bed, and Maddie knew what he was doing, without having to look. She heard him cast his towel aside on to the floor.

Then she felt the pressure as Finlay slowly lowered himself on to her back, pressing himself against her. Through her bathrobe, she could feel his hardness: huge, straining and resting over her buttocks. As they watched the film, he began to gently move above her, moving his hips so that his cock was pressed against her in a simulation of the sex they were watching on the screen.

Maddie's response was an almost automatic reaction to the stimuli she was experiencing; visual, mental and physical. She thrust her buttocks up to meet him, pressing herself up against him and moving with him. Then she relaxed back on to the bed again, lying flat on it and pressing her yearning sex into the bed, trying to give herself some kind of relief from the unbearable tension. She knew that she needed to come, but the delay would make it all the more intense.

Then Finlay's hands were gathering her robe, pulling it upward until he had pushed it over her rump.

Maddie then felt him lower himself on to her again, and sensed for the first time his flesh against her own. With her legs still tight together, he insinuated himself between them, gently pushing and probing to make her open up to him. Maddie tilted her arse into the air, allowing him easier access, and he came into her.

'I wanted to climb down and do this to you right after I saw your performance with Ben in the barn,' Finlay murmured, his cock moving in and out, so slowly. Maddie could feel her buttocks pressing against his lower stomach, and the gentle tap as his balls swung against her thighs. 'I wanted to fuck you like him, only better, and longer,' Finlay whispered.

Maddie groaned and buried her head in the bed,

biting the sheet. She had had no idea that Finlay was attracted to her, and now it was so horny to hear his admissions. She was so stimulated, and she reacted by moving against him with her own rhythm. Their thrusts didn't quite coordinate, and Finlay almost came out of her. He grabbed her by the hips and held her to him as he plunged into her again. He was close to his orgasm, and he halted, twitching within her, while he waited for the intensity to pass. He reached round and began to play with Maddie's clit, caressing her as he began to move again. She reared back against him as she came, and her contractions around his prick triggered Finlay's own orgasm.

Sitting on the bed afterwards, rewatching those parts of the film that they had missed while they were making love, Maddie realised that every single member of the production, apart from Hugh, had been in the movie. Finlay had not appeared, due to his cameraman duties, but Maddie jotted off a mental list and it confirmed that every one else had performed in the film. There was no need to be embarrassed in front of the cast and crew the next day. They all shared the same explicit secret.

Maddie finally plucked up the courage to ask Finlay a question, the answer to which she dreaded. 'Does Ben know about the movie?'

Finlay spluttered with laughter. 'Does Ben know about the movie? Is the Pope Catholic? He's found me a place that does a really cheap deal on copying the master tape on to video, and knows someone who can help with the distribution. He gets a small cut of the profits for his efforts. Ben, that is; not the Pope,' Finlay added with a grin.

'Ha, ha, funny guy,' Maddie smiled weakly. 'I

might have guessed that Ben would be involved in it somehow,' she sighed. 'It wasn't his idea for you to film us, was it?'

'No, it was sheer chance I came across you two. I'm glad I did, though.'

'Has Ben seen it?'

'Of course.'

Maddie silently fumed that Ben had neglected to mention it to her. If she hadn't found out, would he ever have told her about her appearance in a blue movie? She doubted it somehow, knowing Ben.

'It's been quite a night for revelations,' Maddie sighed. 'First I learn that Hugh can be quite a nice guy, and then I see my début as a porn actress.' And I also discovered that Hugh and Finlay are both good fucks, she thought to herself with a wry smile.

Finlay rolled over on to his stomach and regarded her. 'Did I hear you right? You said "Hugh can be quite a nice guy"?' The disbelief was clear on his face.

'Yes. I discovered he did a really sweet thing; that, strange as it may seem, he is capable of behaving altruistically.'

'This is bizarre,' said Finlay, shaking his head. 'I don't believe I'm hearing this.'

'No, really,' said Maddie, determined to convince Finlay. 'He helped this old lady when he was studying at film school in London. He was a real knight in shining armour. He rescued her when she collapsed at the petrol station he was working at, and visited her in hospital; he really looked after her.'

Finlay shook his head. 'I might have guessed it,' he said.

'Guessed what?'

'He's reeled you in with yet another of his lies.

258

Don't believe a word of it. Hugh Shepherd has never been to film school. He did work in London, but not at a petrol station. No way, not our Hugh. Not his style. He told me his life story one drunken night, when he'd had too much to drink and was far less discreet than he should have been. He was involved with a high-class callgirl operation in London for a while, and that's how he got into the film business. He blackmailed some great and supposedly blissfully married Hollywood mogul to whom he'd supplied a couple of girls, and hey presto! There was his entrée into the world of film. Not that he's got very far, since, mainly because Hollywood can recognise lack of talent when it sees it.'

Maddie knew that the Hollywood mogul must be Sam. She wasn't shocked or disapproving. He was only human, after all.

Finlay looked at Maddie thoughtfully. 'What did Hugh tell you about the porno movie?'

'That he'd caught you showing it to the others.'

'So he didn't mention that he's the producer?'

'What?' asked Maddie, confounded.

'When he found out, the other day, he took me aside and told me that he wanted producer's credits and seventy-five per cent of the profits, or he'd take me to court and I'd lose all the profits from the porno movie, and I'd be off *Beneath the Hillfort* for good measure. He said he wouldn't let me work a scam like that at his expense, using his equipment and the production set-up for *Beneath the Hillfort*. I didn't have much choice but to comply. I can't afford to be unemployed, and twenty-five per cent profits from the porno are better then nothing.'

'Jesus! Is coercion and blackmail the only way

Hugh knows how to get things done?' Maddie wondered out loud.

Finlay nodded gravely. 'Yup. Nice guy, isn't he?'

Filming had gone to schedule, and an end-of-term feeling prevailed on the set. There were only a few days of shooting left, and as some members of the crew had to go straight on to work on another project, the day after filming finished, the decision had been taken to hold an end-of-shoot party straightaway. Ben offered the farm as a venue, saying that, with no neighbours, it would be hard to make too much noise or be too rowdy.

Everyone chipped in, and Maddie organised with Grace to get the drinks for the party from the pub. She ordered fruit juices, the ingredients for a lethal punch, some spirits and a couple of barrels of beer. The others entered into the spirit, buying balloons, silly hats and party poppers to take with them. Ben had a friend who, for a small consideration, was willing to provide the sound system and the music for the evening. The organisation had been kept secret from Hugh, as no one wanted him there. Nothing would be more guaranteed to cast a pall on the night's festivities.

Maddie was looking forward to the party. It would be a valuable opportunity to let her hair down. At the start of filming, there had been a lot of after-hours socialising, usually in a local pub or the hotel bar but, as the filming had advanced, things had become so tense on set that the crew and cast were often too tired to party in the evenings, preferring to retire to their rooms and get an early night to prepare for the next day's rigours. Maddie herself often had to work late into the night.

She decided to dress specially as a treat for Ben. She had remembered one of his very first comments to her; and, on one of her rare days off, she had gone shopping in Dorchester. She knew that her outfit would have a devastating effect on him.

On the night of the party, Maddie spent hours getting ready, wanting to make a big impression. She shaved and waxed, filed and buffed and polished, plucked and pampered. She lounged in a bath scented with relaxing oils, and then had washed the soapy suds off in the shower. She washed her hair and cleaned her teeth. Then she cleansed, toned and moisturised, and made up her face; just a light application of make-up, but one that she knew would make her eyes seem bigger and darker, her lashes longer, and her lips fuller. Everything she did was with one aim; to make herself irresistible, a sultry sensual siren.

It was while she was waiting for her nail-polish to dry that Maddie decided to phone Sam Pascali. She was still smarting over Miles's announcement that Sam no longer wanted her to work on *D-Day Dawn*. It simply didn't make sense to her, after Sam's earlier enthusiasm about her previous work and about the prospect of her joining his film, and so she decided to check with the great man himself. She knew that, if it were true, she risked his anger for bothering him; but it was a risk she was more than happy to take. As it was the evening, it would be a decent time to ring Sam in Los Angeles, and so she carefully dialled his number on the bedside phone in her hotel bedroom.

'Maddie, hi!' Sam said enthusiastically down the other end of the line. It didn't sound to Maddie like the sort of greeting she would get if she was off the project. 'Miles said you were unavailable for *D-Day Dawn*, that you were going on to work on another project and didn't want to be involved on mine. Tell me he's kidding. I never did get the British sense of humour.'

Maddie laughed with a combination of disbelief and delight: disbelief in Miles's duplicity and delight at the truth. 'No, it's not true,' she said with feeling. 'Sam, I finish with Hugh in a couple of days. I'm available for the whole pre-production period on your film.'

'Great!' said Sam. 'That Miles is a jerk. Couldn't stand the guy! So I have you for the whole period instead of him – that's real good news! We start next Monday – I'll ring you at your office then; we'll talk things over.'

'Sam, can I ask you about Hugh?' Maddie ventured.

There was a pause on the other end of the line. 'Shoot.'

'What do you think of Hugh? Honestly?'

'Maddie, honey, I wouldn't give him the time of day any more. We had a transaction, it's over now, and I'm never going to have anything to do with that creep again.'

'So you wouldn't pay any attention to what he might say to you about me?'

'Honey, I value you over a thousand Hugh Shepherds. I did what I had to do, and I apologise for the effect on you, but now that's all over. Hugh and I are quits.'

No sooner had he said, 'So long Maddie,' than the phone went dead. Maddie was elated. She was back on track with her Hollywood career. With this news,

Maddie felt she could cope with anything that Hugh threw at her. This party was going to go with a bang.

As everyone gathered outside the hotel to take the balloon-decorated minibus to Home Farm, Maddie checked herself for one final time in the mirror. She was slightly startled by the apparition staring back at her – a sophisticated, elegant voluptuary, with dark coiled hair piled on her head and tendrils becomingly framing her oval-shaped face. She turned and looked at her full-length reflection, admiring the slinky black dress. It was full-length with thin straps that crossed over the scooped back, and a split that went a little way up the back to allow movement, and it was beautiful.

'Jesus, you look fantastic,' George whistled as she walked out of the front door of the hotel to join the others. Maddie blushed with pleasure.

'You're so bloody slim,' Juliet said with a grin as she came alongside Maddie and stroked the black material of Maddie's dress. 'Wow. I thought so. Silk. What's the betting that you get a good seeing-to before the night's out?'

Maddie giggled. 'Here's hoping!'

Sean came up to join them. He slowly looked Maddie up and down. 'What a vamp! Save a slow dance for me, will you?'

'I don't believe it! Maddie, is that you?' Danny shouted from over by the bus.

'Ha-de-ha-ha,' Maddie grinned back, pretending to be offended. She knew that her transformation was all the more startling as, for all the time that she had worked with the crew on the shoot, she had worn scruffy clothes, usually jeans or dungarees, she had gone without make-up, and had worn her hair in a long plait down her back to keep it out of the way. Her colleagues had not seen her in a skirt before, let alone a slinky sheath dress. Maddie was pleased and flattered by the comments she received, from both the men and the women. It seemed her preparations had paid off.

'Come and sit at the back of the bus with me!' giggled Juliet, grabbing Maddie by the arm.

'Now, girls, no mooning out of the back window,' joked Rob.

'No, please do! I'm following in my car!' shouted Finlay, a wicked grin on his face.

The infectious party mood was contagious, and the cast and crew were already drunk on the atmosphere before they even reached the farm. They sang rude songs in the bus as they drove through the quiet lanes; and told ribald jokes, quite a few of them at Hugh's expense. Reaching Home Farm, they piled out one by one and an appreciative cheer rose up. Ben had taken his position as party host seriously. Strings of coloured bulbs were strung across the farmyard, from the stables to the barn, and from the sheds to the farmhouse; and thudding music was reverberating out of the barn.

Maddie was the last one left on the bus. She had kicked off her high heels during the journey, and had had trouble locating them again, as they had slid forward under the seat in front. As she bent down, searching under the seat, she heard Ben asking for her outside. She smiled to herself. She located her shoes, slipped them on, and stood up. Ben hurried up the steps into the bus, and stopped dead in his tracks when he saw her.

'Christ,' he muttered. He walked slowly towards her, looking her up and down.

'Like what you see?' she asked coquettishly, already knowing the answer.

Ben nodded wordlessly. She watched him lick his dried lips and swallow hard.

'Is this for me?' he asked, like a child on Christmas morning, astounded by the extravagance of his presents.

'Just for you,' she whispered.

'How did you know?'

'I remembered a comment of yours. Something about being sensibly dressed for the countryside.'

'A sheath dress and stilettos,' Ben smiled. He came closer, but seemed unwilling to touch. 'I can't believe you remembered that throw-away comment of mine.'

'Throw-away comments often give away more than you realise,' Maddie replied.

'You sussed that it was what gets me going. Thank you. You don't know what this means to me.'

Maddie laughed. 'No,' Ben said, emphatically. 'You really don't. You don't know how horny this is for me, what an effect it's having on me. I can't get enough of it.' He looked her up and down again, his eyes lingering on her feet.

'You can touch, if you like,' Maddie said.

'Not yet. I just want to look.'

Just then, Annie stuck her head around the door of the bus. 'Hey, you two, come and join in the party.'

Maddie followed Ben down the aisle of the bus, watching the delectable movement of his appetisingly close arse. He jumped down the steps of the bus and then turned and held out his arms. 'I'll carry you to the barn. You won't be able to walk on the rough farmyard in those.'

Maddie went down the steps, resting her hand on Ben's shoulder for support. He slipped his arm around her waist and scooped her up off her feet, bringing his other arm up to hold her under her knees.

'Oh, God,' he mumbled thickly, turning his head into her neck. 'You've got stockings on.' Maddie's knees were crooked over his right elbow, and his hand was spread over the silk of her dress at the thigh. Maddie knew that he would be able to feel the tops of her hold-up stockings through the material.

'Specially for you,' she whispered into his temple, smelling his freshly washed hair.

Ben groaned, and caressed her thigh. 'I want you. Now,' he said in a low voice.

Maddie thrilled with the effect she was having on him. It gave her a sense of power, to know that she had reduced this strong man to a quivering wreck.

'Not yet,' she teased. 'We have a party to go to, and you're the host. You can't abandon your guests. Think how rude it would be.'

'I'm thinking of how rude something else would be,' he replied.

'Later,' Maddie said. Ben caressed her as he carried her towards the barn, playing his fingers over the lacy band of her stockings. Once inside, he gently deposited her on to the floor. He had cleared out the interior of the old barn, placing the straw bales like low benches around the edge of the floor, and thoughtfully covering them with sheets so that the straw wasn't too prickly and uncomfortable. At one end there was a makeshift stage, with a sound system and speakers, and a temporary floor had been put down to cover the uneven cobbles of the barn floor. At the other end of the barn was a trestle table

266

serving as the bar. The barn was illuminated by hurricane lamps and the flashing strobes of the disco. The barn was already full with the film cast and crew, as well as the various people they had met during the production and a crowd of Ben's friends from the village.

'Is Callum here?' Maddie asked, scanning the room.

'He's gone off to Scotland again,' Ben replied. 'Why?'

'Just wondered if we'd be repeating the other week's performance,' she said mischievously.

'You'll just have to make do with me, I'm afraid,' Ben smiled, stroking her bare back.

The evening was wild. The release from the stresses and strains of the production and the absence of Hugh had a palpable effect on everyone involved with the film; and those revellers who weren't involved with the film were more than happy to join in the party spirit, as good bashes were few and far between in sleepy Winterborne St Giles. In one corner, Maddie could see Paul chatting to Juliet, one arm up against the wall by her head, pinning her in. Juliet didn't seem overly concerned by her confinement, however. Later she saw that Juliet was deep in an obviously amorous conversation with George, and that Paul had now moved on to working his charms on Patty. Maddie thought that, by the time the night was over, many people would have had some sort of flirtation. From the noises coming from the hayloft, some people were having a damn sight more than that already.

Much later in the evening, the DJ had switched from the pumped-up energy of rave music to mellower, much slower numbers. Sean came up to

Maddie as she was getting a refill of the punch, took the glass out of her hand and put it down on the table, and led her out to the dance floor, which had filled with slow-dancing couples. Maddie was surprised, as she and Sean had a friendly, only slightly flirtatious relationship which had never developed into anything more. Her choice of clothes wasn't affecting Ben alone, she mused.

Sean pulled Maddie close to him, his hands around her, resting just above the curve of her buttocks. She felt his body pressed against hers. She rested her head against his, and they swayed gently in time to the music.

'You're so sexy,' he murmured in her ear. Maddie smiled, and as she looked past the other swaying bodies, she could see Ben standing against the wall of the barn, his arms crossed, a look of thunderous displeasure on his face. He was watching her closely, not taking his eyes off her. Maddie was gratified by the sexual jealousy she had spawned in him. She found it incredibly sexy to be so desired by someone.

The song ended, but Sean did not release her from their close embrace. She could feel him becoming hard against her, and he pressed into her as if he wanted to make sure she had noticed. Another song started up, and Sean swayed against her in time to the music, pressing harder into her now. His hand was slowly slipping from her lower back on to her buttock, and Maddie closed her eyes. The next moment, she felt a hand on her shoulder. She looked up. Ben was standing next to her.

'My turn for a dance, I think,' he said to Sean.

'Not if the lady doesn't want it,' Sean replied, staring challengingly at Ben and making no attempt to release Maddie.

'I'd love to dance with you, Ben,' said Maddie, sensing that the situation might deteriorate if she didn't do something to defuse it. She was sure that both men had probably had enough to drink to be quick to anger, and she wasn't totally sure that Ben would be a clean fighter.

Maddie thanked Sean for the dance, then she opened her arms and accepted Ben as he stepped up to her. Sean walked off, clearly angered by her choice.

Ben held her close as they danced. 'It's funny. I shared you with Callum and there was no problem. I just didn't like the way Sean was making a move on you.'

'What makes you think I'd have accepted?' she asked.

They swayed in time to the music, and Maddie felt Ben against her, just as she had earlier felt Sean. It was interesting to make the comparison between two obviously fit men, but Maddie preferred Ben by far. He was undoubtedly the sexier of the two. She could not deny that there was something of the charming rogue about him, and this was far more appealing than Sean's safe, polite demeanour. She liked Ben's uncontrollable, unpredictable mien: the excitement he generated, and the tension as she waited to see what extraordinary thing would happen next.

Ben leant down to whisper in her ear. 'Let's go. Now.'

Maddie looked up at him, and silently assented. Ben led her by the hand across the floor, and she couldn't help but notice that now it was Sean's turn to scowl from where he was standing by the door. As they reached the entrance, Ben scooped her into his arms again, and carried her out into the night.

This time, in the dark, he was more bold. He slid his hand up inside Maddie's dress, resting his hand on her stockinged thigh, gently caressing her. Then his hand slipped higher, to touch the bare flesh above the lace of the stocking top. Ben carried her across the farmyard and into the house, up the stairs and, kicking the door open with a foot, into his bedroom. It struck Maddie as ironic that, despite the frequency of their lovemaking, she had never before been into his bedroom. Until now, and with the one exception of that time in Callum's house, Ben too had shared her love of sex in unusual places. Maddie smiled. She was always willing to try something new with Ben.

He gently lowered her to the floor. Maddie watched as Ben moved around the room, lighting the candles. She noticed that they were all new, unburnt ones, and wondered whether he had bought them specifically with this seduction in mind. She hoped so.

Ben approached her again, and took her aback slightly by dropping to his knees in front of her, and bowing right down before her. Maddie was going to laugh at the ridiculousness of this gesture, when she felt his hands grasp her ankles, and then realised with a shock that he was rubbing his face against her shoes. Stunned, she stood stock still. She had met fetishists before – Greg with his fixation about her hair, for one – but never a shoe fetishist. And then it occurred to her. Of course, that time on the hillfort when Ben had massaged her feet. She simply hadn't realised at the time, thinking he was spending a long time on the massage because her feet were sore. Now she could see that there might have been a different reason for the tender attention she had received that afternoon.

Ben caressed her ankles, and then slid his hands down over the shiny leather of the shoes, feeling the pointed tips under his fingers and then running his hands back to the spike heels. Maddie was curious, and more than a little turned on by the urgency of Ben's caresses. He looked up at her, and she could see the look of thick lust in his eyes.

'God, these shoes turn me on so much,' he muttered.

Maddie wasn't sure what to do. What did shoe fetishists enjoy?

Ben stood up and hurriedly stripped off his shirt, then unzipped his trousers and kicked them away. Maddie could see a huge bulge under his briefs.

'See what you do to me?' he said, looking down. Maddie moved towards him, and ran her hands over his beautiful, familiar body with a new sense of passion. Their lovemaking had never become stale, but this was injecting another element altogether. She felt thrilled, charged, powerful. To be found so arousing, to have such an effect, to see a man brought to his knees by her body made Maddie gasp with the gathering force of her own arousal.

She placed her hands on the waistband of his briefs, and slowly pushed them down. She could feel his erection catching under the material, and then it sprang free, looking harder and more urgent than she had ever seen it looking before. Ben impatiently shrugged the briefs down his legs and kicked them away. He stood in front of her, naked. In the candle-light, she could see the small pearl of his juices on the tip of his cock, which tapped rigidly against his belly.

Ben stood still, allowing Maddie to look him over, and then came closer to her. He reached out and slowly ran his hands over her dress, feeling the stockings beneath, and swearing gently under his breath. Then he turned her around, and she felt him undoing the zip at the back of her dress. Ben then slipped the straps off her shoulders, kissing the nape of her neck as he did so. He bobbed down behind her as he lowered the dress and held it as she stepped out of it. He carefully draped it over the back of a chair.

There was a pause, and Maddie turned her head slightly to see what was happening. Ben had taken a few steps back, and was staring at her intently.

'Jesus Christ,' Ben said, taking his cock in his right hand. 'Look at you. Tiny little knickers with a bit of lace up the back, and your beautiful arse. My God, those black stockings. And those shoes.' He closed his eyes and shuddered, as he slowly worked himself in his hand.

'You like my shoes?' Maddie asked. She already knew the answer, but she wanted to hear him reiterate his desire again, to hear his fantasies out loud.

'Oh, God, I love them,' he said emphatically, his right hand moving faster.

'What do you want me to do?' Maddie asked.

'I love the feeling of the spike against my skin,' he whispered.

'Lie down on your back. On the bed,' said Maddie, suddenly assuming control. Somehow, she seemed to sense what it was that he needed.

Ben hurriedly complied, and lay looking up at Maddie as she approached. His cock twitched in anticipation, and he moved his hand towards it again.

'Leave that alone,' Maddie commanded, and Ben obeyed.

'Do you like what you see?' she asked, stepping on to the bed and straddling him. She positioned a foot on either side of him, so close that her shoes were touching his skin. She knew that he could see right up her. She lifted one long stockinged leg and lightly pressed the heel into his chest. She didn't want to hurt him. Ben moaned, and she saw when she moved the heel that there was a little red mark on his flesh.

'Oh, God, that's good,' he moaned, his eyes glazed with desire.

Maddie put her shoe on his chest once more, and pressed a little harder this time. Ben grasped her ankle with both hands, and pulled her leg down so that she was exerting even more pressure on him. His hands felt for her shoe, caressing the spiked heel and the pointed toe. 'Jesus, you're so sexy,' he muttered.

Maddie stepped back.

'On to the floor,' she ordered. 'Lie down, on your stomach.'

Ben scrabbled off the bed in his hurry to obey. He lay down, his massive erection pressing into the carpet. Maddie walked over to where he lay prone on the floor, and looked down at him. Ben's head was turned to one side, his eyes closed. She noticed that he was making slight gyrating movements with his buttocks, and she knew that he was grinding his prick into the carpet, dry humping it in an effort to achieve some sort of relief.

'Tell me what you're doing,' he said, in a lust-strangled voice, his eyes still closed.

Maddie smiled, and stood astride him.

'I'm pressing my black spike-heeled shoe into your back,' she whispered. 'Now your buttock. Do you like it?'

'Oh yes,' Ben moaned.

'I'm stepping on to you, one foot and then the other. I'll make you eat the carpet, you're so turned on.'

Ben groaned, and Maddie could feel him moving under her foot, thrusting and pumping with his buttocks.

'Now I'm stepping on to your back with both feet. The heels are digging into you. They hurt, but it feels good.' Ben cried out as Maddie carried out the action she was describing. 'Now I'm going to turn you over.' She stepped off Ben's back and pushed him over with the tip of her shoe. He rolled over compliantly. His cock was enormous: throbbing and angry-looking. He opened his eyes, and gazed up at Maddie again.

Maddie straddled him again, but this time she slowly lowered herself over him, squatting until her livid, pouting sex was almost touching the tip of Ben's penis where it lay just beneath his navel. She could feel her thigh muscles flexing as they supported her. Then she leant forwards, catching her weight on her palms by Ben's shoulders, and she shifted the weight off her feet and on to her knees.

'Put yourself into me,' she whispered to Ben, on her hands and knees above him. He needed no further bidding. He grasped his cock around the base and pushed it back so that it was pointing directly up. As Maddie lowered herself, Ben pushed himself gently into her. She sighed as she felt him gradually filling her, his thick prick warm and hard. His hands reached for her waist, and he effortlessly lifted her up and down over his cock. Maddie's head was thrown forwards, her long hair swaying back and forth as it covered Ben's chest.

Then Ben slid his hands down to her stockings, and he played with them, stroking the sheer material and slipping his fingers under the lacy band. Maddie could feel him thickening and hardening, a signal of the imminence of his climax. She had a wicked thought, and moved her feet so that her heels were pointing down, right over Ben's shins. She jabbed him gently with them, and that was all it took to drive him over the edge. He bucked and roared like some wild animal as he came. Sweat-drenched, they collapsed together in an exhausted heap, and slept.

They woke some hours later, Ben rising to do the milking and Maddie to drive back to the hotel. She was consoled by the thought that there were only two more days of filming and then she would be free of Hugh for ever. As she stepped into the kitchen with her stilettos in her hand, Ben kissed her and whispered, 'Morning, my darling. Has anyone ever told you that you'd make a lovely farmer's wife?'

Maddie looked down at herself in her slinky black dress, and laughed. 'What, dressed like this?'

Ben nodded. 'Dressed any old how. Because, if no one's ever told you, then I'm telling you. Well, asking you, to be more precise.'

Maddie looked at Ben, happiness growing inside her until it felt that it would burst out.

'Well?' Ben asked. 'Will you marry me?'

Maddie kissed him, and whispered her reply, and then kissed him again. Ben lifted her up, and carried her back to the bedroom. The milking could wait; the film could wait. They had some more pressing business to attend to.

BLACK LACE NEW BOOKS

Published in November

FORBIDDEN FRUIT
Susie Raymond
£5.99

Beth is thirty-eight. Jonathan is sixteen. An affair between them is unthinkable. Or is it? To Jonathan, Beth is much more exciting than girls his own age. She's a real woman: sexy, sophisticated and experienced. And Beth can't get the image of his fit young body out of her mind. Although she knows she shouldn't encourage him, the temptation is irresistible. What will happen when they have tasted the forbidden fruit?

ISBN 0 352 33306 5

HOSTAGE TO FANTASY
Louisa Francis
£5.99

Bridie Flanagan is a spirited young Irish woman living a harsh life in outback Australia at the turn of the century. A reversal of fortune enables her to travel to the thriving city of Melbourne and become a lady. But rugged bushranger Lucas Martin is in pursuit of her; he wants her money and she wants his body. Can they reach a civilised agreement?

ISBN 0 352 33305 7

Published in December

A SECRET PLACE
Ella Broussard
£5.99

Maddie is a locations scout for a film company. When a big-budget Hollywood movie is made in rural UK in the summer, she is delighted to be working on-set. Maddie loves working outdoors – and with a hunky good-looking crew of technicians and actors around her, there are plenty of opportunities for her to show off her talents.

ISBN 0 352 33307 3

A PRIVATE VIEW
Crystalle Valentino
£5.99

Successful catwalk model Jemma has everything she needs. Then a dare from a colleague to pose for a series of erotic photographs intrigues her. Jemma finds that the photographer, Dominic, and his jet-setting friends have interesting sexual tastes. She finds their charms irresistible, but what will happen to her career if she gives in to her desires?

ISBN 0 352 33308 1

SUGAR AND SPICE 2
A short-story collection
£6.99

Sugar and Spice anthologies mean Black Lace short stories. And erotic short stories are extremely popular. The book contains 20 diverse and seductive tales guaranteed to ignite and excite. This second compendium pushes the boundaries to bring you stories which go beyond romance and explore the no-holds-barred products of the female erotic imagination. Only the best and most arousing stories make it into a Black Lace anthology.

ISBN 0 352 33309 X

To be published in January

A FEAST FOR THE SENSES
Martine Marquand
£5.99

Clara Fairfax leaves life in Georgian England to embark on the Grand Tour of Europe. She travels through the decadent cities – from ice-bound Amsterdam to sultry Constantinople – undergoing lessons in pleasure from the mysterious and eccentric Count Anton di Maliban.

ISBN 0 352 33310 3

THE TRANSFORMATION
Natasha Rostova
£5.99

Three friends, one location – San Francisco. This book contains three interlinked and very modern stories which have their roots in fairy tales. There's nothing innocent about Lydia, Molly and Cassie, however, as one summer provides them with the cathartic sexual experiences which transform their lives.

ISBN 0 352 33311 1

If you would like a complete list of plot summaries of Black Lace titles, or would like to receive information on other publications available, please send a stamped addressed envelope to:

Black Lace, Thames Wharf Studios,
Rainville Road, London W6 9HT

BLACK LACE BOOKLIST

All books are priced £4.99 unless another price is given.

Black Lace books with a contemporary setting

ODALISQUE	Fleur Reynolds ISBN 0 352 32887 8	☐
WICKED WORK	Pamela Kyle ISBN 0 352 32958 0	☐
UNFINISHED BUSINESS	Sarah Hope-Walker ISBN 0 352 32983 1	☐
HEALING PASSION	Sylvie Ouellette ISBN 0 352 32998 X	☐
PALAZZO	Jan Smith ISBN 0 352 33156 9	☐
THE GALLERY	Fredrica Alleyn ISBN 0 352 33148 8	☐
AVENGING ANGELS	Roxanne Carr ISBN 0 352 33147 X	☐
COUNTRY MATTERS	Tesni Morgan ISBN 0 352 33174 7	☐
GINGER ROOT	Robyn Russell ISBN 0 352 33152 6	☐
DANGEROUS CONSEQUENCES	Pamela Rochford ISBN 0 352 33185 2	☐
THE NAME OF AN ANGEL £6.99	Laura Thornton ISBN 0 352 33205 0	☐
SILENT SEDUCTION	Tanya Bishop ISBN 0 352 33193 3	☐
BONDED	Fleur Reynolds ISBN 0 352 33192 5	☐
THE STRANGER	Portia Da Costa ISBN 0 352 33211 5	☐
CONTEST OF WILLS £5.99	Louisa Francis ISBN 0 352 33223 9	☐
BY ANY MEANS £5.99	Cheryl Mildenhall ISBN 0 352 33221 2	☐

MÉNAGE £5.99	Emma Holly ISBN 0 352 33231 X	☐
THE SUCCUBUS £5.99	Zoe le Verdier ISBN 0 352 33230 1	☐
FEMININE WILES £7.99	Karina Moore ISBN 0 352 33235 2	☐
AN ACT OF LOVE £5.99	Ella Broussard ISBN 0 352 33240 9	☐
THE SEVEN-YEAR LIST £5.99	Zoe le Verdier ISBN 0 352 33254 9	☐
MASQUE OF PASSION £5.99	Tesni Morgan ISBN 0 352 33259 X	☐
DRAWN TOGETHER £5.99	Robyn Russell ISBN 0 352 33269 7	☐
DRAMATIC AFFAIRS £5.99	Fredrica Alleyn ISBN 0 352 33289 1	☐
UNDERCOVER SECRETS £5.99	Zoe le Verdier ISBN 0 352 33285 9	☐
SEARCHING FOR VENUS £5.99	Ella Broussard ISBN 0 352 33284 0	☐

Black Lace books with an historical setting

THE SENSES BEJEWELLED	Cleo Cordell ISBN 0 352 32904 1	☐
HANDMAIDEN OF PALMYRA	Fleur Reynolds ISBN 0 352 32919 X	☐
JULIET RISING	Cleo Cordell ISBN 0 352 32938 6	☐
THE INTIMATE EYE	Georgia Angelis ISBN 0 352 33004 X	☐
CONQUERED	Fleur Reynolds ISBN 0 352 33025 2	☐
JEWEL OF XANADU	Roxanne Carr ISBN 0 352 33037 6	☐
FORBIDDEN CRUSADE	Juliet Hastings ISBN 0 352 33079 1	☐
ÎLE DE PARADIS	Mercedes Kelly ISBN 0 352 33121 6	☐
DESIRE UNDER CAPRICORN	Louisa Francis ISBN 0 352 33136 4	☐
THE HAND OF AMUN	Juliet Hastings ISBN 0 352 33144 5	☐

THE LION LOVER	Mercedes Kelly	☐
	ISBN 0 352 33162 3	
A VOLCANIC AFFAIR	Xanthia Rhodes	☐
	ISBN 0 352 33184 4	
FRENCH MANNERS	Olivia Christie	☐
	ISBN 0 352 33214 X	
ARTISTIC LICENCE	Vivienne LaFay	☐
	ISBN 0 352 33210 7	
INVITATION TO SIN	Charlotte Royal	☐
£6.99	ISBN 0 352 33217 4	
ELENA'S DESTINY	Lisette Allen	☐
	ISBN 0 352 33218 2	
LAKE OF LOST LOVE	Mercedes Kelly	☐
£5.99	ISBN 0 352 33220 4	
UNHALLOWED RITES	Martine Marquand	☐
£5.99	ISBN 0 352 33222 0	
THE CAPTIVATION	Natasha Rostova	☐
£5.99	ISBN 0 352 33234 4	
A DANGEROUS LADY	Lucinda Carrington	☐
£5.99	ISBN 0 352 33236 0	
PLEASURE'S DAUGHTER	Sedalia Johnson	☐
£5.99	ISBN 0 352 33237 9	
SAVAGE SURRENDER	Deanna Ashford	☐
£5.99	ISBN 0 352 33253 0	
CIRCO EROTICA	Mercedes Kelly	☐
£5.99	ISBN 0 352 33257 3	
BARBARIAN GEISHA	Charlotte Royal	☐
£5.99	ISBN 0 352 33267 0	

Black Lace anthologies

PAST PASSIONS	ISBN 0 352 33159 3	☐
£6.99		
PANDORA'S BOX 2	ISBN 0 352 33151 8	☐
£4.99		
PANDORA'S BOX 3	ISBN 0 352 33274 3	☐
£5.99		
SUGAR AND SPICE	ISBN 0 352 33227 1	☐
£7.99		

Black Lace non-fiction

| WOMEN, SEX AND ASTROLOGY | Sarah Bartlett | ☐ |
| £5.99 | ISBN 0 352 33262 X | |

-------✂----------------

Please send me the books I have ticked above.

Name   ....

Address ....

....

....

.... Post Code ....

Send to: **Cash Sales, Black Lace Books, Thames Wharf Studios, Rainville Road, London W6 9HT.**

US customers: for prices and details of how to order books for delivery by mail, call 1-800-805-1083.

Please enclose a cheque or postal order, made payable to **Virgin Publishing Ltd**, to the value of the books you have ordered plus postage and packing costs as follows:

UK and BFPO – £1.00 for the first book, 50p for each subsequent book.

Overseas (including Republic of Ireland) – £2.00 for the first book, £1.00 each subsequent book.

If you would prefer to pay by VISA or ACCESS/MASTERCARD, please write your card number and expiry date here:

....

Please allow up to 28 days for delivery.

Signature ....

-------✂----------------